DRAGONSON

The Third Book of Gwydion

Jenny Sullivan

PONT BOOKS

First Publication—1997

ISBN 1 85902 580 3

Published with the support of the Arts Council of Wales.

Printed in Wales at
Gomer Press, Llandysul, Ceredigion

This book is for
my three beautiful and intelligent daughters,
Kirsty, Tanith Aeron and Stephanie.

One of the advantages of having children is
the friends they bring to enrich our family circle.

This book, therefore, is also for my
'Honorary Sons and Daughters':
Joanna, Amanda and Nice Matthew
Darren (Gwydion), Kerry, Amy and Faye
Sophie and Laura
and last but not least
Jacquie
with all my love

INTRODUCTION

Dragonson continues the story which began with *The Magic Apostrophe* and continued with the *Island of Summer*. It all began when Tanith became a witch on her thirteenth birthday with the aid of a Magic Apostrophe fitted into her name —like this: 'Tan'ith'.

She was accepted into the Circle of the Daughters of the Moon, an ancient group of witches consisting of Tanith's mother and five of her six aunts. She was given a magic pendant, an emerald set in a silver five-pointed star, and the Arianrhod ring which, when touched to the pendant, increases her magical powers.

She was also given the Emerald Spellorium, the family's Good Spell Book, and a crystal scrying ball which helps her to see what is happening elsewhere. Last but not least, she was given Gwydion, a cat which can shape-shift into any creature he wishes but whose real shape is human.

Tanith's Aunt Antonia keeps, locked away in a dungeon in the surprising house in which the Circle meets, the Grimoire, a Bad Spell Book, belonging to Astarte, a bad witch who wants to get it back so that she can have power over the earth and encourage wickedness and ill luck. She has a familiar, a pet magpie, which seldom leaves her side.

The Island of Summer told how Astarte stole the Grimoire and took it through time to Ynys Haf, the Island of Summer, where magic is in every bush, tree and stream, and which bears an uncanny resemblance to Wales. Tanith and her companions travelled through the Door of Time to bring back the Grimoire.

Now read on . . .

MAIN CHARACTERS

Tanith Williams	Now fifteen and facing G.C.S.E.s at Glanllyn comprehensive
Gwydion	Usually a white cat—but also a shapeshifter
Teleri Angharad Probert	Tanith's best friend—known as T.A.
Mam	Tanith's mother
The Ant	Chief Daughter of the Moon—Tanith's Aunt Antonia

(And five other Aunts, who, together with Tanith, form the Circle of Seven)

Mr Howard	Tanith's school music teacher, who is also Taliesin, bard and friend to Great Merlin —but only in Ynys Haf
Heledd	Tanith's older sister
Aunty Fliss	Tanith's Aunt Felicity, now living in Ynys Haf to escape the effects of Alzheimer's Disease, a terrible disease which only affects her in the Real Time world
Nest	Gwydion's half-Tylwyth Teg Aunt who lives in Ynys Haf
Fflur	A wolfhound who accompanied Tanith back from the Island of Summer

—and not forgetting The Baddies—

Astarte Perkins	The Bad Witch
Rhiryd Goch	Evil Lord of Castell Du, who would like to be High King of Ynys Haf
The Great Druid	A Very Evil Druid, whom Tanith and Gwydion left sleeping an enchanted sleep in a cave in Ynys Haf

And now—

Astarte's Great-Great-Ever-so-many-Greats-Grandmother, the Wickedest Witch of All . . . Merch Corryn Du: Spiderwitch!

Chapter 1

'Is that the baby?' T.A. asked, hopefully.

'No. I just checked on her, and she's out for the count, T.A. Anyway, Mam says we mustn't keep picking her up every time she squeaks —she says it's bad for her.'

'Don't see how it can be,' T.A. grumbled. 'If she's making a row, she wants something. Stands to reason.'

'That's what *I* think.' I pinched the last Malteser before T.A. could get her hands on it. 'But Mam said we're only making a rod for Heledd's back when she comes home. And we wouldn't want to do that, now, would we?' I said, grinning wickedly.

The baby we were sitting is Heledd's—born six weeks earlier, just before she and Sion got married. I know that's the wrong way round, but that's Heledd! She's still a dingbat, and when Mam first found out Hel was having a baby, she was tearing her hair out that someone like Heledd would be bringing up her first grandchild —she says she can hardly take care of herself, let alone a helpless baby, but Sion has turned out to be what Mam calls 'a steadying influence'.

Pity he can't give her some brains as well. Look what she called her, after all! Karoline-Adelaide, after (wouldn't you know it!) that blonde girl in that Australian soap. Mam said it was just as well she wasn't a fan of all-in wrestling, or else she'd have called her Boston Crab or Half-Nelson or something! Anyway, Mam being Mam, she put the first bits of both names together, and came up with something we could handle—Kari-Ad (which of course instantly became 'Cariad'). And since she really is a sweetheart, Cariad she will probably always be. Even Hel calls her that now.

The reason we were babysitting Cariad in our house was, Heledd was in Australia. It was kind of weird, actually. She got a letter out of the blue telling her she had won first prize in a competition—a bit of a surprise because she couldn't even remember entering it, although she enters stupid competitions the way some people eat, sleep and breathe. The prize was two tickets for a fortnight's visit to the Land of Oz, a visit to the set of the soap serial, and—best of all as far as Hel's concerned—a walk-on part in one episode. At first she thought she couldn't possibly go, because of Cariad, but Mam said that she couldn't possibly NOT go, and miss the opportunity, and she would be delighted to look after the baby for the fortnight Hel was away. Mam's taken to being a Granny like a duck to water, and I've got to admit, it's not bad being an Aunty, either. Except for the nappies . . .

So there we were, T.A. and me, babysitting, and simultaneously trying to revise for our G.C.S.E. maths exam which (help, help!) was coming up the next Tuesday, and pigging out on chocolate. Mam was at Dad's choir concert, so we were in charge. Trouble is, T.A. is besotted with Cariad, and wants to cuddle her every time she so much as twitches.

'I can tell you, T.A., if you'd seen some of the repulsive nappies I've changed in the last two days, you wouldn't be so keen on her,' I said. 'She's lovely, but she doesn't half pooh her knickers a lot!'

T.A. grinned. 'I notice Gwydion isn't around the way he usually is. Where is he?'

'Gwydion,' I said, helping myself to a Crunchie, 'is doing whatever it is boy-cats do in Spring. Personally I think he just can't stand the noise. As soon as Cariad opens her mouth, he's off.'

'I'm sure I heard her just then,' T.A. said, hopefully. 'Shall I just go up and . . .'

'NO!' I said. 'Pay attention, T.A. I've GOT to get this maths into my brain somehow, and you're my only chance. I want to get at least a C, so I NEVER have to do maths ever again as long as I live. Read me the question, please.'

'The barrel—look, there's a little drawing of a dear little barrel—is a cylinder with radius 25cm and height 84 cm. Find the volume of the barrel. Come on Tanz, you can do it.'

I put my head in my hands. 'I can't. Whenever anyone starts talking about volumes and radiuses and stuff, my mind goes blank. Oh, T.A., I'll NEVER pass maths, I know I won't.'

'Don't be a wimp,' my friend said, sternly. 'Come on, use the calculator. I'll give you a clue: this little pi button here, with the little Stonehenge thingy on it.'

There was a thump from upstairs. T.A. leapt to her feet. 'I'll go.'

'You won't. Sit down, T.A. It was probably just Gwydion coming home.'

'I think we should check . . .' T.A. began, and then we both sat up straight at the unmistakeable creak of floorboards overhead.

'When Gwydion walks,' I said, slowly, 'you don't hear a sound, and Cariad's bright, but even she can't walk around at six weeks old. So who's upstairs, T.A.?'

Strange, T.A. didn't seem quite so keen to go up

and investigate now. 'Could it be your Mam and Dad back early?' she asked.

I shook my head, nervously. 'What, coming in through the bedroom window? No way. Anyway, they won't be in until eleven at the earliest. Come on, T.A., we've got to go up.'

'I'm right behind you,' T.A. said, making sure she was. I picked up the poker, and tiptoed (slowly) up the stairs, T.A. nervously hanging on to my T-shirt. On the landing, we stopped and listened. Everything was silent, although my heart was pounding so hard I felt it ought to show through my T-shirt, like a cartoon character's, and the hair on the back of my neck was prickling. My poker at the ready, I tiptoed towards Cariad's bedroom and slowly, slowly opened the door, ready to beat to death any intruder trying to harm my baby niece.

The curtains were billowing into an empty room, and I huffed with relief that I hadn't had to bash some savage burglar over the head with my poker. Bravery isn't my strong point. The wooden cradle, hand-carved by my Dad for Heledd when she was born, rocked gently in the centre of the room, and the fluffy-clouds-and-sheep mobile suspended over it turned slowly in the current of air from the wide-open window. I turned to tiptoe out again, silently, before Cariad realised we were in her room and started bawling. Then I remembered that when we'd put her to bed, the windows had been open barely an inch at the bottom . . .

I flung myself at the light-switch, and rushed to the cradle. The light cotton blanket was crumpled at the bottom, the mattress bore a dent where a small body had lain, but Cariad was gone.

In the hollow where her body had been was a black, white and iridescent blue magpie feather. And a sinister red and black arrow. My stomach flip-flopped.

'Rhiryd Goch!' I breathed, hardly believing my eyes. 'T.A., this is one of Rhiryd Goch's arrows!'

T.A.'s face suddenly turned pale. 'And that feather means Astarte, doesn't it. Oh, heck.'

T.A. knows I am a witch, she ought to: she shared my last adventure in Ynys Haf, but it kind of scares her. Right now, it scared me, too. Last time, my Aunt and Uncle had been involved in an accident—a tree fell on their car—but this, the Others coming into our home and stealing our baby: this was different, and I didn't know what to do.

But I knew, at least, where to start. I went to the window, stuck my head out, and screamed, 'Gwydion! Where are you? Please, Gwyd, if you can hear me, come home NOW!'

Fflur, my wolfhound, prowling in the garden in search of hedgepigs, which she hates with a passion, heard my voice and hurled herself at the back door, barking to be let in. Otherwise, apart from the old lady next door twitchng her bedroom curtains to find out what the fuss was about, nothing stirred.

'He must be miles away, T.A.,' I said, beginning to panic. 'I can't get hold of Mam, the Ant is away on holiday, all the other Aunts are all over the place— what can I do?'

T.A. suddenly turned on her heel and fled downstairs. Helplessly, I followed her, arrow and feather clutched in my fist. In the kitchen, T.A. was riffling through the phone book.

'What are you looking for? Mam and Dad are in

some church in the middle of nowhere, T.A.. There won't be a phone,' I said.

'No,' T.A. muttered. 'But there's also Mr Howard, remember?'

T.A.'s coolness got my brain together again. Quickly, she found the number, read it out, and I dialled, having to do it twice, because my numb fingers muddled up the number the first time and I got that really annoying recording of some female telling me I'd mis-dialled. I pressed the receiver to my ear, praying that Mr Howard would be there, hearing the ringing tone over and over. Then there was a click, and Mr Howard's voice said, 'I'm sorry no one's here to take your call. Please leave your name and telephone number, and I'll get back to you as soon as I can.' An ansafone! I HATE talking to machines! I took a deep breath. How could I let him know this was a real emergency without any of his flat-mates getting suspicious about him? I clicked my Arianrhod ring against my emerald pendant and thought, hard. My brain was sluggish, but the witch-me was beginning to think clearly.

'Mr Howard,' I began, speaking slowly and clearly, 'this is Tanith Williams. I have a real problem with the homework you set. You know— Taliesin's song? Please phone me back as soon as you can, O.K.? It's VERY IMPORTANT,' I finished. I hung up. 'What else can we do, T.A.? *Think!*'

She thought. 'All I can think of to do is use your scrying ball while we're waiting for everyone to come back.'

Why hadn't I thought of that? I shot back upstairs to my room, and got the ball off the shelf. I hadn't used it for weeks, not since my G.C.S.E.s began at the beginning of May. Yeah, yeah, I know I should've, but there just wasn't time, what with all the revision and stuff. I unwrapped it and stood it on my desk, took a shaky breath and gazed into its depths, sinking down and down into the layers of light. I concentrated hard on trying to follow Cariad, see where she'd been taken, and at last I was rewarded by a faint gleam and something flickering deep down in the ball.

I peered harder, trying to make it out, clicking the silver of the Arianrhod ring against the crystal, making sure that my finger didn't touch its surface and interfere with the magic. Suddenly the mists cleared, and I saw a long, stone-walled, smoky room with huge open fireplaces at each end, lit by candles in iron brackets hanging between jewel-bright tapestries on the walls. A long table was set for a meal, and dozens of men wearing red and black livery sat around it, laughing, eating and drinking. I recognised Castell Du—the great, sinister fortress that dominated Ynys Haf, the Island of Summer. A smaller table stood on a dais above the level of the others, and sitting at it, a woman in a white veil crumbled a piece of bread nervously onto the polished wood, food untouched on the pewter plate before her. I couldn't see her face, because her head was bent over the table, and her veil hid her features.

A door flew open, and in strode a fox-haired, thick-set man, wearing a rich red tunic, a sword at his side and a dagger in his belt. I had last seen him being hustled into a dungeon by Taliesin's men. Rhiryd Goch! He carried a bundle in his arms, and I knew it was Cariad. Her tiny face was screwed up and her mouth was open in a huge 'O'. Even though I couldn't hear a sound, I knew she was screaming blue murder! Rhiryd Goch wore the unhappy expression of a man who hadn't had much to do with babies, and didn't want any more, thank you very much. Mind you, our Cariad does have powerful lungs for such a small person. Her fists thrashed the air, and Rhiryd Goch thrust the baby across the table and into the seated girl's arms. She didn't seem to know what to do either, because she sort of juggled with Cariad, almost dropping her, and the baby's face grew redder and her mouth opened wider. The girl raised her head and when I saw her face, I understood why.

It was Astarte! Her sandy hair squirmed like live wires from under the restraining veil, and her mismatched blue and brown eyes blazed with triumph.

Astarte was back. And she had my niece!

Chapter 2

I sat down, slowly.

'Astarte's back, T.A.,' I told her 'and she and Rhiryd Goch have got Cariad.' Swiftly I covered up the scrying ball and reached for my sweatshirt.

'Where are you going?' T.A.'s face was screwed up with worry.

'After her, of course, what do you think?'

'On your own? You can't, Tanz!'

'I can't let Astarte have Cariad, T.A.! Who knows what she might do to her? And how will we explain it to Hel when she gets back from Australia? "Oh, hi,

Hel, did you have a nice time? Oh, by the way, we've lost your baby".'

T.A. grabbed my sleeve. 'Calm down, Tanz. Don't go galloping off in all directions at once. I'm on your side, remember? I really, really think you should wait until you hear from Mr Howard, or until Gwydion gets back, or your Mam and Dad.'

'I can't! What if they hurt her?'

'Stop and think, Tanz. They won't. Don't you see, they've taken her so that you will follow. Once they've got the baby *and* you, they know your Mam and Aunt Ant will do anything they want—including handing over the Grimoire, the Spellorium, their life savings *and* next week's housekeeping. *Think, Tanz!*'

I sat down, slowly, my sweatshirt half on and half off. I thought. 'I suppose you're right, T.A. I'll wait.' If I'm honest, I wasn't too keen on going through the Door in Time all by myself. I'm a fully-qualified coward, and I worked out ages ago that the longer I stay that way, the longer I'm likely to be around to *be* one. I'm so chicken, it wouldn't surprise me if one day I sprout feathers.

I suddenly became aware that Fflur was going demented at the back door, and went to let her in. She shot past me upstairs, growling deep in her throat, and flung herself through the door of Cariad's room, sniffed at the cradle and then followed an invisible trail to the window. She peered into the darkness and putting back her head, let out an unearthly howl, which echoed off the walls and must have scared every kid in Glanllyn witless. It did the trick, though: a white cat-shape streaked through the hedge, across the grass, up the oak tree in the garden, and in through the open window.

Gwydion sprang onto the small table in the corner and paced, his snowy tail lashing the air, while I explained what had happened. When I'd finished he blinked emerald eyes, leapt lightly to the floor and shimmered, cat-shape becoming blurred, growing, stretching up and up and putting out long legs and strong arms. Gwydion was back.

And grown up. I had to put my head back to see his face, which was now well over six feet above the ground. I just stopped myself from asking him if it was cold up there. This wasn't the time for teasing. He padded across the room in soft leather boots, and bent over the cradle, as if he didn't believe that the baby had gone. His dark face was angry when he turned, and even angrier when I showed him the arrow and the feather.

'Astarte and Rhiryd Goch,' he said, black brows drawing together over clear green eyes. 'We should never have trusted him. We should have known they'd be back.'

I shrugged, helplessly. 'What else could we have done, killed them? We don't do that sort of thing, do we? We're supposed to be the good guys, remember?'

Gwydion's face was stern. 'Yes. But there are times when I wish . . . Oh, never mind. We need Taliesin.'

'Ah,' I said. 'I'm ahead of you there. I've phoned him already, only I had to leave a message on his wretched answering machine.'

Gwydion paced, his arms folded, his hand stroking his chin—which, I noticed, rather surprised, was stubbly and made a rasping sound! 'I don't think we can wait. We'll have to get a message to him somehow to follow us. We've got to get going. That baby is important.'

'Important, how?' I asked. 'She's just our baby. She's important to us, but isn't she just bait? So Astarte can get the Grimoire and the Spellorium, I mean?'

We'd both forgotten T.A., who was watching us, her eyes shining. 'I think I know,' she said, shyly. 'She's the next generation of Daughters of the Moon, isn't she, Gwydion?'

Gwydion noticed her, apparently for the first time. 'T.A.!' He hugged her. 'You're right. Cariad is the beginning of the next Circle. By the time Tan'ith is the Oldest One, there will be six others to join her, and one will be Cariad.'

Now *that* made me stop and think. Me as Aunt Ant, so to speak! Still, that was years away, when I was old. This was now, and we had troubles to sort out.

'If you're going back to Ynys Haf,' T.A. said, shyly, 'please, can I come, too?'

Gwydion thought about it, then shook his head. 'Not right now, T.A. We need you here, in case Taliesin phones back. And someone's got to explain what's happened when Tan'ith's mother and father get back. Let Taliesin and Gwenhwyfar decide. If they think it's all right, then you can come later, I promise.'

'Well, just as long as I'm doing SOMETHING,' she said. 'I couldn't just go home and do nothing, could I? But what are you two going to do?'

'We're going to get to Ynys Haf as fast as we can,' Gwydion said. 'Come on, Tanz. Owls, I think.'

I remembered the spell, and felt myself shrinking down and down. My legs shortened and my feet became strong talons, clicking on the polished wooden floor; my arms became wings, and my eyesight changed into owl-sight. Despite the awful worry about

Cariad, I felt a queer sort of excitement as well. I was going back to Ynys Haf, and adventure.

Two fine tawny owls hopped to the window-sill, and hurtled up into the night sky. It was a comfort to see the great round moon sail out from behind a cloud—the Lady was with us. We flew swiftly to the nearest Door, two stones standing side by side on a hill, landed, and shimmered to ourselves on the short grass beside it. Holding hands, we walked towards it, and Gwydion spoke the few words of Old Welsh which would open the Door and let us through into Once Wales.

Except they didn't. We walked between the tall *meinihirion*—the Old Stones—and came out the other side, still in our Time.

'What happened?' I asked, puzzled.

'Somehow the Others've sealed it,' Gwydion replied, frowning.

'Can they do that?' I asked.

'They just did, Tanz. Come on, let's try the next one.'

But the same thing happened at the next, and the next, and the one after that. Eventually, there was only one door left to try. It was one I hadn't known about before, hidden in the ruins of an ancient castle on a cliff-top above the sea, and it was many, many miles away from Glanllyn, further away than all the other Doors. But it looked *right*, somehow. I knew this one would work. For one thing, it had a strange shimmer about the air between the gateposts, and there was a smell of magic about the place. I stepped forward, eager to be in Ynys Haf, but Gwydion pulled me back.

'No, Tanz,' he said, slowly, 'not such a good idea.'

'What?' I said. 'But Gwyd, this is the only Door left!'

'Exactly.' Then I realised what he was getting at.

'Oh. This is the only one left, so they know this is the only one we can get through, so—'

'So they will be waiting for us on the other side. Look at the ruins, Tanz. Don't they remind you of anything?'

I looked around, thinking hard. Then, like a big electric light bulb going on over my head, I realised that we were standing in the ruins of Castell Du! As soon as we stepped through that Door . . .

Gwydion saw the penny had dropped. 'They'd have us the instant we went through. And then we'd really have a problem.'

A bit late, I remembered I was a coward. Now, if I'd been a normal, brave sort of person, I would have stormed through the Door, hurled a couple of spells at Astarte, zapped Rhiryd Goch with a thunderbolt or something, grabbed Cariad, and come back, all in five minutes. But I was a bit too fond of my skin, and the way it covered me so nicely. I didn't particularly want lots of holes in it, or it to turn green and slimy, anything like that.

'Um. I think we need to wait for Taliesin, Gwydion.' I was surprised my teeth weren't chattering.

Gwydion nodded. 'They won't harm the baby, so don't let that worry you. They want the baby, yes, but they also want the Grimoire and the Spellorium. And possibly, you. I don't think Astarte has a forgiving nature, Tanz, and she wasn't too happy with you when you left her, was she?'

I grinned, remembering the last time I'd seen Astarte, wrapped all round in the Lady's tree, unable to move.

Gwydion laughed down at me, and, I suddenly felt a great big lump in my throat. 'I know this probably isn't the right time, Gwyd,' I said, a bit indistinctly, 'but it's ever so nice to have you back again.'

'It isn't the right time at all,' he said. 'But it's ever so nice to be back, Tanz. I get so tired of being a cat, sometimes. They lead quite boring lives, you know. Except when they're hunting. But come on. I think we'd better get back home and see if we can find Taliesin, and fast.'

We shifted back to tawny owls, and flew home. I was out of practice at flying, after such a long time being just me, and by the time we flew in through the open window of the baby's room and had shifted back, my arms were aching like toothache. T.A., all alone, was sitting in the living room, mournfully eating the last Mars bar. When we joined her, she sprang to her feet, swiping the chocolate from her lips with the back of her hand.

'You're back!' she mumbled chocolatily, then her face fell. 'But where's the baby? Is she all right?'

'She'll be fine, T.A.,' Gwydion reassured her. 'But the Others have sealed off all the Doors except one they *want* us to go through, and so I don't think we'll oblige them, at least not right now. We'll wait until Taliesin comes, and then decide what to do.'

I heard the sound of a key being fitted into the front door lock. 'Mam and Dad are back!' I said, relieved.

Mam came into the living room at a run. 'What's happened?' she asked. 'I knew something was up, I could sense it, so I left your Dad to get a lift back with the accompanist. Gwydion, what's going on?'

It's very hard to explain to a Mamgu that her precious only grand-daughter has been stolen. My Mam was no exception. First of all she flapped around like a chicken, clucking, throwing handbag, hat and jacket in all directions, then, seeing Gwydion's calm face, and thanks to a cup of tea produced by T.A., she stopped panicking and started to think.

'You're right, of course,' she said, 'the worst thing you could have done would have been to go through that last Door. They'd have had you the minute you stepped through. I'd go through myself, and fetch her back, but I think you're right. We need Taliesin. Where on earth can he be?'

The air behind her blurred, and a sudden breeze lifted our hair. 'Here,' said a familiar voice, and Mr Howard—Taliesin—was, at last, with us.

Chapter 3

'I came as quickly as I could,' Taliesin said, 'What's happened?'

'Astarte and Rhiryd Goch have got through the Door in Time,' Mam said. 'I can't understand how Rhiryd Goch managed it, he doesn't have the power. Or he shouldn't have,' she said, her face worried. 'They took the baby and left us this, just to let us know who was behind it.' She held out the feather and the sinister arrow, and Taliesin took it, shaking his head, perplexed.

'Rhiryd Goch's power is with the sword,' he said at last, 'although he's probably got an Honours degree in treachery. But it takes powerful magic to travel through a Door, and Rhiryd Goch doesn't have it. Astarte must have helped him.'

'Hang on,' I butted in, remembering the picture in the scrying ball. 'Astarte didn't come with him. He managed it all by himself. Rhiryd Goch took Cariad. He handed her over while I watched. We've got to do something, Taliesin. I can't bear the thought of her with our baby.'

'If I know Astarte,' Mam said, grimly, 'and I think I do, the first thing she'll do is find a nursemaid to look after her—she certainly won't want a bawling baby around her. And our Cari, even though I love her to bits, has a very powerful set of lungs.'

'And uses them,' Gwydion added, ruefully. 'Cats have such sensitive hearing. You're right, of course. The baby will be perfectly safe, because Astarte means to use her to bargain with. The question is, are we going to wait for her to ask, or shall we go and get the baby back before Astarte asks for a ransom? Whatever it is.'

'As if we didn't know!' Mam snapped. 'She wants the Grimoire and the Spellorium, same as always. She's getting a bit desperate, I expect, knowing you're getting close to your Time, Gwydion . . .' She stopped, suddenly.

'Pardon?' I asked, my ears pricking up. 'What Time? What do you mean?'

Gwydion ignored me, and so did Mam. Typical.

'I think we should go through as fast as we can, while we've got the element of surprise. Tansy and I tried to get through tonight, but all the Earth Doors were closed except for the one in Castell Du. We'll have to go in by the Deep Way, Genny. That's the only one they don't know about.'

'Deep Way?' This was a new one on me. 'What Deep Way?'

'You'll find out,' Taliesin said. 'The question is, who will go?'

I kept very quiet. Although in theory I wanted to go back to Ynys Haf and see Aunt Flissy and Nest again, I also knew it would be *extremely dangerous*, and basically I'm totally against danger, and even more against me being in the way of it. Then I realised everyone was looking at me.

'Not me again!' I howled. 'Why does it always have to be me?'

Gwydion laughed. 'Because you're It, Tanz! Haven't you worked that out yet? The Time will come when you have to take over from Aunt Ant, and since Aunt Ant is a thousand miles away, sunning herself on holiday right now, you're elected. Unanimously. You're the strongest, remember?'

'But I've got G.C.S.E.s next week!' I wailed. 'I've got to revise. Mam, you know how terrible I am at maths. I can't possibly go anywhere now!'

Then I noticed T.A. watching me, a half-smile on her face.

'I don't know what you're grinning at,' I said crossly. 'It's all very well for you, T.A. You don't have to go whopping about all over Time—'

'Rescuing little helpless babies?' T.A. asked, innocently. She knew perfectly well I would end up going. I always did.

I subsided, and sighed. 'Oh, all right.'

Taliesin put his arms round me and squeezed. 'That's my girl. I knew you would. And Gwydion and I will be with you, making sure you don't—'

'Mess the whole thing up?' Gwydion finished, laughing.

'That's IT!' I said, huffily. 'As soon as you're a cat again, Gwydion, you get tuna flavour Kittybits for dinner FOREVER! And you can forget the Jersey milk—it'll be tapwater for you! When do we go, Taliesin?'

'Since your Mam is twitching for her grand-daughter, Tanith, I think it had better be right now. It's late, but the sooner we start off, the sooner we'll be back.'

'So where's this Deep Way thing?' I enquired. 'Do we need the car to get there? I've done so much flying tonight my arms are aching.' Then I noticed T.A.'s face, which was thoroughly anguished. I knew how much she wanted to go back.

'Um?' I tugged Taliesin's sleeve. 'What about T.A.? Can she come?' Her grin was like the sun coming out. Taliesin frowned.

'I don't know. It will be dangerous, and—'

'It was dangerous last time,' T.A. said, hopefully. 'I'm not scared. Even when the Great Druid turned me into a rat, I wasn't scared.'

'Look, T.A., we know how brave *you* are,' Gwydion said, (Was there a little, like, dig at me there?) 'only this time the Circle hasn't met, so the Lady hasn't given permission, and I don't think it's a good idea for you to go without the Lady's say-so.'

'Then can I come and see you off?' she begged.

Gwydion sighed. 'All right. We'll take your car, Genny. It'll be a bit of a squash, but never mind.'

26

It wasn't a long drive, but the roads around Glanllyn looked unfamiliar in the darkness. The car's headlights swept across dark woodland on both sides, and although I knew we were heading in the general direction of Carmarthen, I couldn't for the life of me work out exactly where we were. The road ahead climbed steadily, winding itself round and round a hill until we reached the top. There was a village on the other side: I could see the twinkling orange street lights marching up the hilly streets of houses, but there was nothing remotely resembling a Door, no matter how hard I looked. Gwydion had a torch, but the moon was so bright he didn't really need it. Having the moon around cheered me up: I knew that the Lady was watching, somehow, even if we hadn't held a Circle of the Daughters of the Moon. She would understand that we had to get Cariad back, quickly. At least the Grimoire was safely locked up in Aunt Ant's dungeon, bound with iron and surrounded by water—and magic, lots of it, which was far better than iron bars for keeping unpleasant things safely out of the way!

I still couldn't see any Door. 'So, where is it?'

Gwydion's eyes glittered in the moonlight.

'Wake up!' he said, pointing. 'Look, Tansy!'

I looked.

A hole yawned at my feet, and a flight of steep steps led down into the hill. T.A. squeaked.

'Where did that come from?' she asked.

'Oh, it's been there for the last thousand years or so,' Taliesin answered. 'Give or take a century. But you have to look carefully to see it. And this is the one way into Ynys Haf the Others don't know about.'

'You hope!' I crossed my fingers.

'You'd better get going,' Mam urged. 'Time's going on, and I've got things to do. I have to talk to the Lady, soon, explain why we've had to start without asking her. And you, T.A.,' she added, ruffling T.A.'s hair, 'had better get home to your Mam.'

T.A. sighed. She was disappointed not to be going with us. I gave her a hug. 'Look, toad-face,' I said affectionately, 'I'll bring you back a prezzie, O.K.?'

'O.K.,' she said, trying to smile. 'A stick of rock, or something?'

'Yeah. Peppermint. With "Ynys Haf" written right through it,' I promised.

She hugged Gwydion and Taliesin in turn, and Mam put her arm round her: half to comfort her, and half because she probably suspected that if she didn't hang on to her she might follow us.

Taliesin led, then I went next, and finally Gwydion brought up the rear. Strangely enough, he didn't need his torch down here either. The walls each side of us, and the rocky roof arching over us, glowed with a strange pale light, just enough to see by. Once, I looked back, past Gwydion, and saw that there was darkness behind us and ahead of us too: the light, whatever it was, came with us as if it was escorting us. We went down and down, deeper and deeper inside the hill. I began to imagine we'd meet some little guy in a red suit with horns and a pitchfork any minute!

The air grew cooler, and damper, and water trickled down the walls.

'Where are we?' I whispered, afraid to talk aloud, although I didn't quite know why.

Taliesin turned, smiling. 'Almost there, Tansy.' He stopped before a large wooden door. 'Tell me,' he

28

asked in a matter-of-fact kind of voice, 'what sort of a swimmer are you, Tan'ith?'

The Apostrophe should have warned me, but it didn't. Am I thick, or what? Just as well, though, otherwise I might have started to panic, because once he opened the door, I realised why the walls were damp!

The doorway was full of water. Now logically, if you open a door with a lot of water behind it, the water immediately pours in and wets your feet, yes? Like when you open the washing machine in mid-cycle, and the water pours all over the kitchen floor? Right?

Wrong.

The water just stayed there, as if a giant sheet of cling-film was covering the door. Experimentally, I stuck my finger in. It got wet, and little bow-waves appeared on each side of my fingernail. There was nothing holding the water back. Except magic, of course. More of which crept up on me when Gwydion shape-shifted me into a grey seal.

'Aaark?' I said, twitching my whiskers, gazing fascinatedly at my flippers. My companions shimmered and changed, and one by one we flopped clumsily forward into the green, shivering doorway.

It felt like flying. We streaked through the water, side by side, strong flippers powering us upwards to where the surface glowed with light. One by one we broke through into air, and peered shorewards, three sleek sealheads surveying the land.

On the cliffs above us loomed Castell Du: sinister, forbidding—and very well guarded. Sentries stood on every turret and patrolled the battlements. I remembered the shoreline below the Castle—this was where we had left the Great Druid, fast asleep and snoring, guarded by the awful Oldway Creatures. The tide was so high, crashing against the rocky shoreline, that it almost reached the opening of the Druid's Cave. Not much hope of getting in the back way, then, I thought. Taliesin nudged me, and the three of us submerged again, swimming north along the coast a bit, until we were out of sight of the patrolling sentries when we shimmered and changed, not back to ourselves again, but into three cormorants, rowing out of the water on strong black wings, leaping from grey sea into grey sky.

I could almost smell the woodsmoke from Nest's fire. The *tŷ hir*, the Welsh longhouse that had been home the last time, came into sight. Smoke poured from the hole in the middle of the thatched roof and Gwydion perched beside it, listening, to make sure it was safe. Then the three of us flew down and shivered into ourselves.

Chapter 4

Taliesin's jerkin was of dark brown leather, and his trousers were tucked into leather boots. I was glad of my thick wool cloak, jerkin, leggings and long, heavy skirt over the top, because the air was cold. It felt more like February than early May, which it was back home. I breathed cold freshness unpolluted by factories, motor cars and oil-spills, watching my breath clouding the still air. I had this really funny feeling in the middle of my stomach: excited and happy both at once. I had come home.

Now that is so weird! Walking (O.K., swimming) straight back into danger, and feeling happy about it! I knew, though, that once things started to happen (which they would), they would be nasty things, if past experience of the dreadful Astarte had anything to do with it. Doubtless I'd soon turn back into plain, cowardly old me, and want to go back to my Time, quick.

But right now, I was aching to see Nest, and Aunty Fliss. I listened, hearing indistinct voices inside. I bashed on the door, grinning excitedly at Gwydion, and the voices stopped. But although they had obviously heard, no one came. I knocked again, louder, and this time, someone approached the door.

'Who's there?' asked a familiar voice.

'It's us, Aunty Fliss! It's us!' I yelled, and at last I heard the latch being lifted, the scraping sound of a heavy bar being lifted and bolts being slid across, before the door finally swung open and Flissy stood in the doorway.

'Oh, Gwydion, Taliesin, *Tansy*,' she whispered, and burst into tears. I put my arms round her. What on earth was the matter? Surely the awful Disease hadn't caught up with her? Not in Ynys Haf? Then Nest appeared behind her, and joined in the hug, and we all cried and hugged until Taliesin and Gwydion, wearing identical expressions of 'Good grief, *women*!' bundled us all inside and closed the door. Once we'd stopped crying, we looked at each other.

'You've grown, Tansy!' Aunty Fliss said, wiping her eyes on her pinny. 'And you, Gwydion! You're huge!'

31

Nest looked up at her nephew, her tiny half-fairy figure looking even smaller now. 'Dragonson!' she said, softly. 'Dragonson, at last.'

That reminded me. 'What—?' I began, remembering the question I kept trying to ask.

Taliesin interrupted. 'Flissy? Where is Iestyn?' His voice was gentle, as if he already knew the answer wouldn't be pleasant.

Iestyn, the chief person in the little village lying under the shadow of Castell Du, had fallen like a ton of bricks for Aunt Flissy when I'd last been here, and when I'd left, I'd had a pretty good idea that they'd get married—or whatever the Ynys Haf equivalent was.

Flissy's eyes filled. 'Rhiryd Goch took him,' she said, fishing for her hanky in her pinny pocket. 'He took all the village men and locked them up in the dungeons of Castell Du. He won't let them go.'

'How—?' Taliesin began, angrily, but Nest reached up and undid the twisted silver brooch pinning his cloak.

'Questions after,' she said. 'First, *dewch i mewn*, warm yourself, and eat.'

Nest may have been half Tylwyth Teg, but the other half was definitely Welsh Mam—like mine, she fed everything that moved! We followed her through into the main room of the *tŷ hir*. Two huge shapes launched themselves at us, and the wolfhounds, Brân and Garan, my Fflur's brothers, covered all three of us with wet licks. Since both of them could put their front feet on Taliesin's shoulders quite easily, and did, this sort of distracted us for a while, until we'd got them calmed down again, and then we sat beside the fire and ate and drank, Nest and Flissy bustling about serving us. Nest was being wise: while Flissy was busy, she wasn't getting upset, and when we were satisfied and the dirty dishes had been cleared away, we heard what had been happening in Ynys Haf.

'You tell it, Nest,' Flissy said, 'I'll only get upset. Honestly,' she said, half laughing, half-crying, 'that great lummox of a man was always under my feet until I agreed to marry him, and even more under my feet when I did, but I miss him now he isn't here. Our house seems so empty without him.'

Nest patted her hand. 'Of course you miss him. And you are welcome to stay here with me until he comes back. It's better that we should be together.' She turned her attention to Taliesin. 'But how did you know to come? I have been trying to send a message through the Door, but you are here before I've even thought of a way.'

'Rhiryd Goch took the baby, Nest,' I said. 'We came to get her back.'

'Baby?' Flissy asked, puzzled. 'What baby?'

'Well,' I began, grinning from ear to ear, 'just after we got back from Ynys Haf the last time, Hel fell in love with the boy next door—remember Sion Bobi Thomas, Fliss?'

Flissy's mouth fell open. 'Sion Bobi? Never! That spotty little—'

I laughed. 'He's not so spotty now, Aunty Fliss. Or little. Anyway, they had this baby—Karoline Adelaide—'

'Cariad,' Gwydion put in.

'Cariad, a dear little girl, and then they got married—'

'Oh, trust Heledd!' Aunt Fliss commented.

'—and Sion and Hel went to Australia on a trip, and

we were looking after Cariad, and somehow Rhiryd Goch got through the Door in Time and stole her. So we've come to fetch her back.'

'Well, I never!' Flissy said, whether because of Heledd/Sion/Cariad or Rhiryd Goch I'm not sure.

Nest, however, was less fascinated by family news. 'Rhiryd Goch? He went through the Door?'

I nodded. 'Yes. We can't work out how, but he left us one of his arrows and a magpie feather to let us know who'd done it.'

Nest shook her head. 'But he doesn't have the power! He couldn't possibly get through unless someone—' She stared at Flissy, who stared back.

'Unless someone loaned him a moon-time's power!' Flissy finished.

'Astarte,' Gwydion said. 'But even Astarte must have known that lending Rhiryd Goch her magic was a very, very dangerous thing to do. Rhiryd Goch is an ambitious man.'

'You can *lend* people *magic*?' I said, astonished. 'How?'

'The way the Lady did with T.A.,' Nest explained. 'She just gave her a little bit, just enough for her body to cope with being shape-shifted, and for her not to be too surprised at the magic she saw. But if Astarte did it for Rhiryd Goch, she must have loaned him an awful lot for him to get through a Door. And now that he has it, he keeps it for a whole month. And *that* could be very dangerous indeed. For everyone.'

Taliesin chewed his lip, thoughtfully. 'We're going to have to be careful,' he said. 'The men who helped us last time? All taken?'

Flissy nodded, sadly. 'Every single man who stood

against him, taken in the middle of the night from their wives and children. All locked up in Castell Du with Iestyn. So we are all on our own, this time, Taliesin. Just the five of us.'

'Well,' I said, putting on a brave face that felt kind of wobbly, 'five of us are more than a match for Astarte and Rhiryd Goch's lot. We're the good guys, remember? And this time they haven't got the Grimoire, so we don't have to worry about having to find that. All we have to do is get Cariad back, let Iestyn and the others out of the dungeons—' Suddenly I noticed that everyone was looking at me.

'—leap tall buildings at a single bound, and save the planet Earth?' I finished, feeling stupid.

'Something like that,' Gwydion said, grimly. 'I think we need to talk to the Lady. She'll know what to do.'

Flissy sighed. 'Do you think we haven't tried? We've done just about everything we can think of to summon her, but something seems to be blocking us.' Her face brightened. 'But with Tan'ith here, and you two, maybe . . .'

'We can try,' Gwydion said, comfortingly. 'Your bowl, Aunt Nest?'

Nest fetched the heavy wooden bowl from the shelf, and tipped in herbs and powders from various packets and papers, then took a burning twig from the hearth and dropped it in. Creamy smoke billowed and spread, filling the upper part of the longhouse, wreathing the heavy wooden beams and spreading into the sleeping-loft, but there was no sign of the Lady. I peered through the fragrant smoke at Nest on the opposite side of the fire, seeing her face become more desperate. This was awful! Almost without thinking, I grasped my emerald pendant with the hand that wore the Arianrhod ring, and heard the tiniest click as they met. Instantly, I saw a blurry, familiar shape in the smoke. I don't know what made me do it, but I reached through the smoke with my ring hand, felt something more or less solid, grabbed it—and hauled, hard!

There was a loud clap of thunder, and outside, the heavens opened, rain pouring down so hard that it came through the smoke hole, and the fire hissed and spat in the hearth. But when the noise stopped, and the smoke cleared a little, the Lady was with us. I'd literally pulled her through into Ynys Haf.

She looked as she had when I'd last seen her; slim, beautiful, holding her wonderful staff that budded and flowered constantly, the tiny white blossoms starry against the thick green leaves. Her black hair was bound with starlight, and she brought with her a calmness that we needed.

'My Lady,' Taliesin said, kneeling, and Gwydion followed. Flissy, Nest and I curtsied. It was hard not to—she was royal if anyone was!

'Well done, Tan'ith,' the Lady said, her voice deep as a low harp. 'Without your quick thinking, I would not be here.'

'What is happening, Lady?' Nest asked. 'We have tried and tried to find you, but every way was closed to us.'

'And the Doors in Time were all barred, Lady,' Taliesin added. 'There is a powerful magic at work.'

The Lady nodded. 'Someone freed the Witch Astarte a week ago, and the evil powers of the Others have been growing ever since.'

'Rhiryd Goch got through a Door,' Gwydion said, 'and he's taken the baby.'

She frowned. 'The laws of magic are being twisted,' she said. 'This must not happen. The war between good and evil must be fought by the rules. But someone is breaking them. Astarte is powerful—but not quite powerful enough to bar *my* way between worlds. So, who?'

Taliesin stirred, as if a thought had struck him. 'Lady,' he began, and then stopped. 'No, it can't be.'

'Speak, Taliesin,' the Lady encouraged.

'Lady, you know that the Dragonson's Time is coming,' he said.

There it was again. I opened my mouth to ask, then shut it again. No one would answer me anyway. No one ever did when I asked that question. They always changed the subject. But sooner or later they'd have to tell me. I'd *meant* to ask it last time we were in Ynys Haf, but Gwydion had turned back to Cat before I could do it. *Why did everyone keep calling him Dragonson?*

The Lady turned her gaze full on Gwydion. 'I had almost forgotten,' she said, and smiled. 'You have certainly grown up, Shapeshifter. It is, indeed, almost time. And Taliesin, I think that you are right.'

'What?' I howled, forgetting myself. 'Right about what? Will you all please stop talking in riddles!'

Gwydion grinned. 'I'm getting older, Tansy. Fairly soon I will have repaid my debt to old Merlin, and I hope he'll let me off being your Cat. But someone else, if I'm not mistaken, would like me not to get any older. *She* would have the power to free Astarte, so that she could lend Rhiryd Goch the magic he needed to take Cariad.'

'Who?' I asked.

'Merch Corryn Du. Spiderwitch. What Aunt Ant is to your Circle, Merch Corryn Du is to Astarte's. She was my father's enemy, and would destroy Ynys Haf entirely rather than see me rule it. What do you think, Taliesin?'

Taliesin nodded. 'You're right. She's powerful enough to break the Lady's spell. Astarte's tried to get the Grimoire back and failed twice. The Spiderwitch must be getting desperate. Lady, what are we to do?'

The Lady's eyes flashed with anger. 'That—woman has been a menace for all her many lives. She shall not have Ynys Haf. She must be stopped once and for all. I can give you power, Tan'ith, but I cannot fight the battle. Merch Corryn Du should not interfere, either. Only Astarte and Rhiryd Goch should be against you. But already the Magical Rules have been twisted. Tan'ith, you must not fail!'

Oh, right. Two socking great males, one each side of me, and who's It? Me. Wouldn't you know it? Rats. I swallowed, hard.

'I won't fail, Lady, I promise,' I said, my heart wibbling down to my stomach.

'Then we must get to work,' the Lady said. 'First, we must free Iestyn Fawr.'

'Yes, please!' Aunt Flissy said. 'Oh, yes please.'

Chapter 5

The Lady paced, frowning. 'I can give you a piece of my staff, Tan'ith, and you have your own magic, of course. But what else? How can I arm you?'

I was sort of hoping she'd suggest a sub-machine gun or something, but of course she didn't. Our battles weren't fought with ordinary weapons—and yes, I know we're the good guys, darn it!

'You will need more than just the twig. This time,' the Lady said gravely 'there will be great danger.'

I could have done without that. 'So what sort of weapon, Lady?' I asked, still hoping for thunder-bolts.

She reached into the folds of her robe and brought out a small book: its cover seemed made of light. The Spellorium glowed green as cold fire, but this little book made me feel that my fingers would go straight through if I touched it, like trying to hold moonlight. When I took it, a tiny electric shock shot up my arm.

'Ow! What's that?' I yelped, almost dropping it.

'Llyfr Ynys Haf,' she replied. 'It holds the secrets of the Island of Summer, and it has been in my keeping for a thousand years. Guard it well. And know it, Tan'ith. Memorise the rhythms of Ynys Haf, her creatures, her waters, her skies and her seasons, because until you know them as well as you know yourself, you will not know Ynys Haf.'

All this and G.C.S.E.s, too?

A book and a twig. *Real* firepower! Ah, well. I hoped the Lady knew what she was doing.

She was fading, and gradually she disappeared, back into the billowing smoke still pouring from Nest's bowl. The room seemed very dark without her, and I felt as flat as Boxing Day.

Gwydion broke the silence. 'Tanz,' he said, and there was a grin in his voice. 'You've got some homework to do.'

'Yeah,' I said, gloomily. 'Thanks a bunch, Gwydion.' I laid the Lady's branch on the table, settled myself beside the fire, and opened the little book.

I needn't have worried about memorising what I read. Every word stayed in my brain as if it had been burned in with a laser. Wow, if only it'd been Maths instead of Magic! Move over, Einstein! While I read I felt the magic of Ynys Haf creep over me: the warmth of the earth, stirring lazily towards spring, and the power that pushes new leaves out of winter-dead bark; the warmth of a wild bird's egg, new-laid in a nest, and the squirming of soft, new-born creatures. The wind was like rock beneath my wings, and the power of it was at my back. The sun warmed me, the rain blessed me, and the icy, crystal purity of new snow dazzled my eyes.

When I closed the little book, all the light had fled the cover. I stared, bemused, wondering what had happened to it. Had I done something to extinguish it? But then I realised that the light was in me, now, instead. I held out my hand, expecting to see light sparkling through my veins, visible on the surface through the skin, like bubbles of spring water in a glass, but my hand looked ordinary, like always, with my bitten little fingernail (I keep one to nibble on when I'm worried, O.K.? Just the *one*). But I had the strangest feeling that if I went outside, kicked off my boots, and wriggled my toes into the brown earth, I might take root, and put out branches and leaves. The Lady had given me Ynys Haf: I was Ynys Haf and Ynys Haf was me. It certainly put G.C.S.E.s into perspective! I felt as if I'd been reading for just a few minutes, but the *tŷ hir* was shadowy, and rushlights sputtered in their wooden stands. Aunty Fliss was up in the sleeping loft making a bed for me, and Taliesin and Nest had disappeared. I hadn't noticed them go. Only Gwydion was still there, at his old place beside the fire, the wolfhounds heaped at his feet like hairy, snoring hearthrugs. He was sharpening his knife on a whetstone, bringing the blue metal to a wicked razor edge.

'Gwydion,' I said, and he looked up.

'Finished?' he asked. I nodded. 'And how do you feel, now?' He watched me intently, as if my reply was very important.

I stretched. 'I feel as if I've come home to where I've always belonged, where my granny, and great-granny, and great-great-granny lived. Right back to *ap* Adam and *mab* Eve. If you know what I mean.'

He smiled. 'I know exactly. I feel the same way myself.'

'Only this *is* your home, Gwydion,' I reminded him. 'Mine's the other Time, remember?'

'Is it?' His expression was strange.

I opened my mouth to say 'Of course it is,' but the words wouldn't come. The little book had changed me, although I wasn't sure how. I started to feel—oh, I don't know—as if the Lady had tricked me or something. Then felt ashamed when I realised that actually, she'd given me a wonderful gift: I could be properly at home in two places now.

41

Gwydion watched me, probably reading my mind. Mam always says that my face is an open book. No wonder she can always tell when I've been up to no good.

The door of the *tŷ hir* opened, and Taliesin and Nest came in, well wrapped against the night air. Gwydion jumped up, disturbing the dogs.

'Well?' he asked. 'What happened?'

'After we've eaten supper, Gwydion,' Nest said firmly. 'I need a hot drink and a rest. Then we'll talk, after.' Her honey-coloured eyes rested on me. 'Did you finish the Book, Tan'ith?'

I nodded, and she stared into my eyes for a long moment. It felt as if she was trying to see inside my head. then she smiled. Whatever the test had been, I got the feeling I'd passed!

We ate a savoury stew and thick chunks of bread, finishing up with some of last Autumn's apples from the store. One of the amazing things about Ynys Haf is the way quite ordinary food tastes extraordinary: apples are like sweet wine, and the honey mead tasted of flowers and long-ago summers. I had to loosen my belt when I'd finished eating, feeling fat and round, full as an egg. Flissy, Nest and I cleared up, while Taliesin and Gwydion banked up the fire and settled the cows in the byre for the night with fresh water and sweet hay. Then we sat around in the firelight and made plans.

'I've talked to Anwen who does the laundry at Castell Du,' Nest laid logs on the fire and sparks crackled and flew. 'Apparently Astarte's got a young woman looking after the baby. Anwen said that you mustn't worry, she's good at her job, knows what she's doing. She's got a baby herself, and she's feeding both of them. Cariad will be fine—at least, until Astarte's got what she wants.'

'We'll see she doesn't get *that*,' I said, grimly. 'What about Iestyn and the others?'

'Ah.' Taliesin shifted in the high-backed settle. 'There we have a problem. They are locked in a dungeon, according to Anwen, although they haven't been harmed. They aren't exactly comfortable, but they are being fed, so for the moment they're safe enough.' He picked up a stray piece of wood and tossed it into the fire. Brân moved uneasily at the sudden flare. 'Our main problem is that Astarte has put some kind of barrier around Castell Du. I shapeshifted and tried to get inside, but I was thrown back. Until we can break that barrier, we can't get in, and we certainly can't get Iestyn and the others out.'

'A barrier? What, like a force-field, you mean?' Taliesin nodded. I stretched out my toes to the warmth of the fire. 'So what can we do?'

'Tomorrow,' Taliesin replied, rubbing Garan's ears, making him close his eyes ecstatically, 'we shall go back, and take you with us, Tan'ith. Armed by the Lady, you will be able to tell what Astarte's done.'

Now, at this point I should have started to twitch, right? Turned pale green and shaky and started wishing I was somewhere else, preferably a long, long way away? But I didn't. I wasn't scared. Maybe the Lady's Book had fixed my worry-wart. Maybe I was getting braver as I got older. Weird, or what?

Chapter 6

Next morning, mind, I felt a bit different. Not *scared* exactly, but sort of fizzy and butterfly-ish around my middle. When we'd eaten, Taliesin, Gwydion and I shape-shifted into starlings, Nest opened the door of the *tŷ hir* and we flew out, circled once to get our bearings, and then headed for the castle, sinister on its crag above the sea.

The closer we got to the Castle, the stranger the air felt—sort of thick and silky. We landed in a small stand of trees at the foot of the hill, and, once we were sure no one in the Castle could see us, we shifted back to ourselves. It was odd. In one place among the trees, the air felt fine, but in another, it felt different, a bit like finding a warm patch when you're swimming in a cold sea, you know? The Castle was surrounded by a thick blanket of unpleasantness and we couldn't seem to get past it. The closer we got to the Castle, the thicker it got. Someone, somehow, was stopping us getting inside.

Gwydion slipped deeper into the trees, away from the invisible barrier, and Taliesin and I followed.

'What can we do?' I asked. They both looked at me. Taliesin raised his eyes to heaven and Gwydion sighed.

'We were hoping,' Taliesin said, absently scuffling the toe of his boot in the leaf-mould, 'that you could tell us!'

'Me?' I said, 'why me?'

'Because you are Ynys Haf now, Tanz,' Gwydion said, shaking his head and speaking slowly, as if he were talking to a half-wit. 'You have the Book! Ynys Haf herself will tell you what you have to do. Tune in to Ynys Haf, Tanz!'

'Tune in?' I said, crossly. 'I'm not a transistor radio, Gwydion.' And then I realised that I kind of *was*. I just hadn't been *listening*, that was all. Once I realised and—oh, all right Gwydion—tuned in, things changed. My feet tingled: I could feel every earth-worm, mole, and beetle underneath; underground streams stroked my soles, Ynys Haf's every tiny vibration was tuned in to *me*! When I closed my eyes, I felt dizzy, as if I was floating in space.

'Ah,' I said, opening them quick before I fell over. The feelings were like pieces of jig-saw, but I didn't know which bit went where. I took a deep breath, put my hands on the bark of the nearest tree, and closed my eyes. Roots squirmed down, tiny tendrils stretched and wriggled through brown loam, and a tunnelling mole wove its single-minded way between the roots— towards Castell Du! I let go the tree and grinned.

'There's a barrier right round Castell Du, but luckily Astarte seems to have forgotten the under-ground bit. There's a mole heading for the Castle right now, underneath Astarte's magic barrier. So if we shift into something small and burrowy, we can get inside too, no problem.'

Within seconds we were small creatures in dusty velvet coats, virtually blind, but with a totally amazing sense of smell! I sniffed: earthworms! Yum! Fat-and-pink-and-wriggly-and-juicy! We dug swiftly down towards the castle, efficient little digging machines, dodging roots, poking our hard noses into the soft earth, pushing our way onward with determined, spade-like front paws. I found out that moles are grumpy little creatures. I pushed away at the cold earth, and mostly what I felt was this filthy temper!

Anything that got in my way was going to get bitten, very hard. Luckily, nothing did. Except an earthworm. Which I ate. I don't think I'm ever going to eat spaghetti again . . .

Our three side-by-side tunnels reached the castle walls almost at the same time, and, sensing each others' vibrations, Taliesin and I dug towards each other until we met in Gwydion's hole, in the middle, where we had a conference. Moles couldn't dig through thick stone walls, but there were some handy cracks that would certainly let in something a bit smaller—a beetle, say. Eventually, after a lot of scrabbling-in-the-dark, we found ourselves in a network of passageways underneath Castell Du.

They weren't very nice passages, even for beetles. They were cold, and dank, and dark. Doors led off every few yards, thick dungeon-type doors with iron bars. Taliesin, Gwydion and I scuttled towards one and peered through the gap under the door. The cell was filled with men, but none of them was Iestyn, so we scuttled along to the next, and the next. At last, there was Iestyn Fawr. He was thin and his dark beard was black against his pale face. My Mam would have reached for her saucepans and her bakestone, straight away, to feed him up. Iestyn lay miserably on a heap of straw, chained to the wall by a metal cuff around his ankle. I shot under the door towards him, and ran into a drift of stale straw—which saved my life.

Where there are dungeons, there are usually rats . . .

The big brown brute leapt across the floor at me, but caught a wisp of straw instead of me, missing me by the width of my left feeler, that's all! I scrambled for the door, and safety, but the rat was fast, and I

46

could smell its horrible breath right behind me. And then the rat lost interest in me, because Gwydion had turned back to Cat, and was advancing on it with a hungry look in his slitted eyes. I shut mine, quick, and when I opened them again, the rat was stretched out dead on the floor, long yellow teeth protruding from its half-open mouth, and Gwydion was shimmering into human form. Taliesin and I followed suit, quickly, and Iestyn, grinning from ear to ear, struggled clanking to his feet.

'My Lords, Lady Tan'ith!' he said, and Taliesin laid his finger across his lips.

'Softly, Iestyn Fawr,' he whispered. 'There are ears about.'

Iestyn nodded. 'Someone should keep watch. The guards will be back soon.'

Taliesin went to the door and peered out, checking the passageway in both directions, while Gwydion and I squatted down beside Iestyn. I kept a wary eye out for rats, but I think Gwydion probably gave off enough essence of Cat for them to stay well away.

'What happened, Iestyn?' I asked, and the big man frowned.

'Well, Lady, I've been sort of keeping an eye on that Astarte since you left. She've been well tucked up for best part of a year, now, and right unhappy she've been about it, too. She don't talk much, you understand, but she don't half *look*!' Iestyn chuckled. 'Anyway, there I was down by the Door a bit ago, and I noticed the leaves of the Lady's bush was getting a bit limp, like. I gave it a bit of a water, see if I could perk it up, but the next time I went there it looked even worse. Last Wednesday sennight, I went and had another look, and blow me if the bush wasn't dead as that rat over by there, and the Witch standing next to it as cool as you please. "Ah, Iestyn Fawr," she says, and next thing I know I'm stuck to the ground like I've tooken root myself! She insulted me a bit, and then a little while later, along comes Rhiryd Goch and—' He stopped, and looked uncomfortable. Gwydion and I exchanged glances.

'What, Iestyn?' Gwydion asked, and Iestyn shook his head.

'Herself, Dragonson. You-know-who. All thick black hair, and nasty, beady black eyes. Her. You know.' Iestyn didn't seem to want to say the name. 'Tell you what, I'm not ascared of much, Taliesin, but Herself . . .' He shuddered. 'Even that Astarte don't give *her* any back-chat, and she'm related, look!'

'Merch Corryn Du!' Gwydion said, softly. 'The Lady was right.'

Iestyn went pale. 'You said her name, Gwydion! Now there'll be trouble.'

Gwydion smiled, but there wasn't a lot of ha-ha-ha about it. 'Astarte must be desperate if she's had to bring in the Spiderwitch. She's not your usual cuddly granny, is she?'

Iestyn still looked thoroughly unhappy. 'Begging your pardon, Gwydion,' he said, 'but are you sure you're strong enough to fight Merch Corryn Du, the daughter of the Black Spider? She's a terrible powerful woman.'

Taliesin spoke from the doorway. 'Don't worry, Iestyn. Tan'ith has the Lady's Spirit of Ynys Haf. The Power is in her, now. Can't you tell?' Iestyn turned his head and Looked. I *hate* being stared at! Then he smiled, his big face crumpling with relief.

'Now you tell me, Lord Taliesin, she do have a shiny sort of look.' He reached out and patted my shoulder. 'You'll do it, then, Tan'ith. Even Merch Corryn Du is no match for you if you've got the Power.'

I sighed. Other people went to primary school, comprehensive school, did their G.C.S.E.s, their 'A' levels, and went to university, no problem. Like following signposts straight down the road, no messing. And then there was me, bang in the middle of revising for my G.C.S.E.s, finding myself in the Island of Summer, having to take on Astarte again, and her spidery great-great-ever-so-many-greats-Granny into the bargain. Is that fair? It's all very well being magic, but all it seems to bring me is problems. I can't use it for anything useful, like learning chemical formulae, or the horrible rules of mathematics, or French vocabulary. It just means I keep getting into sticky situations with nasty people. Who'd be a witch, I ask you? And what about this new enemy? Was she *really* spidery? I don't like spiders. I crossed my fingers and hoped it was just a name, and she didn't actually have eight hairy legs and fangs dripping with venom . . .

Gwydion had been watching my face, and I think he knew what I was thinking, because he was grinning. I felt myself go red. 'Shut up!' I mumbled.

'Didn't say anything!' he said, smirking even more irritatingly than before.

'No, but you thought it,' I said, crossly. Iestyn, bemused, rattled his chains, reminding us that while we were bickering, he was still attached to a very cold, damp wall.

'We'll get you out,' Gwydion said, 'but it will mean some—er—adjustments . . .'

49

'All of us?' Iestyn scrambled to his feet, his chains rattling; 'I won't go without my lads, Dragonson, I . . . Adjustments?' he said, suspiciously. 'What do you mean, adjustments?'

'All of you,' Gwydion replied. 'But you'll need to change.'

'Change how?'

'Well, we had a bit of difficulty getting in,' Gwydion said, 'because of a barrier of magic around Castell Du. We had to tunnel underneath, you see, Iestyn, and then come in through the walls. And if we're to get you out, then you all have to go back out the same way . . .' Iestyn's eyes went big and round, and he had started to shake his head when Taliesin hissed a warning from the door. We all three shifted quickly back to beetles, and scuttled into Iestyn's pile of smelly hay to hide.

Heavy footsteps echoed in the passageway, a key turned in the lock, and the barred door groaned open, revealing the stocky figure of Rhiryd Goch. Iestyn, pretending sleep, lay in his straw. Rhiryd Goch strode across the dungeon and kicked Iestyn hard on the leg. Iestyn sat up, slowly, rubbing his eyes.

'Wake up, *mochyn*,' Rhiryd Goch growled. His skin was tanned dark against the fox-red hair, reddish-brown eyes glittered, and his nasty, thin mouth was framed by what my Mam would have called a 'tiddy little beard'. If you can imagine a shortish, muscular, much, much nastier Henry VIII, that's Rhiryd Goch! Iestyn shifted back out of kicking reach.

'Still here, I see?'

'Where else would I be, your Lordship?' Iestyn rattled his chains. 'With these on, I'm not going far, am I?'

Rhiryd's foot lashed out again, and I started to get cross. Iestyn was now my uncle-by-marriage, and nobody picks on my family!

'Keep a civil tongue in your head, *mochyn*!' Rhiryd snarled. 'Haven't you realised yet that you are bait? The tethered goat to draw the wolves? When the Bard, the girl and the Shapeshifter come for you, we'll have them. So sit quietly, goat, and bleat as much as you like. The sooner they hear you, the better. And when we've got them, and made them give us the Grimoire and the Spellorium, and Ynys Haf is mine—why, then we'll slit the goat's throat, just for fun.'

I took a deep breath, and concentrated. I could feel my temper building, and I was trying very hard to remember a good zapping spell—and then Gwydion wrapped his feeler round mine, silently communicating through our joined antennae. 'No, you idiot! Not now. CALM DOWN, TANSY!'

Reluctantly, I calmed, fizzling a bit with fury, but I knew Gwydion was right. We had to get Iestyn and the others out and find Cariad first, and then I'd sort Astarte out—permanently. This would be the last time I'd ever let her interfere with *my* life. Eventually, after another kick and a bit of a prod at Iestyn with his sword, Rhiryd Goch went, and the three of us shifted back again.

'I don't care how you get me out,' Iestyn said grimly, 'just do it, all right? Just don't tell me, first. Surprise me, like.'

'The other men are in two other dungeons,' Gwydion explained. 'We'll shift you, then we'll go and explain to the others, and then the whole bunch of us will get out the way we got in. Will they panic?'

51

Iestyn shook his head. 'I don't think so, Taliesin. They know magic, even if not personally, themselves, like. They won't panic.' Taliesin changed Iestyn to a large black beetle, and the four of us scuttled next door, shifted, and explained to the dungeon full of startled villagers what was about to happen. Then, followed by a small army of black beetles, we poured under the dungeon door, and into the second cell, where we made more beetles. With me leading the way, we headed for the crack in the wall and freedom.

I stuck my beetly head into the crack and stopped. The air was thick, treacly, and foul. The barrier now reached *below* the walls of Castell Du. We couldn't get out. We were trapped.

Chapter 7

Gwydion ran into the sticky air at about the same time as I did, and backed out of the crack in the wall just as fast. Behind us, queues of beetles ran into each other like cars in a traffic jam. Tiny voices said 'watch out, clumsy,' and 'mind my foot, you oaf!' and just plain 'ouch!' in beetletalk. They milled about, a glossy black moving pool, and I realised that if Rhiryd Goch or one of the guards happened along, they'd soon know something was going on.

'Quick, back to the dungeons, everyone, while I think what to do,' I said. Obediently, the lake of black beetles became a river, pouring back into the cells, where Gwydion and Taliesin changed everybody back. Now that I had time to look at them, there were some familiar faces—especially small, round, grumpy Sion ap Sion, who had been so unenthusiastic about me last time I'd visited Ynys Haf. Sion was huddled together with another man, his hair so fair that it was almost white. They were talking, and Sion wore a bad-tempered, disbelieving expression.

I got cross. 'If you're going to say that little short haired girls with spotty dapples on their faces ain't no good in a crisis, Sion ap Sion,' I snapped, 'let me point out right now that (a) I am no longer little, (b) my hair is no longer short, and (c) I may have freckles but I also have the Lady's power. So if you've got anything to say, say it so we can all hear it, or shut up, all right?'

Sion went bright scarlet behind his vast, droopy moustache. 'I weren't sayin' nothin' nasty, Lady! I were just saying to Eifion Gwyn here how fortunate it is, like, to have you with us again.' The white-haired man looked startled.

'*I* knows, Lady,' Sion continued, 'that while you be with us, us'll be all right. I 'spect,' he said, but he wouldn't meet my eyes. Behind his back, Gwydion winked.

'Now,' I said severely, 'If you'll all be quiet for a minute and let me—um—use my powers, I'll try and find some way of getting us out of here.' It didn't cross my mind for a minute that I was taking over from Taliesin and Gwydion without so much as a by-your-leave. The Lady's power had not only made me braver, it had also made me dead bossy. (Although T.A. would probably say I was bossy enough before.)

I shut my eyes, and concentrated, holding the Arianrhod ring against the emerald pendant. First, my toes tingled. Then, the feeling crept up my spine. The sounds of the castle faded away, and I could hear the rustle of trees outside, the movement of creatures in long grass, the clap of a flighting pigeon's wings, and the squeak and rustle of a harvest mouse building a nest in a cornfield. And then, clearer than any of the other sounds, came the sweet sound of rushing water, becoming louder and louder until it took over my whole head.

I opened my eyes. 'Gotcha!' I said, and grinned. 'We should have thought of this before, Gwydion. Astarte forgot that some things go deeper than dungeons. Right in the middle of the courtyard there's a nice, deep well, with an lots and lots of nice, fresh H_2O sloshing round in it.'

Eifion Gwyn cleared his throat. 'Aitchtoowoe?' he said uncertainly. 'Beggin' yer pardon, Lady, but we 'as mostly water in our wells, Lady. If you don't mind me sayin' so.'

'Sorry, Eifion. I meant water. I was just being clever, that was all.'

'I see what you're getting at, Tansy,' Gwydion rubbed his chin, 'but we've still got to get this lot through the castle, out into the courtyard and down the well—without anyone noticing.'

I hadn't thought of that. Taliesin rested his arm lightly across my shoulders. 'I think Tan'ith is right, that's the way out for us, but we'll need to be careful how we go. How many of us are there?' He counted heads, quickly. 'Twenty-one. Right. If we divide into three groups of seven, Tan'ith will lead one group, Gwydion the second, and I shall lead the last. We shall need to change you back to beetles until we get over the rim of the well, and then into something, um—' I knew what he was getting at.

'Something that can get through the well safely,' I finished for him. They were only just getting used to black beetles: frogs might be the last straw! 'Right, ready?' I gave Sion ap Sion my Best Stare. 'Are you coming in my group? Or don't you trust me enough?'

Sion ap Sion smiled weakly. He was much too nervous of me to refuse, and Gwydion snorted with laughter, which he rapidly turned into a cough. Gathering the seven twitching men around me, I made them link hands, black-beetled them and led them towards the crack under the door. On the threshhold I paused, peering up and down the corridor to make sure no one was coming, and then we all scuttled out along the wall.

We made good use of whatever cover there was, scrambling one at a time behind tapestries, through rushes, along cracks at the bottom of walls, and at last, even under the long skirt of a serving woman who probably would have had seventy different sorts of conniption if she'd known that eight black beetles were scuttling along under her clothes! Unaware, she took us safely to the Great Hall, full of scratching, fighting dogs, and off-duty men-at-arms swapping tall stories, unstringing bows, polishing armour and sharpening various unpleasant-looking metal weapons. At the far end of the hall the door to the inner courtyard loomed, and beyond it was the well. A flash of black and white wings caught my eye, and I saw, just to the right of the door, Astarte and a cluster of chattering, sewing women. I wasn't exactly *scared,* but my beetly heart thumped a bit when we got close. She hadn't changed much: I wondered how tall she was these days, but couldn't tell because she was sitting down. She was still gingery, and rat-faced, and still had those weird odd-coloured eyes. She hadn't changed much. She was sitting on a stool, looking downright miserable, which made me feel good. Anything that made Astarte miserable was fine by me. She crouched at the feet of a strange, black-haired woman, seated in an ornate high-backed chair, the magpie cockily perched on the back. As I scurried past I sneaked a peek from under the dusty hem of the serving-woman's dress.

The strange woman was thin, and sat very straight. Her thick black hair was wound around her head in a massive coil, as if she'd taken a medium sized python, tied it in a knot, plonked it on her head and stuck long jewelled pins in it to anchor it. Her skin was pale, almost greenish, as if she didn't often see sunlight, and she was eating something with a longhandled spoon from a deep golden dish. In between mouthfuls, she was wagging her spoon angrily at Astarte, telling her off, and the more she nagged, the more miserable Astarte became, and the happier I felt, which was probably rotten, but I don't care. Anyone as horrible as Astarte Perkins deserves to be miserable. The swish of the servant's skirt and the distance made it hard to eavesdrop, but I could hear the woman's low voice hissing on, and Astarte replying 'Yes, Granny. No, Granny.'

Granny! It was the Spiderwitch! I almost tripped over my front pair of legs trying to turn round to get another look, but it was too late. We were at the door to the courtyard. The servant went into the dairy, so eight beetles crouched in between the cobblestones blinking in the sunlight. The well was about three metres away, and waving my antennae for the others to follow, I headed for it, and led the way up the low wall. At the top, I looked around to make sure no one was watching, and changed us all into small green frogs. 'Ribbit!' I said, meaning 'Jump!' Six frogs obeyed: Sion ap Sion sat on the edge like a weedy kid afraid to jump into a pool. I hopped across to him and ribbited at him severely. He shut his eyes and stayed there. He looked quite funny, because somehow the spell had missed a bit of him, so there was this frog with a HUGE moustache! Then, out of the corner of my eye I spotted movement in the doorway to the Great Hall. A big black and white bird swooped towards us, iridescent blue flashing beneath strong wings. 'Magpie!' I ribbited frantically, and shoved, hard. Sion plummeted down the dark well, croaking frantically the whole way, and belly-flopped into the water at the bottom. I leapt after him, and the magpie perched on the rim of the well, squawking angrily at a missed meal.

The water was cold, and I swam round in the dimness until I'd found all seven frogs, then dived down and down, the others following me. The well was fed by spring-water, and we followed the icy, pure stream underground until we reached the source, a few hundred yards outside the castle on the lower slopes of a mountain. As the last frog popped out I changed us all back, and then we waited for the others. It seemed ages before Gwydion arrived with his lot, and the sun was beginning to go down by the time Taliesin and his, including Iestyn Fawr, arrived. The men were pleased to be out, and there were lots of hugs and slaps on backs, that sort of stuff. Then Sion ap Sion, looking as if every word hurt, spoke up.

'I has to say I'm thankful, Lady.' He rubbed his

nose, making it redder than ever, and his moustache quivered. 'I don't 'spect we could've got out of there withouten you. Leastways, not so quick, like. But now I've said my piece, I'm a-goin' 'ome.'

I opened my mouth, but Gwydion beat me to it. 'Fine, Sion ap Sion. And tomorrow morning, or maybe even tonight, Rhiryd Goch's men will batter your door down and take you again. Now THAT would be a waste of our time, Sion ap Sion, wouldn't it?'

Sion ap Sion blushed, polishing his bald head with his hand. 'Well, we can't sleep in no woods, my Lord, that's for sure. We'll catch our deaths, this weather. 'Tis on'y early Spring, after all.'

'He's right, Gwyd,' I said. 'Is there anywhere else they can go?'

Gwydion looked at Taliesin, and raised his eyebrows. Taliesin shrugged. 'Up to you, Gwydion.'

Gwydion stared at his shoes for a bit, and then gave me a curious look. 'There is a place,' he said. 'But it is not a place to be entered lightly. But I promise you will be safe there—if you swear never to speak of it once you leave.'

Sion ap Sion turned pale. 'Not—?' he said.

Taliesin nodded. 'It is the only place in Ynys Haf where Rhiryd Goch and Merch Corryn Du can't get at you. So either you take your chance and sleep cold, Sion, or you stay in warmth and safety.'

'Safety is as safety goes,' Sion ap Sion muttered.

Iestyn interrupted. 'Taliesin's right. We'll be safe there, and then our wives and children won't be worrying about us. It's my decision, Sion ap Sion, and yes, on my head be it, before you say it! The Cave it is, Gwydion.'

58

Cave? Gwydion and Taliesin led the way up the mountain. Walking was puff-out-of-breath at first, then ow-I've-got-a-stitch, and finally, it was downright climbing boulders that looked like bodybuilders on steroids, muscling their way out of the bare earth. They had a no-nonsense look about them, those boulders. My knees were wobbling like jellies by the time Taliesin stopped. A great, smooth boulder stood in his way, and he stepped aside to let Gwydion go before him on what was only a path if you were 99% mountain goat.

Gwydion went up to the boulder, put his right hand on the left side of it, and pushed. Not hard, just the gentle sort of push you give a door to shut it not too noisily. And the boulder *moved*! It rolled aside, revealing a dark cave-mouth.

'Move over Aladdin, here comes Gwydion,' I muttered, impressed. Gwydion stepped into the entrance of the cave, and Taliesin and I followed.

Inside the mountain was a castle. Honest! A whole castle, inside a massive cave. Turrets, battlements, everything, all hidden away! The drawbridge was down, and walking towards it, I had this urge to hang on to Gwydion's hand, or the hem of Taliesin's jerkin, or maybe even both, but I gritted my teeth and pretended I wasn't scared stiff.

The castle had an un-lived-in look about it. Where Castell Du was obviously full of people—close up you could see washing flapping on the battlements, people hanging out of turret windows shouting at other people, children swinging on the drawbridge chains and chucking lumps of mud at guards, people going in and out with carts full of vegetables and stuff, and hunters coming back with clusters of dangling dead bunnies, or a deer slung across their saddle, busy, busy, busy. But this castle breathed silence.

'Does Sleeping Beauty have anything much to do with this place?' I muttered, and Gwydion grinned.

'Not exactly. But have you noticed the battlements? And the gatehouse?'

I looked. Now that he mentioned it, there was a weird sort of thick, rounded bulge around the top of the castle walls, which went from the left-hand turret to the one on the right, and then wound to the top of it, ending in an arrow-shaped spike. The gatehouse was huge and triangular, with curious pointy white things top and bottom. It was, I gradually realised, the open mouth of a very realistic looking stone dragon, seen from the side, so that visitors had to walk from one side of the mouth to the other, across the teeth, to get into the courtyard. The neck, body and tail wound round the castle as if it was protecting it. There is NO WAY, I said to myself, that I'm going in there.

Strangely, however, I carried on walking. At the top of the drawbridge I stopped. I didn't want to walk inside those huge, gaping jaws, even if the dragon was made of stone. The walls of the gatehouse were red, like the inside of a mouth, but there was a courtyard beyond. Gwydion put his arm round me.

'Remember that question you've been meaning to ask for so long?'

'The "Dragonson" question?'

'That's the one.'

'You're going to tell me you're a dragon's son.' I looked at him, uncertainly. 'You can't be. Can you?'

'Why? I can be anything else I want to be!'

My legs got wobblier. We passed through the awful,

jagged gatehouse. I didn't want to believe that my Gwydion had anything to do with a place as terrible as this.

The strange thing was that, as we neared the end of the tunnel, the feeling changed. It stopped being scary, and empty, and lifeless. I heard voices, laughing, which grew louder, and stamping, blowing horses, and hawks squawking in the mews. I opened my eyes. There was sunshine, even though that was impossible inside a mountain. The courtyard was full of people. Smiling people. They moved aside to let us pass through, and the women bobbed into curtsies, and the men, shuffling and grinning, doffed their hats. Eifion Gwyn and Sion ap Sion weren't quite clutching each other, but looked as if they'd rather like to.

At the foot of a flight of steps into the great tower of the castle, Gwydion stopped. The huge iron-bound and heavily studded door at the top swung open, and Gwydion dropped to one knee.

'Nhad!' he said, joyfully.

Chapter 8

Pardon? Excuse me? *Esgusodwch fi?* His Father?

In the doorway waited a tall man. His cropped hair, although there were silver streaks in it, was dark, and his eyes shone vividly blue, as if lit from within. And now I knew where Gwydion had got his nose from! They were very, very alike—except that Gwydion's father was kind of transparent . . .

He was *there* all right, but *not there* at the same time. A bit like a hologram, but more so. Gwydion rushed up the steps three at a time. They stared at each other, and then the older man smiled.

'You've grown, my son,' he said at last, his voice deep as a bell. 'Are you better behaved than you used to be?'

Gwydion blushed. Taliesin, who had followed him up the steps, dropped to one knee and bowed his head respectfully, although I could see he was grinning.

'I can vouch for him, DragonKing. He is everything you would wish in a son, and you can be proud of him. Even Merlin is ready to forgive him at last.'

'And has the Time come? May I sleep?'

'He has one more task, sire, and then you may rest.'

Gwydion's father turned his head to look at me, standing at the foot of the steps. 'You are Tan'ith?' I nodded. 'And you? Have you the courage to help my son reach his destiny?'

It was out before I could think, honest. 'No Sir. I'm scared stiff. I'm not brave. When God passed out brave, I was last in the queue, and there wasn't much left by then.'

He let out a great shout of laughter, and I turned red.

'Well, Gwydion? Is she a coward?'

Gwydion ran down the steps, grabbed my hand and towed me up. 'She's a fully paid up member of the cowards' union, Nhad, but I'd trust her with my life.'

Close up, Gwydion's father wasn't quite so scary even if he was see-through. His eyes were bright and kind, and had those little lines in the corners that only come from laughing a lot. My Dad has them too. I found a bit of courage from somewhere. 'I may be scared, Sir,' I said, 'but it's my niece that needs rescuing, and I won't let Astarte have her. Or the Grimoire and the Spellorium, either—I suppose that's what she wants as a ransom. It's what she usually wants.'

The tall man looked steadily at me. 'I can see that you have the Lady's powers, Tan'ith. If she has given them to you already, so far ahead of the appointed time, then your enemy is not only Astarte. Your own magic is more than enough to deal with someone like her. So who, Gwydion?'

'Merch Corryn Du, Tad. I think she has lost patience with Astarte, because she used Rhiryd Goch to kidnap the baby, and to do that . . .'

'To do that,' Gwydion's father's dark brows came together in an angry scowl. 'To do that, she has given him magic. So Rhiryd Goch keeps that power for one full moon's passing. That worries me. But not as much as Merch Corryn Du. She is the one you must fear, Tan'ith. Don't ever forget that. She is the real enemy. Only when she is gone will Ynys Haf be safe.'

I took a deep breath. 'I'll do my best, I promise. We must get our baby back first, though.'

Ddraig Ynys Haf gazed at me steadily, as if he was trying to read my mind. Then he smiled. 'Now, Gwydion, who are your companions?'

Taliesin answered. 'The good men of Ynys Haf we rescued from Rhiryd Goch's dungeons. If they go home he will take them again. Will you give them your protection, please?'

Gwydion's father turned his head and looked thoughtfully at the silent huddle of men at the foot of the steps. He really was incredibly like Gwydion. He also apparently had the same sense of humour. He spotted Sion ap Sion trying to hide behind Eifion Gwyn, and not succeeding because his enormous whiskers stuck out so far.

'Sion ap Sion? Come here, Sion ap Sion. Let me look at you.'

Sion, his knees wobbling so hard I could see them shake, tottered obediently up the steps.

'*Yma*, DragonKing,' he said squeakily, like a four-year-old starting school, then said it again, louder, trying to make his voice deeper so he wouldn't sound quite so terrified. 'HERE, DragonKing,' he boomed unconvincingly.

'Do you seek shelter with me, Sion ap Sion?'

'Um. Yes. Please, Sire.'

'Aren't you afraid, Sion ap Sion?'

Sion ap Sion munched his moustache unhappily. 'Yes, my Lord. I s'pose. But I ain't safe outside, either, am I, thass fer sure. Lord Taliesin says I'll be safe in by 'ere, so I s'pose I'll be all right.' Then he obviously had an idea. It was like a cartoon light bulb going on over his head. 'If you says I'll be all right, DragonKing, sire,' he said craftily, 'then I cert'nly will be, won't I? Nobody's goina argue with you, look.'

Gwydion's father shook his head solemnly. 'You're safe with me, Sion ap Sion. But—' He bent down close to Sion's ear '—be careful of the gatehouse dragon. He hasn't been fed for a while and he has a passion for small, round, bald men with big moustaches. He eats them like pickled onions.'

Sion ap Sion gulped and turned pale. 'Beggin' your pardon, my Lord, but can I go inside now? Please?'

DragonKing stood back and threw out his arm. '*Croeso i Gastell y Ddraig!*' he called, loudly enough for the waiting men to hear, 'Welcome to Castell y Ddraig. You have my protection, and it is gladly given. Come inside.'

The rescued men trooped slowly (and sort of unwillingly) up the steps and into the castle, and Gwydion, Taliesin and I followed them. Once inside, they were surrounded by servants and men at arms, some obviously old friends.

We were in a great hall, hung with tapestries and lit by huge coloured windows, so that the sun shone through the bright glass in fractured sections of colour, lying like jewels on the tables and rush-strewn floor. A vast Irish wolfhound loped towards us and sniffed suspiciously at my ankles. I didn't mind him sniffing— I just hoped he didn't want to *taste!*' He didn't: when I sat down he flopped contentedly at my feet. He was the same brindled brown as Fflur. I wondered if she was missing me.

The hall was full of soldiers and servants, just as the Great Hall at Castell Du had been, and they were doing much the same things: polishing, sharpening, gossiping, gambling. Unlike Gwydion's father, they were real people, there was no doubt about that, they were all there, not transparent and ghostly . . .

The hair stood up on the back of my neck and I went Very Cold. I looked at Gwydion. He was staring at me, steadily. His father was speaking to a burly man in the corner, giving orders. 'Gwyd,' I began, shakily, 'is he?'

'My father has been dead for nine hundred years, Tan'ith, treacherously poisoned by Rhiryd Goch's father. I am the Dragonson. When I am ready, I will be DragonKing in his place.'

My hair wasn't showing any signs of lying down. 'If he's dead, Gwydion,' I whispered, 'then how come . . .?'

Taliesin overheard. 'This is Ynys Haf. The Lady comes and goes at will: you know that. DragonKing is long dead, but until Astarte and Rhiryd Goch are driven from Ynys Haf for ever, he cannot rest. That is our task, to free him. This time, we must finish Astarte and Rhiryd Goch once and for all. That's why the Lady gave you the Book: she has almost nothing left, barely enough to protect herself. She can't help you this time. All she can do is watch. It's up to you, Tanz. You're strong enough. Are you brave enough?'

'I'm brave enough to deal with Astarte and Rhiryd Goch,' I said, 'but what about Astarte's Great-Great-Granny? What if she's given Astarte the same sort of powers the Lady's given me? What then?'

Gwydion leaned on the table, staring at his hands, clasped in a shaft of brilliant blue sunlight slipping through the window. 'I don't think she will, Tanz. Look at the dumb things Astarte's already done!'

'What, lending Rhiryd Goch her magic?' Gwydion nodded.

'Yes. The thought of him with half an hour's magic is bad enough. Rhiryd Goch with a whole month's worth is scary. No, Spiderwitch won't trust her.'

'So that means,' I said, slowly, 'that we have to fight Astarte, Rhiryd Goch, AND the Spidery Great-Great-Granny from Hell, right?'

'Right!' Gwydion said grimly. 'Think you can do it, Tanz?'

I started to think about it, and then decided, the same as usual, that I wouldn't, not right then, anyway.

66

If I *thought* about it, I might just roll up in a ball like a hedgepig and want to go home.

'Probably not,' I said. 'But I'll have a jolly good go. Nobody pinches my little niece and gets away with it!'

We were interrupted by a girl, bringing us almondy biscuits and sweet apple wine. I tried to forget that I was sitting in a dead king's castle eating bickies: the whole thing was so unreal, I couldn't wait to get back to T.A. to tell her! We left afterwards, and walked from the sunlit, impossible courtyard out through the dragon-mouth gate into the dark outer cave. I touched the great coils of the dragon's neck (when I was safely outside!) and was relieved to discover that it wasn't warm or scaly, but cold and smooth as marble.

Outside the cave, Gwydion, Taliesin and I shape-shifted into foxes and set off towards the *tŷ hir,* running swiftly through the woods and along the edge of fields on silent pads, our glossy brushes streaming like flames behind us. When we arrived, we shifted back, and bashed on the door to be let in. Flissy opened it, her face anxious.

'Are they safe? Is Iestyn—'

I gave her a hug. 'Iestyn's fine, Aunty Fliss!' I reassured her. 'They're all safely out, and tucked away where Rhiryd Goch can't get them.'

'Where?' she asked, and I opened my mouth to tell her, but Gwydion interrupted.

'They are safe, Fliss,' he said softly. 'They are with my father.'

Flissy's mouth fell open, and she went pale. 'In Castell y Ddraig?' she whispered. 'Will I ever have him back again?'

'Of course you will,' Taliesin chimed in.

'DragonKing is sheltering them: as soon as it's safe they can come out, I promise. We may need their swords before this is done. And besides, Sion ap Sion is there, and he would drive a saint to drink.'

'And my father is no saint,' Gwydion muttered.

'That he is not,' Aunty Fliss agreed. 'Your father, Gwydion, is—was—is—a brave man, but in his youth he had a very bad temper, and even now he doesn't suffer fools gladly.'

'Which is why he handed me over to Merlin to bring up when Mother died,' Gwydion said, grinning.

Taliesin chuckled. 'Unfortunately Merlin's temper is even shorter than your Father's.'

'Which is how you ended up being my Cat!' I said. 'What did you do to Merlin to tee him off, Gwyd?'

Gwydion shook his head, pretending to be ashamed. 'All I can tell you, Tanz, is that it involved his best socks, two large cabbages, a bucket of water and a toad.' He grinned, remembering. 'A big toad. That was a long time ago, though. I'm so well-behaved now I can hardly believe it.'

'Neither,' Taliesin said dryly, 'can I.'

*　　*　　*　　*

We were sitting around the table late in the afternoon, making plans to get Cariad out of Astarte's clutches, when I heard a strange noise. It seemed to come from outside my head—and inside it, both at once. 'What was that?' I asked. 'I heard something.'

The others stopped talking and listened.

'What?' Gwydion looked mystified. 'I didn't hear anything.'

'Neither did I.' Taliesin said. 'What was it, Tanz?'

68

I frowned, trying to think. 'It sounds daft,' I said, 'but it sounded just like someone—um—opening a can of Coke! That sort of "phsst" noise, you know?'

Gwydion looked puzzled. 'What would make that noise? You must be imagining it, Tanz.'

I shook my head. 'I didn't. I heard something.'

Nest, who had been milking the cows at the byre end of the *tŷ hir,* came in to the people-end carrying a wooden pail of milk. 'Don't forget that Tansy has the Power of Ynys Haf,' she said mildly. 'If she says she hears something, she hears it. Whatever it was.'

We all sat round and looked at each other.

Nothing happened.

'You must have been mistaken, Tanz,' Gwydion said after a while. 'There's nothing.'

Nest brought pottery beakers for us and filled them full of mead. I picked mine up and sipped it. Then I noticed there was a spare beaker on the table, and Nest, a small smile on her face, was filling it from the jug.

'Why . . .?' I began.

Someone bashed on the door.

Chapter 9

We all stared at each other. 'Open it,' Nest said. 'I think you've got a visitor.'

'Who, me?' Mystified, I went to the door, lifted the heavy latch and pulled it open.

A seriously weird person waited outside. It wore a big grin, a purple T-shirt, jeans and a sideways baseball cap, and it carried a bulging Tesco carrier bag.

69

'Hiya, Tanz!' T.A. said, 'your mouth's open. You look just like a goldfish. Can I come in?'

I shut my mouth and stood aside to let her in. 'How——? Why——? What——' I spluttered.

'You only need "Who?" and "When?" and you'll be able to write the perfect essay-according-to-Miss Lloyd-Jones, Tanz,' T.A. said, cheekily. 'Oh, Nest, it's lovely to see you again. And Aunty Fliss, and Brân and Garan.' She put down her carrier bag and braced herself for the onslaught as the dogs launched themselves at her, licking and whining. 'It's brilliant to be back! Hiya, Gwyd, hi, Taliesin.'

Gwydion and Taliesin looked at each other. 'T.A.,' Taliesin said very slowly, as if he was trying to hold on to his sanity, 'what are you doing here?'

T.A. fended off Brân's wet tongue and shoved at Garan, who was trying to sit on her lap. 'Wow! You know, it was the weirdest thing! I was really down because you left me behind. I kept worrying and worrying about you. I got this peculiar feeling that you might need me for something—even if it's only biting a Druid's toes, Tanz! I was lying in bed, and all of a sudden there was the Lady! Right in my room, lighting it up, the way she does, you know. I thought I was dreaming, but I pinched myself, and I wasn't. Look, Tanz, there's the bruise, see?' She showed me a dark mark on her arm.

'Get on with it, T.A.! You can show me your bruises later.'

'Oh. You might be a *bit* sympathetic. Well, anyway, the Lady said that you'd made a mistake, leaving me behind. She said I had a part in it all and had to follow you. So here I am!'

Gwydion, Taliesin and I all looked at each other. 'T.A.,' Gwydion said, gently. 'How did you get here? The Doors between the worlds are sealed, remember? Except the Deep one we came through. So how?'

'It was AMAZING! The Lady gave me a bit of her staff—she said I had to give the rest to you, after, Tanz— then she made me close my eyes and Think Ynys Haf. I had to remember the nicest bit I could think of, and concentrate really hard. So I thought about that morning when Aunty Fliss and Nest turned back the winter and made it spring, overnight. Remember how beautiful it was? All green and blue and dewdrops glinting in the sun. And next thing I knew, phhht! There I was, in the woods behind the *tŷ hir*. No time door, no flying. Just sort of "beam me up, Scottie"! And here I am. I walked down through the woods. Phhht! Just like that!'

'Phhht!' I said triumphantly. 'I knew it!'

Nest chuckled. 'I don't think that was what you heard, Tansy. I think T.A. brought something with her. Right, T.A.?'

I stared at T.A. Then I remembered what it was that we'd missed more than anything last time we were here. 'Big Macs, french fries and—'

'Coke!' Gwydion and Taliesin said together.

T.A. blushed. 'I had a quick slurp when I arrived in case Taliesin or Gwydion made me send them back. I only drank half, I saved the rest for you.' She took a plastic bottle from her Tesco bag and handed it over. I guzzled it, gratefully. You can get withdrawal symptoms if you go too long without junk food, you know?

Taliesin looked stern. 'And what else have you got in there, T.A.? You know you shouldn't really bring anything here that hasn't been invented yet.'

She opened the bag. 'I brought some presents and stuff. Fishing inside, she brought out a paperback book. 'This is for you, Nest. I found it in a little shop in Lampeter.'

When I saw the title, I hid a grin. It was a modern English version of "*The Herbal Remedies of the Physicians of Myddfai*". Nest took it, solemnly, leafing interestedly through it. She was much too kind to tell T.A. she had the original in her carved oak chest!

'And I brought some Doggychox for my lovely boys!' she said. 'Here, Brân, here Garan!' The hounds sniffed suspiciously at T.A.'s outstretched hands, and then decided to try them. Brân spat his out, but Garan was hooked, and tried to climb inside the bag, nose first. T.A. gave him a few more, then put the bag on the table. 'Not too many, bad boy!' she scolded, 'you'll rot your teeth!'

'And for you, Aunty Fliss,' she fished in her bag again, and brought out a huge bottle of rose-scented bubble bath, a container of washing up liquid, a packet of soap powder, and last of all, a can of bug spray. I laughed when I saw the last present. Aunty Fliss hated creepy-crawlies with a passion, and having the cows sharing the *tŷ hir* with us meant that there were usually a lot of them about.

'It's all right, isn't it?' T.A. said anxiously. 'I got the non-C.F.C.s sort of spray can, so they won't pollute the atmosphere or make holes in the ozone layer or anything.'

Aunty Fliss grinned. 'Honestly, T.A. These are the nicest presents you could have brought me.'

'The question is, how is T.A. going to help us?'

Taliesin wondered aloud. 'If the Lady sent her, she's obviously important in some way.'

'I expect we'll find out eventually,' Gwydion said. 'In the meantime, we wait.'

'And make plans to rescue Cariad.' I passed the coke bottle back to T.A. for her to finish the last bit. 'I expect Rhiryd Goch and Astarte know we're back by now—since we rescued Iestyn and the others. The question is, will they keep the magic barrier around the castle, or will they let it down to lure us in there?'

I suddenly realised T.A. was staring at me. 'What? Have I got a smut on my nose? Have I turned green? What're you looking at, T.A.?'

'Oh. Sorry. It's just—well, Tanz, you're kind of different. You've got a—I don't know, a *shiny* sort of look about you. A bit like the Lady, you know? You look more sort of grown up, too.'

Nest patted her hand. 'The Lady has given her the Book of Ynys Haf. It's inside her. She has the Lady's power, at least for a while. In fact, she more or less is the Lady, until she's finished what she has to do, T.A. But she's still Tansy, underneath.'

'No,' T.A. said, still staring at me. 'She's Tanz on top. It's underneath she's different.'

I was trying to decide whether I was hurt or not. 'You're still my best friend, T.A.'

'Yeah!' she grinned, and I knew everything would be O.K. 'Toadface.'

'Ratface!' I replied, and we pulled faces at each other.

'Honestly!' Gwydion sighed. 'You two!'

'But it's really, really great to be here,' T.A. said.

'Anything that gets me away from G.C.S.E. revision has GOT to be good.'

'Oh, crumbs! G.C.S.E.s! I'd forgotten all about those! How long have we got until—'

'The dreaded maths? When I left, two days.'

'Aaaargh!'

'You know perfectly well you've got all the time in the world,' Gwydion chipped in. 'In Ynys Haf you know it's elastic. It stretches out as far as you want it to.'

'That's all very well, but I'm hardly revising, am I?' I complained. 'And I really, really need to revise maths.'

'Don't worry about it, Tansy,' Taliesin said. 'Mr Pugh Maths-and-Science says you're not as thick as everyone thinks you are.'

'Thanks a lot,' I muttered.

Suddenly the dogs leapt to their feet, growling, as someone rapped sharply on the door.

'It's like Cardiff Station in rush hour in by here today,' Flissy complained. 'Now who's that?'

'What if it's Rhiryd Goch, looking for Iestyn?' I whispered, going cold and shaky, and Flissy stopped half way to the door.

'Quick, shift!' Gwydion ordered, and I grabbed T.A.'s hand and shifted the pair of us into sparrows. Followed by Gwydion and Taliesin, we flew swiftly up to the roof-beams and perched, our eyes watering in the smoke from the hearth and the sputtering rushlights.

Flissy opened the door, cautiously, and peered out. From where we were, I couldn't see who was outside, but then Flissy ushered in a plump young woman, wearing a shawl over her head.

'It's all right,' Flissy called 'it's Mali—from the village.'

One by one we flew down and shape-shifted back to ourselves. Mali squeaked and put her hands over her eyes when Taliesin appeared first, and didn't look as the rest of us changed. Nest patted her shoulder. 'It's all right, Mali. They're all back as they should be now. There's nothing to be afraid of.'

Mali moaned softly. 'I get scared with magic, Lady Nest, you know that. I don't mind it a long way off, but it frights me awful close up to!'

Flissy poured her a beaker of mead. 'Sit down, Mali. What is it? It must be something important, I know how nervous Taliesin makes you.'

Mali blushed. She was pretty, although she was a bit on the chubby side. Her dark hair was tied back in a neat bun, and she had lovely eyes, brown and deep as river water. Something told me that she wasn't quite as nervous of Taliesin as Flissy imagined: in fact, I think she rather fancied him. She kept on looking up at him under her lashes.

She sipped at her mead. 'I got some news, Lady Nest. You know I do the washing for the Castle? Them men-at-arms, I wish they'd change their socks a bit more often. They're disgusting by the time they gets to me. Honest, Lady, I—'

'What was the news, Mali?' Gwydion gently prompted.

'Oh. Yes. Sorry. Well, I was changing the linen in that Astarte's chamber this morning and I overheard her talking with Rhiryd Goch. I don't like that Astarte. English, she is, and shouldn't ought to be queening it here in Ynys Haf. That Rhiryd Goch's a nasty piece of work, too, but at least he's Welsh. Well, on his mother's side he is. I heard tell his grandfather was a wolf and his granny a vixen, which would account for the red hair and that. It's not good when a Welshman turns against his own, and I think—'

'Mali!' Flissy and Nest said sternly.

'Pardon? Oh. That Astarte knows you're here, Lady Tan'ith. And Dragonson and Taliesin. She's not happy, either. I don't know how you got them men out of the dungeons, but I'm awful glad you did. It's not right, keeping a yuman bean in a place like that. Catch their deaths, they will, all cold and damp and nasty. *Ach y fi!*' she shuddered.

'And?' Taliesin was getting cross.

'Oh. And they've tooken the babby away from the Castle. She isn't there any more, and the babby's nurse isn't, either.'

Flissy and I looked at each other, panic-stricken. 'Where have they taken her?' I asked.

'Don't know, Lady. I tried to find out, but I couldn't hang around too long in that Astarte's chamber, they was getting suspicious. I asked the nursemaid's sister, but she didn't know. Ever so upsetted, she is, she got really attached to the little 'un while her Megan was seeing after her. Noisy little thing, mind. Got a good pair of lungs, that babby.'

We'd forgotten to hide the brilliant pink plastic bottle of bubble bath and the aerosol container, and Mali spotted them. 'Is them magic?' she whispered.

Nest hid a smile. 'Very powerful magic, Mali. You must forget you've seen them. And now it's time for you to go, before anyone finds out you've been here.' She gave Mali a small parcel of herbs and a basket of

76

vegetables to take home to her mother. 'We know how hard it was for you to come here, Mali, and we're very grateful. You were brave. Now go back home and don't worry. Everything is under control. Now that the Dragonson is here, everything will be all right again, I promise.'

Mali slipped out of the door, pulling her shawl up over her head, and Flissy dropped the latch behind her.

'Now what?' T.A. asked.

Chapter 10

'We have to find Cariad,' I said. 'Nest, where's the scrying bowl?'

Nest fetched the beautiful, dark wooden bowl and filled it with water from the jug. She waited until the water stilled and then stirred it with her fingertips. The surface rippled like molten silver, and then calmed again. I sat back and waited for Nest to bend over it, but she stood back.

'You do it, Tan'ith.'

'Me? Why me? It's your bowl!'

Gwydion shifted in his seat. 'Tan'ith, you still haven't quite got the message, have you? You are the Lady, amazing as that might seem to anyone who knows what a dingbat you are. You're the strongest of all, even stronger than the Lady herself, at the moment. If anyone can find the baby, it's you.'

I seemed to be spending a lot of time with my mouth open lately. I shut it.

'Come on, airhead,' Gwydion said. 'Scry.'

Still not quite believing it, and not feeling in the least bit Lady-like, I bent over Nest's bowl. My breath rippled the surface of the water and I tried not to breathe on it, but holding my breath made me feel dizzy, so I shut my eyes. When I opened them again, the water in the bowl had changed. It was dark, dark, dark. And then a pinpoint of yellow light appeared, as if someone had lit a single candle. The light got bigger and bigger, and I was looking at a huge chamber with rough stone walls like the inside of a cave. It was filled with dark, heavy furniture, and in the middle of a pool of light, in a high-backed chair, her feet resting on a footstool, sat Astarte's Great-great-grandmother. She obviously didn't believe in dieting, because once again, she was eating something with a long spoon from a golden bowl. She finished whatever was in the bowl, and then helped herself to more . . . First, she put in three great spoonfuls of golden honey, then poured in thick cream, and then—my stomach *wriggled* in horror—a huge ladleful of live bumble-bees, the nice furry kind, like flying teddy-bears. I backed away from the bowl. 'She's eating bumble-bees, Gwydion!' I exclaimed, horrified. 'Why don't they fly away?'

Nest answered. 'Because their wings are gone. She caught them in her web. She's the Daughter of the Black Spider—remember?'

Suddenly I felt very sick and very scared. O.K.— Merch Corryn Du—but *I hadn't realised that she actually was SPIDERY!* Now if there's one thing that really, really spooks me, it's spiders. It's something about the gruesome way they scuttle across the floor, and their long, black, hairy legs, and their general *spideryness*. It's—ugh. 'I think,' I said shakily, 'that I'd like to go home, now.'

Gwydion put his hand on my shoulder. 'Tansy, you can't, you know that. How can you leave Cariad in HER clutches? You know you are strong enough to defeat her—the Lady has seen to that. You just need to be brave enough.'

My lips felt stiff. 'That's the hard bit, Gwydion. (a) I hate spiders, and (b), I'm not a bit brave.'

T.A., desperately trying to think of some way to buck me up, dived into her Tesco carrier bag again. 'Look, Tanz. Have a Crunchie. It'll cheer you up. And here—' she rummaged in her rucksack, leaning against the wall. '—here's the sprig of the Lady's staff. She told me to give it to you, but I forgot until now.' She shoved the piece of twig towards me. I took the twig, but couldn't face the Crunchie. The bright yellow middle reminded me too much of old Spiderwitch's disgusting pudding . . . I held the twig miserably in my fingers, perfectly certain that, twig or not, I wasn't going to be much good to anyone if spiders were involved.

Last time I'd been given a piece of the Lady's staff, it hadn't felt like anything except twig. A very special twig, a twig that budded, blossomed, and fell, and budded again in seconds, but very sort of twiggy. This time, as soon as I touched it, I felt the Lady's power come fizzing through my fingertips, up one arm and down the other, like an electric shock, and I yelped and nearly dropped it. You know the way they put those round electric things on people's chests to jump-start their hearts? Well the Lady's twig jump-started my courage. I felt brave now. Me!

I took a deep breath. 'Don't worry, Gwyd. I can do it. I think I know why T.A. was sent: without the Lady's twig I'd have been too scared to try, but She's sent me her courage as well. Right. Now we'll see if we can find Cariad.'

I stirred the bowl briskly, getting rid of Spiderwitch and her horrid eating habits. When the water stilled, however, we were back in the same place, but in a different corner of it. There was a carved wooden crib, and in it lay a small familiar figure. For once, Cariad wasn't screaming, she was playing with a toy dangling from a string over the crib. It was a large, black, hairy spider, and she chuckled delightedly, waving fat arms and legs, as she batted it to and fro. I hoped it was a toy spider, and not a real one . . . The back of the crib was carved with an intricate web, and carved wooden butterflies were stuck to it. Perched on the high wooden canopy was a large black and white bird, interestedly watching baby and spider.

'That's disgusting! I hope she isn't going to be marked for life by all this!' I said indignantly. 'Giving our baby spiders to play with and putting her in a spidery old crib! I'm going to have WORDS with Astarte Perkins.' I calmed down a bit. Cariad was obviously happy enough, and well-fed. 'O.K. We've found our baby. But where is she?'

'I know.' Nest's small, pointed face was pale. 'The Spiderwitch is keeping her under Cadair Corryn Du. Inside her mountain. And the only way to get her out is to go in and find her'

I *still* wasn't scared. 'O.K. So we've got to go after her. I can do that. I'm not scared any more.'

'That's good,' Gwydion said, grimly. 'Because it isn't

going to be pleasant. First, though, we've got to get into the castle and sort out Astarte and Rhiryd Goch.'

'Why?' I was puzzled. 'If we finish off the old bee-chomper first, we can soon sort out the one with the technicolour eyeballs.'

Taliesin picked up a wooden spoon and twirled it absentmindedly between his fingers. 'The only person who knows where Spiderwitch is, is Astarte. So first we've got to capture her, then we've got to make her tell us how to get to the Mountain. And that, Tan'ith, is not going to be easy. We have to *make* her talk.'

'Easy,' T.A. pulled a fierce face. 'First we pull her hair, then we kick her shins, then we offer to pull out all the hairs on her legs, one by one. She's probably got very hairy legs.'

'Great idea,' Gwydion ruffled her curly black hair matily, 'only, we're the good guys, T.A., remember? We can't do nasty things like that.'

'That's not fair!' T.A. yelped. 'They do! They were horrible to Nest, for a start.'

'And Rhiryd Goch kicked Iestyn and locked him up in a dark dungeon,' I agreed. 'Can't we torture Astarte just a little bit?'

'No, Tan'ith, we can't.' Nest gazed moodily into the scrying bowl, watching Cariad's plump legs waving in the air. 'We aren't like them, and if you try to be, then you will be bringing more evil to Ynys Haf.'

I subsided. 'I suppose you're right. So how do I get the information out of her? Ask her politely? "Now, Astarte dear, please tell me how I can find your Dear Old Great-Granny? Sure she'll tell me. Not.'

Gwydion shrugged. 'I expect once we've got her

something will come to mind. But first, we need to get her, remember?'

'And for that,' Taliesin put the spoon down and slapped his hand on the table, making me jump, 'for that, we need to get Iestyn and the other men to help us. We have to get inside the Castle unseen, overpower the guards, fix Rhiryd Goch, find Astarte and make her talk.'

'Just like that!' I said.

'Just like that,' Gwydion agreed.

It had grown dark outside, and owls were hunting, the triumphant 'kee-wick' that announced the death of something small and furry echoing through the trees. There was nothing we could do until daylight, and so we sat around the fire catching up on news, Taliesin stroking silver strands of music from his harp, his beautiful voice lulling us to calmness.

I was still trying to get used to the idea that I was (if only temporarily) the Lady. I hoped she was safe, since I had her power, and was hidden somewhere secure, where no one could get at her, because without that power, she would be almost helpless. I looked down at my hands, seeing my bitten fingernail (well, I can't be expected to give it up altogether—but I'm *cutting down*, O.K.?). I didn't *look* different, but I certainly felt it. I couldn't believe how confident I felt! Sort of 'stand back, folks, SuperTanz is coming through!' And powerful! Like I could bend iron bars and leap tall buildings at a single bound sort of thing. I felt eyes on me, and looked up to see Gwydion watching me. He had an odd expression on his face.

'What?' I demanded.

'Nothing. Only—tell me, Tanz, are you still worried about your G.C.S.E.s?'

82

I didn't have to think about it. 'Nope. I'll worry about those later. Right now I've got Cariad on my mind.'

Later, when I was up in the sleeping loft trying to get comfortable on the scratchy straw mattress on the wooden floor, I hoped she wasn't lonely, or frightened, or getting nappy rash or anything. I scowled. Just wait until I got my hands on Astarte and Rhiryd Goch . . .

Next day Taliesin, Nest and Flissy and I went about our chores in the *tŷ hir*, sweeping, dusting and washing clothes the hard way (they still hadn't invented washing machines). I filled the mangers for when the cows came in at night, and Gwydion mucked out the byre and spread fresh straw. Even though there were going to be some nasty things happening soon, it still felt so good to be back. The most amazing thing about having the Lady's power was that everything, all my senses, seemed sharper somehow. The colours seemed brighter, my hearing was so keen I could hear an earthworm tunnel under my feet, and the magic of Ynys Haf seemed to call out to me, recognise me, say 'Hey, Tanz, so this is where you belong!' I knew I didn't, of course, I had to go back to school quite soon and sit those lousy exams, but right then I had this lovely peaceful-welcome-home sort of feeling.

During the night, I'd had an idea, and over breakfast I shared it with the others. 'D'you think Mali would help us?' I asked, munching on an apple. 'Because I think I know how to get into Castell Du without having to fight.'

Gwydion paused, a chunk of cheese halfway to his mouth. 'You do? How?'

83

'Well, Mali washes the men-at-arms' smelly socks and stuff, doesn't she? If she will do it, who better to slip something into their bedtime cocoa but Mali? Or their morning coffee. Or their playtime milk and bickies. Then they'd all fall asleep, we wouldn't have to fight, and nobody would get hurt, would they?'

Flissy stared at me. 'Of course! Why didn't *I* think of that?'

'It's a good idea,' Nest said thoughtfully, 'but it would be better if we put a spell on their clothing. Everyone wears clothes, but not everyone eats and drinks the same thing, let alone at the same time. The trouble is, Mali is such a twittery little chatterbox I wonder if she would be able to manage it without telling everybody.'

'She would if you and Tansy went to talk to her.' Flissy began to clear away the dishes. 'You'd probably have to promise her something, mind.'

'Like what?' T.A. asked. 'She ought to do it for love of Ynys Haf.'

'She probably would, if you put it like that, but some people work better with just a little honey to sweeten things,' Flissy said, scraping plates into the compost bin.

'Don't talk about honey.' I shuddered, remembering the bumble bee pudding. 'I think it's a good idea, anyway,' I said. 'When shall we go, Nest?'

Nest took off her apron. 'No time like now, Tan'ith. And I think I know just what Mali would like to— um—encourage her to help us.'

The cottage where Mali lived wasn't far, and so we walked through the woods. Spring was late, but definitely on its way: buds were popping out in that wonderful limey green of new leaves, and the birds were going demented in every bush. Mali's cottage was small compared to the *tŷ hir*, but spotlessly clean. Outside, long clothes lines strung between trees held row upon row of shirts, socks, tunics, woolly jerkins and baggy sort of tights thingies. Mali was round the back, poking white cloth boiling in a big cauldron over a stone firepit. She brushed a stray lock of hair from her face with the back of her hand, saw us, and curtsied.

'Lady Nest!' she squeaked. 'And Tan'ith! Fancy you coming to see me. There's an honour!' She dried her hands on her pinny. 'Will you come inside and take some ale?'

'No thanks!' I said, quickly. I didn't like the taste of that stuff. But Nest said she would, and so we went inside the tiny, dark cottage. A very old lady, so wrinkled that she seemed to be made of crumpled brown tissue paper, sat in a corner, spinning on a wheel, the hum and click of it soothing and rhythmic.

'*Pwy sy wedi dod*, Mali? Who has come?' she called out.

'It is Nest, Mam. And the Lady Tan'ith.'

'*Croeso*, Nest, *cariad fach*!' The old lady beamed, her face crinkling even more, her white hair like dandelion clocks. 'That old stuff you did give me for my rheumaticals worked wonders, look! I can spin again, now!'

'I'm glad I could help. But you must forgive me. I will come and see you again soon, but now we must talk with Mali.'

Mali, looking nervous, fetched stools and poured ale into wooden goblets. She stood nervously at the end of the table, twisting her fingers in her pinny.

'Sit down, Mali, we've got something to ask you,' Nest said gently. 'We need you to do something for us.'

As Nest explained, Mali's eyes grew rounder and rounder. 'Who, me?' she squeaked at last. 'Ooo! I couldn't do nothin' like that, Lady! Not me! They'd catch me at it, and beat me, and torture me, and lock me in a dungeon an'—'

'*Taw a dy lol!* Don't talk rubbish!' The quavery old voice from the corner was stern. 'Pull yourself together, girl. You be careful, and keep quiet and don't chatter, and no one will know it's you. You should be honoured to do it for Ynys Haf!'

'That's all very well for you to say, our Mam,' Mali muttered. 'It's not you what has to risk your life delivering magicky socks and stuff, is it now? I got my living to think of, as well.'

Nest leaned forward and patted Mali's hand. 'If you do this for us,' she said softly, 'you shall have your heart's desire.'

'My—' Mali's eyes narrowed. 'How do you know about my heart's desire?'

'Nest knows everything,' I said mysteriously. 'Every. Single. Thing.'

Mali looked worried. 'Everything?' Nest nodded.

'Heart's desire, look, promise?'

'Heart's desire,' Nest agreed.

'What do you want me to do?'

Nest explained, and then she and I went outside to the washing blowing on the line. I took out the sprig of the Lady's branch and walked along the lines, touching each dangling garment with it, and thinking 'sleeeeep, sleeeeep, sleeeeep'. I didn't worry about it working— I had the Lady's magic. I knew it would. The laundry was dry, and so when we'd finished enchanting it we helped Mali sort and fold it, and pack it into baskets to take back on her horse and cart.

When we'd finished, Nest turned to Mali. 'Now,' she said. 'Which particular heart's desire do you want?'

Mali looked cunning. 'I thought you said you knew everything, Lady Nest.'

'I do. You have many heart's desires—some you don't even know about yet,' Nest replied calmly. 'Which one, Mali?'

She grasped her pinny firmly in her fists and shut her eyes as if she knew that what she wanted was beyond the bounds of possibility. It probably was. 'I-want-Taliesin-for-my-own-true-love,' she gabbled.

I groaned. Come back Heledd, all is forgiven, I thought. Nest didn't bat an eyelash.

'If you're sure that's what you want, Mali, you shall have him as soon as this little problem with Ynys Haf is sorted out.'

Mali gaped. 'I shall?'

'Certainly.'

I couldn't believe what I was hearing. I stared at Nest. She was promising Taliesin to Mali?

'Honest?' Mali still wasn't convinced.

'Honest. You know that the *tylwyth teg* don't lie.'

Mali beamed. 'He's ever so handsome.'

'He is,' Nest agreed. 'It's such a shame—but no, never mind. I promised you your heart's desire, and your heart's desire you shall have.'

'What?' Mali asked suspiciously. 'What's a shame?'

'Well, he does have this terrible habit,' Nest smoothed a folded shirt on top of a basket. 'But I don't expect you'll mind. Not since he's your heart's desire. What's a little problem like that if you've got your heart's desire?'

'Whaaaat?' Mali said, jumping up and down. 'What habit? What little problem?'

I began to see where Nest was heading, and hid a smile.

'He's one of the Old Ones, Mali. You know that.' Mali nodded. 'And he's a shapeshifter.' Mali nodded again. 'I'm just not sure how you'd cope with that side of things. You'd never know whether you were married to a bird, or a fox, or a rabbit—'

'—or a bug, or a snake, or a rat,' I went on.

Mali's eyes were popping out. 'Is it too late to change my 'eart's desire?' she asked, plaintively.

'No, of course not,' Nest said, patting her shoulder. 'How about that nice Dafydd ap Rhodri?'

'How did you know about him?' Mali gasped.

'Nest,' I said smugly, 'knows everything!'

Chapter 11

Mali delivered the washing first thing next morning. We had to hope it would work, because until we actually got inside Castell Du, we wouldn't know. I wasn't worried, though. I had so much confidence I felt nothing could go wrong.

But first, we had to get the men back from Castell y Ddraig. We would still need them to guard the enchanted men-at-arms, even if they *were* asleep And of course, since we weren't exactly in the hygienic nineteen-nineties with showers, and hot and cold running water out of taps, probably not all of them would change their shirts and socks every day, or even every week. Month. Or year . . .

Gwydion shapeshifted into a peregrine falcon and flew out the door of the *tŷ hir*, scimitar wings cutting the air, hurtling upwards, his grey-blue plumage and barred chest dwindling into the sky in the direction of the Dragoncave. About an hour later, T.A. spotted a flock of starlings circling overhead. They came in to land, shrieking and squabbling as only starlings can. As soon as the starling that was Iestyn Fawr changed back, Flissy ran into his arms, and I looked away, not wanting to spoil their reunion by peeking. I noticed that one of the arriving starlings had a bald head and a curious moustache of feathers sticking out above its beak. 'Hello, Sion ap Sion,' I said, as Gwydion shapeshifted him. He was complaining, as usual.

'Look, I knows that spotty-dapple girlie thinks she do know everything, but that Mali won't do things right,' he muttered. 'On'y a washergirl, that one, and none too bright in the 'ead. An' what if she do lose her nerve, like? We could all get killed, an' tortured, an' locked in dungeons, an'—.' His moustache quivered, and although he had been shape-shifted back, he was still flapping his arms.

Nest patted him on the back. 'Calm down, Sion. Mali won't let us down. And Tan'ith will be watching her very closely.'

This was news to me. 'I will?'

'It would make sense, Tanz,' Gwydion said reasonably. 'If you shapeshift and go into Castell Du at the same time as Mali, then you can keep an eye on

89

her, can't you? Make sure she doesn't make any mistakes—or start to chatter and let things slip.'

'And you'd better get going,' Nest suggested. 'Mali normally takes the washing back at around noon, and the sun is almost overhead already. If you shift into birdshape, you can follow her without her knowing. You can go in the main entrance, because if Mali can get in, you can, too.'

I took a deep breath and concentrated. I felt myself shrinking, my arms sprout feathers, my feet change into claws, a small, sharp beak replace my mouth and nose. I hopped to the doorway, spread my wings and flew towards Mali's cottage. She had already left, and I had to flurry to catch up with her, then, when I spotted her piled donkey-cart on the mud-track road leading to the Castle, hedge-hopped alongside, a small, friendly robin, too small and insignificant to notice.

As we neared the Castle, I noticed that the air had lost the thick, turgid feeling of Astarte's magic barrier: since we'd got the men out and Cariad was elsewhere she'd obviously decided she didn't need it any more.

Mali drove the patient grey animal up the steep slope towards the drawbridge, and I perched on top of one of the clothes baskets while she spoke to the sentry. Mali *was* a chatterbox. A steady stream of words poured from her, and the sentry rapidly gave up trying to follow her conversation and just waved her through the archway into the cobblestoned, bustling inner courtyard. At the door to the great hall, Mali climbed down from her cart and began unloading washing, carrying it inside where servant girls took it from her and set it on one of the long tables running down the sides of the hall. No one noticed the robin on the roof-beam.

90

A man in a brown jerkin wandered over and started fishing in one of the baskets, and Mali slapped his hand away. 'Just you wait, now, Wil Traed Mawr. Once Angharad an' me has sorted it, you can have your washing. Don't go crumplin' it up with your dirty fingers.' The man grinned, and ambled away, and Mali and Angharad began to sort the piles of clothing. When they'd finished, Mali collected dirty laundry in the empty baskets, and loaded them into the cart for the return journey. I flew outside the gate with her and landed on the cart, intending to hitch a lift back to her house, but the smelly socks were so awful I decided to fly!

Back at Mali's cottage I waited until she'd unloaded and gone inside, and then, out of sight of the windows, shape-shifted, not wanting her to realise I'd followed her. I knocked at the cottage door, and she opened it. Her ancient Mam was dozing in her chair, her mouth open, loud snores coming out.

'Oooh!' Mali patted her hair. 'I done it, Lady Tan'ith. I delivered the laundry like you said. I hope I'm not goin' ter get in trouble now.'

I shook my head. 'You won't. I know you've done what we wanted you to, Mali, and I'm grateful. You've helped the Lady, and Ynys Haf.'

'Thass as maybe, look.' Mali folded her arms. 'But Lady Nest promised I should have my heart's desire, din't she? I haven't got it yet, have I? An' I did what you asked, din't I? So when do I get my reward, like?'

'Right now.' I took a small green bottle Nest had given me out of my jerkin pocket. 'All you have to do is get this potion into whatsisname—Dafydd ap Rhodri. Put it in a drink, or in his soup, something like that. And then you'll have your heart's desire.'

Mali took the potion and stared at it, suspiciously. 'That's a very little bottle, Lady Tan'ith, beggin' your pardon, innit? Dafydd's a big man, nearly two beansticks tall, and fine set up, as well. Is this yer little bottle goin' to be enough?'

I put on my best scowl. 'That potion, Mali, is one of Lady Nest's finest. *One drop* will fix him. I must go, now. Thank you for your help, Mali. But I must warn you. You mustn't say one word about what you did, not to anyone. If you do—' I thought frantically for something horrible enough to scare even talkative Mali into silence '—if you tell anyone, and I mean anyone, Mali, the potion won't work, you won't have your heart's desire, and you'll very likely get dreadful zits—all over your face.'

Mali looked puzzled. 'Zits?'

'Boils. Pimples, Carbuncles—and Spotty Dapples!'

I think she believed me! I said goodbye and left, deciding to walk back to the *tŷ hir* rather than shapeshift again, partly because it was a nice day, and partly because I wanted to think about something. I wasn't entirely certain that giving Mali a love-potion for Dafydd ap Rhodri was—well—fair. What's the word? You know—ethical. I mean, she may have fancied him rotten, but was it right to make a poor, unsuspecting male fall helplessly in love with someone as totally dim as Mali? Wasn't it taking away his—I don't know—his free choice? I still hadn't forgotten the awful results of the love-potion I'd fed Heledd's boyfriend, and what had happened after. I shuddered, remembering Mam ticking me off after that! She'd said that it was wrong for us magical people to meddle in ordinary people's lives, and that things had a way of

92

going terribly wrong if we did. And now we'd done exactly that.

The long shape of the *tŷ hir* appeared through the trees and I speeded up, anxious to get back.

Nest was in the byre, milking, the steady swish of the milk gushing into the leather bucket acting as a rhythm section to the song she was singing to the cow. I went round the front end and stroked the inquisitive, velvety nose. The cow snuffled at my hand, then returned to the manger full of hay.

Nest looked up. 'Something troubling you, Tansy?'

'Mmm.' I leaned on the wooden rail and looked at my hands. 'I know we've got to get Cariad back and save Ynys Haf, but I'm a bit worried about Mali and that Dafydd ap whatsisname. Is it fair to make him fall in love with her? Are we allowed to do that? Isn't it meddling in people's lives?'

Nest grinned up at me, pure mischief lighting her eyes. 'It would be. It would be the sort of thing we really shouldn't ever do—if we'd done it.'

I was puzzled. 'If we'd done it? I just did it, Nest. I handed over the potion, and Mali's going to pour it in his cocoa, and bob's-yer-uncle, right?'

'Wrong.' Nest straightened up, brushing a strand of dark hair back from her face with her forearm. 'What you gave Mali was a little green bottle full of honey and water.'

'But isn't that cheating?'

'Tansy, I know Mali's heart's desire. I also know that Dafydd ap Rhodri has been in love with Mali for ages. Only he's so shy he won't go near her, and Mali, being traditional, is waiting to be asked. What will happen is that Mali will have to go to *him* to get the

93

"potion" into him, and then Dafydd will pluck up courage—especially since he's survived Castell Du, being shapeshifted and a stay in Castell y Ddraig, he'll be feeling amazingly fearless—and Mali will assume it's the potion working, and encourage him, and before long Mali will have her heart's desire!'

I started to giggle. 'That's cheating, Nest! I didn't think the *Tylwyth Teg* cheated!'

'We don't. But we're the sneakiest folk you'll ever find anywhere.'

When Nest had finished milking and I'd helped her turn the cows out into the pasture and refill the mangers for the morning, we went back into the people end of the *tŷ hir* to start getting supper. T.A. was up in the sleeping loft, tidying, and Gwydion, Taliesin and the other men were out secretly visiting wives, girlfriends and children in the village and collecting weapons left behind when the men had been captured by Rhiryd Goch. I wondered if Dafydd ap Rhodri was with them, and if Mali would seize her chance.

Nest gave me a pile of leeks to chop, and I remembered Mam's electric food processor with longing as the pungent fumes stung my eyes. T.A. came down the ladder and was given the job of slicing carrots. By the time the men came back a vast venison stew (back to eating Bambi's Mam, folks!) was bubbling on the fire.

The *tŷ hir* was filled with sleeping bodies that night, and I peered over the edge of the loft, looking at the rows of humped, snoring bodies scattered all over the floor. It sounded like a church organ gone berserk down there! Brân raised his big head and looked at me, his strange, light eyes friendly.

Nest woke me early, and together we crept into the back of the *ty hir* away from the snores so that we could scry what was happening in the Castle. We knew that the men at arms changed duties at six: half of them would get dressed (we hoped in clean clothes!) and go on duty, and the other half would go to bed.

I'd hoped that the other half would put on nightshirts, but I quickly found out that they didn't. Those that didn't sleep fully dressed except for their armour just undressed to their baggy under-knickers, or to nothing at all (I shut my eyes for that bit!) and got into their beds. Which meant that half the men— about thirty of them, fully armed—and Astarte and possibly Rhiryd Goch, whom we hadn't been able to find yet—would be fast asleep but not at all enchanted. We'd need the village men, all right!

One by one, they began to wake, and Nest, Flissy, T.A.and I got them breakfast. It's weird, isn't it, that even though Flissy and I are Daughters of the Moon, and I have the Lady's powers, and Nest is half *Tylwyth Teg*, and T.A.was—well, if nothing else T.A. was a *bit* magic for the time being, we females still ended up doing the cooking! *And* Sion ap Sion complained his porridge was burnt! If it was, it wasn't my fault. There aren't any switches to turn down the heat on an open fire.

While we were collecting bowls and cutting bread, I asked Nest which of the men was Dafydd ap Rhodri. She pointed out a tall, gangly young man, the sort Mam would call 'a yard and a half of pump water' with big, awkward hands, a red face, and hair like yellow straw sticking out all round his head like a thatched cottage.

'What, him?'

'Him.'

'Not much of a heart's desire, is he?'

Nest chuckled, then stared me straight in the eyes. 'Not compared to yours, certainly.'

'Mine?' I was startled. 'I haven't got a heart's desire, Nest.'

'Yes you have. You just haven't realised it yet.'

Rubbish, I thought. Nest and her mysteriosity! How would she know?

'I,' she said softly, as if reading my mind, 'know everything. Remember?'

We cleared away the dishes, and left Aunty Fliss, T.A. and Nest to wash them. T.A. muttered a bit, but when I promised I'd do them after the evening meal, she subsided.

Taliesin, Gwydion and I led the men outside and checked that they were properly armed. Then we shifted them back into starlings and, changing ourselves, flew towards the Castle. The sun was warm, and fat clouds like piles of whipped cream floated around the sky. It felt good to be out and flying, and it was a pity we had to go into the Castle and start tangling with the baddies. I suddenly realised I wasn't afraid. Now that, as Mam might have said, was a turn-up for the book! This was the point at which I usually started clucking and flapping, pure chicken, and all I was actually feeling was slightly cross that I couldn't stay out all day enjoying myself doing aerobatics! We reached Castell Du, and our small army flew up to the battlements, where Taliesin told them to wait while he, Gwydion and I had a look around. We shapeshifted into mice, and scuttling close to stone parapets, keeping to the shadows, made our way around the battlements to check on the sentries— who were all still wide awake.

'The magic didn't work!' I groaned. 'What do we do now?'

'It's not like throwing a switch, Tanz.' Gwydion stopped and washed his whiskers. 'If they all fell over as soon as they got their socks on, then the ones who were still getting dressed would get a bit suspicious, wouldn't they!'

'I suppose so.' We were crouching next to a fat sentry, who was leaning on a long, sharp-looking pike thingy. He scratched his head, pushing his leather helmet up to do it. He yawned, and then, slowly, slowly, his eyes drifted shut, and he fell asleep, snoring gently, standing upright against the wall.

Chapter 12

'Right,' Gwydion said. 'That's the first. If we wait a while, they'll all drop off, one by one.'

We loitered in a dark corner at the top of a twisty stone staircase until Gwydion was fairly sure that every sentry with enchanted socks on would have dozed off. Then we scuttled back to where the flock of starlings perched, twittering and arguing, and shape-shifted us all back.

'Right,' Taliesin adjusted the scabbard of his short-sword. 'The first thing we have to do is tie up the sentries. That way they can't wake up and come looking for us.'

Sion ap Sion muttered something to Eifion Gwyn, and I saw Mali's heart's desire, Dafydd, nodding agreement.

'Have you got something to say, Sion ap Sion?' I asked, coldly. He was really beginning to bug me. 'If you have, then please say it so we can all hear. It's rude to whisper, you know.'

Eifion Gwyn, his white hair gleaming in the shadows, pushed in front of Sion ap Sion, who was scowling at me.

'Begging your pardon, Lady, but me and him thinks us ought to finish 'em off while us've got the chance. No sense tying 'em up, look. If us gets rid of 'em now, us won't 'ave no problem with 'em in the future, will us?'

Sion nodded in agreement. 'Stands to reason, look!' Dafydd said.

Taliesin stroked his chin. 'I can see the sense in what you're saying, Eifion Gwyn, and you, Sion ap Sion, but if we start killing people unnecessarily, we'll end up as bad as they are. And bad people can't rule Ynys Haf. And if we are as bad as Rhiryd Goch and his men, then we won't be worthy of Ynys Haf, will we?'

Dafydd ap Rhodri thought hard, then turned to Eifion Gwyn. 'Lord Taliesin's right, Eifion Gwyn. If we don't have to kill 'em, we shouldn't, look. So let's just get on with tying 'em up. You can tie 'em up *very tight* if you like, if it'll make you feel better.'

Sion ap Sion uncoiled a rope from his shoulder and took out a small, sharp knife. 'I *will* tie 'em up tight, Dai. An' I'm goin' ter use big, uncomfortable knots, I am, look.'

I hid a grin. 'That's great, Sion ap Sion. Right.

Everybody ready? Meet back here when the job's done.'

Taliesin slipped off towards the sea-coast wall of the Castle, and Gwydion and I went to the South wall, where the sentry, a dreamy smile on his face, was still leaning, fast asleep, on his pike. I carefully removed the weapon from under his chin, and Gwydion caught him as he fell. We tied him up (securely, but not too tightly) and left him snoring happily. We did the same to four more sentries, and then slipped back to the meeting point where the others were beginning to gather.

Dafydd ap Rhodri drew his sword and waved it about. 'Say the word, Dragonson, and we're ready. To the death for Ynys Haf.'

'Ah.' Gwydion carefully caught the blade of the sword and pushed it gently down. 'We aren't going crashing into battle, Dafydd. We're going to try to keep as many of us safe as we can. And if you charge into the great hall waving a sword about and shouting, then you are going to attract a lot of attention and end up very dead very soon.'

Dafydd frowned. 'I ain't goin' to creep around like no bandit, Dragonson. I'm a warrior, I am. I never went round stabbing nobody in the back, and I ain't goin' ter begin now, look.'

Gwydion put his arm across his shoulder. 'Nobody's asking you to, Dafydd. But we have magic, and if we use it wisely, then less blood will be spilt on both sides. Right?'

Dafydd nodded, reluctantly. 'Magic.' He looked faintly worried. 'Ah, magic. Well, Dragonson, to tell you the truth I'm getting a bit fed up with bein' beetles an' frogs an' stuff. Couldn't I be something a bit more—I dunno—heroic, like?' His face brightened. ''Ow about a wolf, now. I'd be a good wolf. I could leap on their backs snarling and tear 'em limb from limb before they even got their swords out.'

'You'd be an amazing wolf, Dafydd,' I agreed. 'I mean, it totally terrifies me just thinking about it. But don't you think a wolf in a castle might be—well—a bit sort of *noticeable*? And once you're spotted, it wouldn't be five minutes before every hunting man in Castell Du was chasing you. Mind,' I frowned, and tried to look serious. 'if we change you into a wolf, you'd be a wonderful decoy, wouldn't you! Everyone would be so busy chasing you with sharp swords, and long spears with blades like razors, and knives, and bows and arrows, and—'

'Ah,' Dafydd swiped his hand back through his hair, making the thatch stick up in all directions. 'Perhaps you're right, Dragonson. What did you have in mind, like?'

'Actually,' Gwydion replied, 'I thought cats. There are lots of cats in Castles, to keep down the rats and mice from the stables. If we're careful, no one will notice a couple of cats.'

'They'll notice twenty-four of 'em, though,' I said.

'Yes. So we'll have to go in groups of seven, like before. One of us will go with each group, we'll find where the men are, and then shapeshift them so that we can overpower them and tie them up.'

'Can't we . . .?' Sion ap Sion said, hopefully, taking his knife out of his belt.

'No!' Gwydion, Taliesin and I said together.

We shapeshifted them, and ourselves into an army of

100

moggies, and divided ourselves into groups of eight. Taliesin took Sion ap Sion, I took Eifion Gwyn, and Gwydion took Dafydd ap Rhodri, so that we could keep a close eye on them, and then we poured, a twisting river of multi-coloured fur, down the staircase where we divided and went our separate ways. I led my group into the guardroom where the sentries that had just come off shift had collapsed onto their mattresses on the floor. It was a small, hot, smelly room, with just one arrowslit high up on the wall letting in daylight. There were eight sleeping men. Silently, I shifted my small band back to human shape. Eifion Gwyn's white hair shone like a snowy owl's in the darkness. And out of the corner of my eye I saw him slip his dagger from his belt. I was at his side in an instant, and whipped it from his hand. 'No!' I said. 'No bloodshed, Eifion Gwyn.' Two at a time the sleeping men were overcome, and when they were all tightly tied, we shifted back to cat-shape and went on to the great hall. One or two men were lying around playing dice, or talking, but there were eight others sitting in a group drinking ale and eating, their weapons close to hand. I knew we would never manage to take them all out at once. Then I remembered the Lady's twig. I told the other cats to spread themselves out in the hall, and try to blend in. Eifion Gwyn spotted a mouse, and shot off after it, but the mouse was too quick, fortunately. But his swift pounce drew the attention of some of the soldiers, so that the other cats were able to slip unobtrusively into the hall under tables, on windowsills, curled beneath chairs, to watch and wait. And nobody notices a cat, keeping still. Eifion Gwyn sheepishly sat in the straw and, the way cats do when they're embarrassed, began busily washing himself.

I slipped across the hall and down the stairs into the buttery, where there would be village women. Sure enough, in the cool room where the great round cheeses were stored, three of the village women were at work, churning butter and turning the cheeses so they'd mature evenly. While their backs were turned, I shape-shifted. One of them turned, and startled, squeaked aloud. 'Shh!' One of the village women I recognised—I think her name was Angharad—grabbed her arm and shook her. 'It's the Lady Tan'ith! Be quiet. Do you want to give her away?'

The one who had squeaked pulled her apron over her head and burst into tears.

'Sorry, Lady Tan'ith,' Angharad said, putting her arms round the weeping girl, 'only she was looking after the babby, and now they won't let her see it except three times a day to feed it. She's all of a to-do, she is, what with missing it, and getting took out in the middle of the night. Smack on midnight, it is, and next morning she's still got to get up, same as always. She don't know if she's coming or going. What's happening, Lady? Are our men safe?'

I nodded. 'They're with me. They're all safe, and we're trying to overcome the sentries without setting off any alarms. We need Astarte. Where is she?'

'Sooner you get that one and sort her out, the better,' Angharad said, folding her arms. 'She's a nasty piece of work, she is. Not a nice bone in her body! She's sleeping late, like always. What with her Great-Great-Granny come to stay, she's up all hours of the night. Merch Corryn Du goes out as soon as it's dark, and we don't see hide not hair of her until dawn!'

'Right. Angharad, can I borrow your skirt,

headscarf and pinny? I need to get out in the hall without being recognised.'

Angharad untied her white headscarf and pinny, and passed them over. The skirt and the apron-strings went round me twice, since Angharad was roughly the shape of a cottage loaf, and I arranged the headscarf to hide my face and hair. I borrowed a wooden tray and some leather beakers, filled a large earthenware jug full of ale, took a deep breath, and ventured back up the stairs to the great hall. Outside the door, I took a small piece of the Lady's staff from inside my jerkin and slipped it into the jug, where it floated on top of the liquid.

I went to the two men first, thinking that it would be less noticeable if they fell asleep, and put beakers down and filled them with ale. One of the men put his arm round my waist and I clouted him swiftly round the ear, making the other one laugh. The clouted one, muttering, picked up his drink and swigged it. Within minutes first one, then the other, fell asleep.

Now the table with the men playing dice and talking. Eight of them. I put the tray down on a table and filled the beakers with ale, and, keeping my head down so that they wouldn't see my face, I put seven down in front of seven men who picked them up and swigged absentmindedly. I put the last beaker down in front of the eighth man. He caught my left wrist as I picked up the heavy tray and turned to go and before I could stop myself, I looked up, straight into the tawny eyes of—Rhiryd Goch!

'You aren't Angharad!' he said, suspiciously. 'Wait a minute. Don't I know you? You're—Guards!' He stood and yelled at the top of his voice, still hanging on to my wrist while I tried to pull free. Of course, none of the Guards came, although one of his drinking companions at the table looked up blearily.

'Thass orl ri', my Lord. She'ss pretty 'nuff,' he managed, before keeling over and falling fast asleep with his nose in his bread and jam.

Rhiryd Goch looked at me, his face dark with anger. 'What have you done, Moonwitch?'

'That,' I said, cheekily, 'is for me to know and you to find out.'

'And I will, don't worry,' Rhiryd Goch snarled, dragging me off in the general direction of the dungeons 'I shall make you tell me anything I want to know.'

Ve haf vays of makink you talk! I thought. I didn't like the general idea of being locked up and tortured, it didn't sound like a nice way to spend a sunny afternoon at all. But Rhiryd Goch was bigger than me, and he was holding me tightly. Then I remembered the tray, which was still in my right hand.

Now I *know* we aren't supposed to use violence. *I know,* all right? But what else could I do? I raised the tray over my head and brought it down on Rhiryd Goch's head.

Byoinnnng. Goodnight, Rhiryd Goch. He went face down in the straw. From all round the room cats converged on me, and I shape-shifted them back so they could tie up the sleeping—and unconscious, in Rhiryd Goch's case—men-at-arms.

As soon as Eifion Gwyn was back in human form, he started. 'Oh, very nice, I'm sure. "No weapons, Eifion Gwyn. We're the good ones, Eifion Gwyn. No bloodshed, Eifion Gwyn." All right for some people, though, innit?'

I put my face very close to his. 'Look, Eifion Gwyn. There was nothing else I could do, all right? If I hadn't bashed him he would've . . .'

'He would've been overpowered by all of us, if you'd thought to change us back,' Eifion Gwyn said bitterly. 'No thought, some people. Always thinking of themselves.'

'I forgot you were there, O.K.?' And I had, too. Like I said, nobody notices an unobtrusive cat. And I'd gone and broken Taliesin's no violence rule. I glanced guiltily at Rhiryd Goch, who was tightly trussed up like the others. He had a huge bump on his head, and he was snoring loudly, but he seemed to be all right. Unless he's got concussion, I thought. Or a fractured skull. And dies.

Gwydion's voice came from behind me. 'All done?'

I nodded, miserably. 'Yes. Only I went and bashed Rhiryd Goch over the head. I'm sorry. I didn't think.'

Gwydion knelt beside the fox-haired man and examined him. 'He'll be all right. Hardest head in Ynys Haf, Rhiryd Goch. He'll probably wake up with a bit of a headache, but that's less than he deserves. He stole Cariad, Tanz, remember?'

I remembered, and felt a bit better. But I'd let my concentration slip when I panicked. I'd have to take more care in future.

Taliesin appeared with his seven men. 'Where's Astarte?'

Angharad appeared in the stairway from the buttery wearing a large white cloth wrapped round her.

'Oh, sorry, Angharad. You want your skirt back.' I stepped out of it and handed it over, together with her headscarf and pinny. 'Which is Astarte's room?'

'You just let me get dressed, Lady Tan'ith, and I'll

take you up. Time that young madam got her come-uppance.' She scuttled down the stairs to the buttery and reappeared tying her apron a few minutes later. 'This way.' She led the way out of the great hall on the seaward side, across a courtyard and up a flight of spiral stairs.

At the top of one of the square turrets looking out to sea were two chambers. The door to one stood open, and the room was dark and sinister.

'That's where Merch Corryn Du sleeps,' Angharad whispered, 'when she's here. And I can tell you, I'm rightly glad when she isn't. That one,' she pointed to the closed door 'that's where Astarte sleeps.'

'Right. You'd better go back downstairs, Angharad. You'll be safe there,' Gwydion suggested.

Angharad looked disappointed. 'Aw. I'd hoped . . . Can't I stay if I keep quiet? Nasty piece of work, that Astarte. Not polite with the servants, you know? I'd really like to see her get her just desserts, so I would.'

Taliesin turned her firmly around and pointed her down the stairs. 'I'm sure you would, Angharad. But there's likely to be magic flying around, and sometimes magic has a kind of permanent effect on people. And I wouldn't like to see you end up as a frog or a snail. Right?'

Angharad scuttled down the stairs. 'Right, my Lord!' she said, her voice echoing up behind her.

Gwydion stepped forward and put his hand on the great iron latch to Astarte's room . . .

Chapter 13

Big letdown. She wasn't there. There were an awful lot of dirty clothes, though, scattered all over the place, and a jug of mead had been upset on the wooden floor so that it had dribbled between the planks and dried to a sticky mess. The bed hadn't been made, and on the table beside it was a bowl full of sticky sweets—not, I was relieved to see, honey-dunked bumble-bees. In the darkest corner a large cage covered in a grubby skirt stood on a table. Using the very tips of my fingers, I lifted the skirt to see what was inside the cage. The magpie's beady eyes stared malevolently back at me. For once the magpie was somewhere Astarte wasn't.

'Oh.' I was disappointed. (See how brave I was? There was a time when I'd have been relieved she wasn't there.) 'So where is she?'

Gwydion looked round the room, curling his lip in distaste. 'How can anyone be so messy? This is disgusting.'

My room at home may have been untidy. Well, it was, actually. But it certainly wasn't dirty. And there may have been clothes and stuff everywhere, but I knew where everything was, and it was regularly mucked out once a week. This room didn't look as if it had seen broom or duster in a month of Sundays.

Taliesin picked up a discarded skirt from the floor, wiped a chair with it, and sat down. 'Not the world's tidiest person, I agree. But where is she?'

'If we get back to the *tŷ hir,* we can use the scrying bowl,' I suggested.

'Which would mean a wasted journey if she's

107

somewhere in Castell Du and we just haven't found her yet.' Gwydion was pacing the floor, thinking. You can always tell when Gwyd is thinking, because you can hear the wheels going round.

Taliesin bent over and picked up the skirt he'd used as a duster. 'What about you using your divining powers, Tanz?'

'My what?'

'Divining powers.'

'Didn't know I had any.'

'You didn't before the Lady gave them to you,' Taliesin said. 'What you do is hold something that belongs to a person and concentrate on it. And then you should get a picture of where they are.'

I surveyed Astarte's skirt dubiously. 'Do I have to actually *touch* the beastly thing? Can't I just look at it, very hard?'

Gwydion sighed. 'Yes, you have to touch it. Unless you'd rather use her comb, or her hairbrush, or her chamber pot . . .'

'Yuk. Pur-*lease!* O.K., give me the skirt.' I took it gingerly between my fingers and closed my eyes, concentrating. Nothing happened. I took a firmer grip and got a hazy, wobbly picture. It looked vaguely familiar, and then it clicked into focus sharp as a T.V. screen. It was T.A., outside the *tŷ hir*, bending down towards something. Then she picked up whatever it was, turned away, and went back indoors. With her back to me, I couldn't see what she was carrying, so I opened my eyes.

'What?' Gwydion asked.

'Well, I've just seen T.A. outside the *tŷ hir*,' I said uncertainly. 'She picked something up and carried it inside, but her back was towards me and I couldn't see what it was.'

Taliesin grabbed my shoulders. 'You saw T.A.? Then Astarte is close to her. Close your eyes and turn around, Tan'ith, quickly.'

I did as I was told, and grabbed the yucky skirt tightly. Suddenly I was in front of T.A., and I saw that nestled down in her arms was a small, shorthaired white kitten. 'Oh. It's O.K.,' I said with relief. 'It's only a kitten. Probably one of the woodshed cat's. Nest said she'd had a litter a couple of weeks back.' I watched T.A. go through the byre end of the longhouse and into the people end, still holding the kitten under her chin and cooing at it, although I couldn't hear her of course. Still no sign of Astarte, though. Nest and Flissy weren't there, either, and I remembered that they'd gone visiting village wives to reassure them that they would have their husbands back fairly soon. Garan and Brân must have been out, too, or T.A. wouldn't have risked taking the kitten inside. It jumped from T.A.'s arms and scampered up the rungs of the loft ladder, turning at the top to stare down. It was a strange-looking animal, its snowy fur so short and fine that around its (very large) ears it looked almost pink where the skin showed through. It wouldn't have won any prizes at a pretty kitty show. Especially since . . .

It also had one blue eye, and one brown.

'Aaaah!' I shrieked. 'It's Astarte! Astarte's the cat! And T.A.'s alone with her!' I dropped the skirt and started rushing round all over the place like, as Mam would have said, a chicken with its head cut off.

Taliesin grabbed me as I panicked past him. 'Calm

109

down, Tan'ith.' His voice was stern. 'Remember your power comes from the Lady. Take a deep breath and *think*.'

I took a deep breath and hauled myself together with a huge effort. 'T.A. is at the *tŷ hir,* and Aunty Fliss and Nest are out. Astarte is inside, hiding up in the sleeping loft. She's obviously hoping to get the drop on us when we go back.'

Gwydion sat on the chair Taliesin had just vacated. Funny, nobody seemed to want to risk sitting on her disgusting bed! 'So what you've got to do is get back there, quickly, before T.A. takes it into her head to feed Astarte some milk.'

I was puzzled. 'Feed her? Why? What would that do?'

'Well, she's already invited Astarte into the *tŷ hir*, which gives her some powers over our house; if she feeds her too, she gets a whole lot more. If Astarte's up in the sleeping loft, it's likely she hasn't thought of that, or she'd be twining round T.A.'s ankles, yowling. So you'd better get back there, speed of light.'

I suddenly noticed the 'you' in the middle of all that. 'Me? What about you two? Aren't you coming?'

Gwydion thumped me on the arm. 'Come on, Tanz. Don't forget how brave you are. Taliesin and I have unfinished business here, remember? If we leave it to Sion ap Sion and his lot, most of the men-at-arms will probably wind up just a little bit dead. So it's up to you, Tanz, I'm afraid.'

Oh, great. Then I remembered the Lady's powers. Yay, SuperTanz!

I shape-shifted into a peregrine falcon and soared

out of the tall, narrow windows, flying fast and low towards the longhouse, faster than I'd ever flown before, powerful wings cutting the air, the trees and bushes below rushing past in a green blur. I landed on the thatched roof of the longhouse and hopped towards the chimney-hole, flapping my wings to clear the smoke away. I couldn't see much, but with my extra-sharp hearing, I heard . . . With a squawk of panic, I took off again, and hurtled through the window-space in the sleeping loft, perched on the edge of the platform and looked down.

T.A., bowl of milk in hand, was calling 'Here, kitty! Come on, puss? Come on pussy-wussy!'

Even in a confined space, and even for a peregrine falcon, my power dive was spectacular. The sort of dive that small boys go 'Nyaaaaaaaaaaarrrrrnnneeee-aaaoooo' over, playing aeroplanes. Well, I was impressed. I knocked the bowl of milk out of T.A.'s hands with one wing, and, talons outstretched, landed on Astarte-the-Cat's back. She hadn't heard me coming, and with a dreadful yowl she shot straight up in the air, odd eyes blazing, flipped over, did a double somersault like an Olympic gymnast and landed facing me, hissing. I wasn't scared. She was a cat and I was a bird, but I was a Big, Tough Bird, with Attitude. I spread my wings, menacingly, puffed out my feathers and opened my hooked beak. Out of the corner of my eye I saw T.A., openmouthed, sitting on the floor, covered in spilt milk.

I suddenly realised that Astarte was changing. She was getting bigger. And bigger. And bigger. She had done Gwydion's panther-trick. I suddenly felt like a very small bird, and thought fast.

Astarte, her tail lashing, her blue-and-brown eyes fixed on me, sank low on her haunches, preparing to pounce. Funny, my brain had just left by the back door. I couldn't, on the spur of the moment, so to speak, think of anything that could beat a large, ferocious panther. Then I did. Fleas, contrary to most people's opinions, *do* have brains. At least, I did. I sprang high into the air, landed on Astarte's furry back, scuttled into the long hair and began to bite. Instantly, Astarte lost interest in everything except dislodging me. She scratched, scratched, and scratched some more, and I kept dodging, and running, and running and dodging, nipping away, avoiding razor sharp claws cutting through the fur, thoroughly enjoying myself, because that's what fleas like best. I discovered that biting, although it's something fleas have to do to live, is apparently also a major sport, like rugby or ice-hockey, for fleas. I wondered if they scored a point every time a claw missed them. According to a sporty-looking flea that rushed past me, sidestepping a claw, I was doing quite well. 'Lovely footwork there!' he hollered in flea-talk. 'Well played, old girl!'

However, I couldn't scuttle about all day playing bite-Astarte's-bottom. But now at least I had time to think. I turned into a wasp, shot out of Astarte's fur, homed in on her nose and *struck*.

'Yeeeeowwwwlllll!' While Astarte was otherwise engaged rubbing her nose with her paw, I shape-shifted back to me, shifted Astarte into a large cockroach, picked her up and put her on the table with a bit of the Lady's staff lying across her middle. While the twig was on top of her, she wasn't going anywhere. Tugging off half a dozen leaves, I quickly found Nest's sewing kit, threaded the bone needle with silk and stitched the leaves into a small circle which I slipped round the cockroach like a belt.

'Are you O.K., T.A.?' I helped her to her feet and wiped the milk off her face.

'No thanks to you, Tanz,' she grumbled. 'You nearly gave me a heart attack, pouncing on me like that!'

'Better a heart attack than Astarte in charge, T.A. What on earth possessed you to pick up a weird-looking cat? Especially one with blue and brown eyes, for gosh sake?'

T.A. straightened her jerkin. 'When I picked it up, Tanz, for your information, Tanz, you rotten know-all, Tanz, I didn't notice it had blue and brown eyes. So there, Tanz.'

'All right, all right. She bewitched you. But if I hadn't divined you . . .' I was showing off.

'Divined me? What on earth are you on about now? What's divined?'

I explained, and T.A. looked suitably impressed. 'Wow. I'll have to be careful where I leave my socks, won't I?'

My urgent business now was Astarte. When I shape-shifted her back from cockroach she was NOT a happy teddy.

'Speaking of smelly socks, you really should change your clothes more often, Astarte. And if you eat sweeties in bed, you'll get toothache. I hope.'

The belt of leaves was around her waist. She held her hands above her head and screeched 'Gerritoffme! Aaaaagh! Gerritofferme—NOWorELSE!'

113

'Or else what? You're in no position to threaten me, Astarte Perkins. If you stop and think about it.'

She stopped. And probably thought. Her weird eyes went glazed, and I knew she was trying to shape-shift, or hurl a spell. I also knew that the leaf belt was stopping her. Now, if I could only find out from her where Spiderwitch had taken Cariad before the others came back, they'd not only be amazed, they'd be grateful and impressed, and—. I looked at the expression on her face. Was she going to tell me? Somehow, I didn't think she was.

'Right, Starty-warty,' I said menacingly, 'tell me where my niece is.'

'Shan't.'

'Tell me. Or else.'

She sneered. 'Or else what? You won't hurt me! You lot are the good guys, remember? Good guys aren't allowed to hurt people. So what are you going to do, *scare* me to death?' She made her voice all high and babyish. 'Ooh, ooooh, help, help. I'm soooo fwightened. Not. Go take a running jump, Moonwitch.'

She had me there.

'She's got you there, Tanz!' T.A. chipped in.

'Shut up, T.A. I'm thinking.'

Astarte sat down beside the fire. She looked disgustingly *calm*. It wasn't fair. I had her in my power but I couldn't do anything at all. She should have been begging for mercy. She wasn't.

'Suppose I turn you into a frog?' I suggested.

'Been there. Done that.'

'How about a rat?'

'Been there. Done that. Got the T-shirt. Look.

114

There's nothing you can turn me into that scares me. Nothing at all. And you know you can't hurt me. So what can you do? Not a lot, that's what. So you might as well let me go before my Great-great-Granny finds out you've got me. She might get mad at you, and you wouldn't like that, one bit. She might send a plague of spiders. Big ones, with fangs and long black hairy creepy-crawly legs . . .'

Now that scared me. I, Do, Not, Like, Spiders. Not at all. Didn't show it, though. 'Your Great-great-Granny doesn't have a high opinion of you, does she? Every time I've seen her she seems to be telling you off. And I have to say, she has disgusting eating habits. Bumble-bees, cream and honey. Yuck. Don't the legs stick in her teeth?'

'Oh, stop it, Tanz!' T.A. shuddered. 'You're making me feel sick.'

Astarte glared at me. 'You've been spying on us!' She tossed her gingery, straggly hair. 'Well, I knew that.' I knew she was lying. I could tell because her lips were moving.

She tossed her gingery hair. 'Great-great-Granny was only pretending to be angry with me because— because—' she was thinking fast '—because she knew you were watching! So there!'

I laughed. 'Oooh, Astarte, look at your nose.' I turned her into Pinocchio and made her nose, which was already red and throbbing from my wasp-sting, grow six inches.

'I duppode you thigk thad's fuddy,' she said, crossly. 'Dop it.'

I shrank her nose again. 'You see, I can upset you, Astarte,' I said. 'You're going to tell us what we want

115

to know eventually. So you might as well give in and get on with it.'

'Get lost,' she said. 'There's nothing you can do to hurt me. So take your silly magic and —throw it in the sea. There Is Nothing You Can Do. So there.'

She had me, didn't she? There *wasn't* anything I could do, was there? I was stuck.

'We'll wait until Gwydion and Taliesin get back. They'll think of something. *Then* you'll tell us.'

Astarte smirked. I wanted to kick her. But I wasn't allowed to. Darn it.

'Hang on, Tanz,' T.A. stood up, a slow grin spreading over her face. 'I've got an idea. I think I know how to make her talk.'

She went to the sleeping loft ladder, climbed up it, and disappeared for a few minutes. Then she came carefully down again, holding something in her hand. She held it up.

It was—

Chapter 14

—a feather. I recognised it: it was white and black, and Rhiryd Goch had left it behind in Cariad's cot when he stole her.

'And what are you going to do with that, T.A.? Poke it up her nose?'

'Har-de-har-har-har. Very funny. You aren't thinking, Tanz.' She shook her head so that her black curls flew. 'When you and me fight, how do I always win?'

116

I thought about it. 'You don't always win. You usually cheat because you sit on my stomach and . . .' I could feel the grin spread across my face. I switched it off before it reached my ears. 'Oooh, T.A., what a dreadful mind you've got!'

'I have, haven't I! Shall we?'

'Why not!'

Astarte was staring at us, looking confused and, I was happy to see, slightly worried.

'You're bigger than me, T.A. You hold her, I'll do it.'

T.A. lifted up the end of Astarte's bench, so that she slid off it and collapsed in a heap on the floor. Then she sat on her stomach. 'Go on, Tanz. Let her have it.'

'What do you think you're doing?' Astarte blustered. 'You can't hurt me. You aren't allowed, remember?'

'Oh,' I said, evilly, 'we aren't going to *hurt* you, 'Starty-warty! Not at all.' I knelt down beside her and with one mighty tug, yanked off both her shoes. 'Pooh! T.A., you got the best job after all! Astarte, I wish you'd change your socks occasionally!' I caught hold of the toes of her smelly socks and pulled them off. T.A. handed me the feather and . . . Well, guess. There aren't many people who can stand having their feet tickled. Fiendish or what?

'Aaaaaaaaargh! Stop it!' she shrieked, wriggling and making T.A.'s hair bounce.

'Keep still, Astarte,' I said severely, 'you nearly tipped T.A. off, then.'

T.A. pinned Astarte's shoulders to the floor. 'Are you going to tell us where the baby is, dog-breath?'

'No! Get off me. Or I'll . . .'

'You'll what? You're a bit short on magic, Astarte,

117

remember? You loaned it to Rhiryd Goch. *Big* mistake.'' I wiggled the feather on the sole of her foot.

'No, stoppit, ow, oo, aaaaah, eeeek, nooooo!' She thrashed around, and almost managed to dislodge T.A. again, so I sat on her legs with my back towards T.A.'s. And I tickled, and tickled, and tickled, and tickled and she shrieked, and howled, and wriggled, and moaned, and threatened lots of things she wouldn't be able to do until she got her magic back in a month's time. At long last she said 'All right, all right, I'll tell you.'

'Promise? Or—' I got off her and waved the feather under her nose.

'Stop tickling me and I'll tell you where the baby is.'

'Right.'

T.A. got off her too. 'You'd better,' she warned. 'Otherwise we start again.' Astarte whimpered and crawled onto a bench. She put her head in her arms on the table. I almost felt sorry for her. Almost . . . Then I reminded myself what a thoroughly nasty piece of work she was.

I pulled up a bench and sat opposite her. 'Right. Now, where has your Great-Great-Grandmother taken my niece?'

Astarte lifted her head a little so that her blue eye peered out from under a tatty tangle of gingery hair. 'If I tell you, you aren't allowed to tell Granny I told you. She'd be furious with me.' Astarte shuddered. 'At the very least.'

She was right, there! 'So where, Astarte?'

She sighed and sat up, pushing her hair back from her face. T.A. twiddled the feather under her nose, threateningly.

'All right, all right. She's in her cave. Half-way up

118

Cadair Corryn Du. There, I've told you.' And then she laughed a nasty little laugh. 'Won't do you any good, though. You'll never find her. Although she might find you . . .'

I scowled. 'Am I supposed to be scared? Dream on, Astarte. So. She's in the mountains. We'll find her, *dim problem.*'

'If you find her, Goodwitch, it will only be because she decides to let you find her!' She laughed. 'Are you sure you want to?'

To be honest, I didn't, much. Spiderwitch gave me the heebie-jeebies. But she had Cariad, and so we had to find her and get our baby back. 'That's the difference between you and me, Astarte. I care about my family. You don't care about anyone but yourself. You've left your parents and your brother in our cavern for nearly four years now— you've never once tried to rescue them.' I thought about the candlesticks and the transistor radio sitting in the dark place under Aunt Ant's house. 'Mind, if I had a brother like Dreadful Wayne, I don't think I'd bother, either.'

Astarte sneered. 'I'm supposed to care? Dream on, Goodwitch. People like that aren't important.'

'You really aren't a nice person, are you, Astarte?' T.A. said sternly. 'But we're going to beat you in the end, don't worry.'

Astarte didn't even bother to look at her.

'What's going on?' Flissy's voice startled me. 'Oh, good heavens, it's Astarte.'

'Yup!' I said, smugly. '*And* she's told me where Cariad is.'

'It won't do you any good,' Astarte hissed. 'You won't find her unless Merch Corryn Du lets you.'

Nest came in then, and stopped short when she saw Astarte sitting sullenly at the table. 'How did she get here?'

'Came here to do some mischief, didn't you, Astarte? Thought she'd weasel her way into the *tŷ hir* by making T.A. think she was a sweet little kitty-cat. But we got here just in time. And thanks to T.A., we were able to find out where Great-great-granny-spiderchops has taken Cariad.' I waved the feather under her nose. 'By the way, T.A., why did you bring this with you?'

T.A. scowled ferociously. 'Because I'd already decided to poke it right up Rhiryd Goch's nose and pull it out his ear if I got the chance. *And* follow it with the arrow. Just for taking our Cariad away like that.'

I giggled. 'You poke, I'll pull.' Then I got serious. 'That's again you've helped, T.A. Bringing the feather, and knowing how to get the information out of Astarte. The Lady really sent you for a reason, didn't she!'

Flissy frowned worriedly. 'How *did* you get the information out of Astarte, Tan'ith? You didn't hurt her, did you?'

'Hurt her, Aunty Fliss?' I put on my innocent face. 'She was just tickled to death to tell us, honest she was!' And T.A. and I collapsed in a heap, snorting with laughter.

When the others came back, we all ate supper (yes, we gave Astarte some, but she didn't seem to have much appetite) and then, once she had been tucked up for the night, snoring like a large gingery pig, we discussed our next step, sitting around the fire, the dogs lying on our feet.

120

Gwydion picked up a piece of wood and threw it into the flames. 'We may know roughly where the cave is, but if Merch Corryn Du has used magic to conceal the entrance, then we'll never find it. Her magic is strong.'

'And dangerous.' Taliesin was looking thoughtful. 'She must know by now that we have taken Castell Du, so she won't go back there. She'll stay in her cave and wait for us to go to her.'

I swallowed. 'Are we going tonight?'

Gwydion glanced at me and grinned. 'No. You don't have to be brave again just yet. Tonight we're celebrating, Tanz. Now Rhiryd Goch and his men are safely locked up in the dungeons of Castell Du, our victorious little army is planning a feast. They haven't seen their ladies for rather a long time, and the chance of a party in the great hall of the castle is too good an opportunity to miss.'

We all went, T.A. and me wearing gorgeous dresses Flissy produced from her trunk (I had a feeling they hadn't been there until she 'remembered' them—I think they were magicked for the occasion, because they fitted us perfectly). We discussed what to do with Astarte, but Nest said that she would be perfectly safe left behind so long as she was wearing the girdle of leaves from the Lady's branch. Only magic could remove it, and Astarte didn't have enough magic left to manage half a spell, let alone a whole one.

What a pity the obvious snag didn't strike any one of us! We were all too busy thinking about the party.

We hardly recognised Castell Du when we got there. Mellow light streamed from every window and out of the gatehouse, and the sentries on the gate were our sentries, who smiled and welcomed us in. The heavy doors and portcullis were open wide, and the drawbridge was down. In the great hall log fires burned, fresh straw mixed with dried lavender had been strewn on the floor, the Castle ladies were busy setting tables, and decorating the walls, and the men, fresh from the Dragoncave, sat about in their best clothes, drinking mead, laughing a lot and watching their wives prepare food for the feast.

Only Sion ap Sion was missing. There wasn't a Mrs Sion ap, and so he had volunteered to guard the prisoners. Gwydion pulled a face. 'Can he be trusted?'

Eifion Gwyn overheard. 'He can, my Lord. He knows the likes of us don't hurt our prisoners. We is the Side of Right, we is. We has the Lady on our side.'

'That we do, Eifion Gwyn!' Nest replied. 'My goodness, he's changed his tune, hasn't he?' she whispered, then nudged me. 'Look, Tansy!'

Mali was approaching Dafydd ap Rhodri with a goblet of wine. From the nervous expression on her face I knew it was Nest's 'magic potion'. She tapped Dafydd on the shoulder, and he turned, saw Mali and leapt to his feet almost sending the goblet and its contents flying into the straw. His big face went scarlet, and his hair seemed to take on a bristly life all of its own. Mali fluttered her eyelashes at him, and he took a huge slurp of wine to cover his embarrassment.

Then the wine began to work, and his new-found 'I visited the Dragoncave and survived' courage appeared. He tugged Mali to sit beside him and put his arm around her. Mali looked over her shoulder at Nest, all smiles . . .

'See?' Nest chuckled, 'instant heart's desire!' We

were still giggling when dinner arrived, great steaming platters of roast beef, venison, lamb, pork, chicken, (but not turkey, because that hadn't been invented yet), vegetables, fish, fruit, sweetmeats, custards, pies—so much food that we ate until we were fat and round, like piglets. We sat at the high table, because we were the guests of honour, and had the best of everything, served first, which was a good thing because I was starving!

'I could almost—*almost*—do without Big Macs when there's food like this about!' T.A. said, licking cream from her fingers. The women cleared away the dishes and refilled our goblets, and Taliesin took his harp into the centre of the hall and ran his finger across the strings. He played fast songs, slow songs, happy songs, sad songs, and one or two rather rude ones that all the men joined in the choruses of. He had just launched into a love song, and I was half-listening and half-watching Mali and Dafydd gazing cow-eyed at each other when something caught my eye.

The straw on the floor between the tables was *moving*. Fascinated, and ever-so-slightly tipsy, I watched the layer of straw move across the floor as if something small was running underneath it. I watched it quite closely, until it was a few feet away from me, and then I nudged T.A., who was sitting next to me. 'Look, T.A.!' I said. 'Hic. The straw's—hic—*moving*!'

We watched, fascinated as the moving straw continued right up to me, when it turned left and headed for Gwydion's toes. I bent down to peer under the table, and so did T.A.

'Oh!' she said. 'It's a mouse.'

123

'It's a—hic—very funny-looking mouse,' I said, doubtfully. 'It's got a bald head.'

'And HUGE whiskers!' T.A. said, and collapsed in a giggling heap.

The mouse ran up Gwydion's left leg and scrambled onto the table, where it jumped up and down, squeaking hysterically. Gwydion, who had also had rather a lot of giggle-juice (mead tastes so lovely, it's easy to forget how potent it is!) stared at it.

'That,' he said, seriously, 'that is a mouse. Yes, it definitely is. It's a mouse, you know. It is. It's a mouse.'

Suddenly, I felt my giggles fade away. 'No, Gwydion. That's not a mouse. That's . . .'

'Sion ap Sion!' T.A. and I said simultaneously.

'Who was guarding the prisoners,' Gwydion said, jumping to his feet, instantly sober. He shape-shifted Sion, who carried on leaping up and down on top of the table and squeaking at the top of his voice for half-a-minute, until he realised he wasn't a mouse any more.

'That Rhiryd Goch escaped!' he shouted. 'He turned me into a mouse, he did, then legged it. He's got away!'

I groaned. What was wrong with our brains? Astarte was helpless because she'd loaned out her magic, wasn't she? And who had she loaned it to? Rhiryd Goch, that's who.

Which we had completely forgotten.

Chapter 15

That sort of finished off the party. We looked in the dungeons, and searched the castle from battlements to basement, but Rhiryd Goch had gone. His men-at-arms were still safely locked up—he hadn't bothered to shape-shift them and release them, and one or two of them seemed a bit fed up about that.

'If 'is Lordship do come in by 'ere,' one of them muttered, 'I'll smack 'is Lordship's ear'ole, so I will. Loyalty do go two ways, loyalty do, but precious little do 'e show we, look. Not so much as a backward look or a "'ow yer doin', lads?" were there?' His companions shook their heads. 'No, 'e was off out of it like a rat up a drainpipe. I've a good mind to join Lord Taliesin, I 'ave. 'E do take care of 'is men, 'e do.' The men sharing his dungeon shuffled and stared at their feet. Most of them probably agreed with him, but none was actually prepared to desert in case Rhiryd Goch *did* come back.

'You think about it for a bit,' Taliesin suggested. 'When you've spent a day or two down here, if you're still of a mind to be one of my men, then we'll discuss it.'

The men in the cell exchanged glances. 'Fair enough,' one said, and several of them nodded in agreement. In a couple of days' time they would be able to see which way the wind was blowing—our direction or Rhiryd Goch's!

Back in the great hall, men were buckling on swords and awaiting orders.

'What we goin' to do, Lord Gwydion?' Eifion Gwyn asked. 'We goin' to ride out and fetch Rhiryd Goch back in chains?'

''Eavy ones!' Sion ap Sion muttered darkly.

'It would be good if we could,' Gwydion agreed, 'but since we don't know where—or what—he is right at this moment, we can't, can we?'

'The first thing he'll do,' I said, thinking hard, 'probably, anyway, is rescue Astarte. He knows he is already in Spiderwitch's bad books because he borrowed Astarte's magic and didn't give it back after he'd kidnapped Cariad. I doubt if he wants to face old spiderchops without Astarte. Not that she'll be much help. Loyalty isn't her strong point, either.'

Belatedly, I remembered that Astarte was alone in the longhouse. Gwydion obviously had the same thought. We stared at each other, then shape-shifted swiftly and two barn-owls hurtled out of the great hall, through the courtyard doors and up into the night sky.

The wind had risen, and we were flying into it. It pushed like a giant hand against my wings, and by the time the *tŷ hir* came into sight I was getting tired of pushing back. We swooped down. The door was open, wind howling through it, blowing the rushes and disturbing the cows.

Astarte, of course, had gone. 'If only we'd left the dogs behind,' I said.

'If we had, they wouldn't be alive now,' Gwydion said grimly. 'Look.'

The longhouse looked as if a whirlwind had been through it. The table was overturned, chairs were smashed, and Nest's scrying bowl had been thrown on the floor. Its magic had saved it from breaking, luckily, but T.A.'s gift, the Book of the Physicians of Myddfai, had been torn in shreds and scattered like snow. The great oak chest that held the original had been over-

126

turned, but the book was still inside, luckily unharmed. Everything else that could be damaged had been.

We surveyed the wreckage of Nest's neat house, and at that moment, Nest and the others arrived, shapeshifting from owls. The half-fairy covered her mouth with her hands when she saw the damage, and sat down, quickly. Aunt Fliss put her arms round her. 'Never mind, Nest. We'll get this place tidy again, don't worry.'

'We'll all help,' T.A. said, still pink with excitement from being shapeshifted.

'And then,' Taliesin said grimly 'then, we'll scry Rhiryd Goch and Astarte in Nest's bowl. And get after them.'

So we rolled up our sleeves and got on with it. What made Nest maddest was that they had been so *wasteful*: they'd sloshed milk all over everywhere, tipped flour into the milk until the floor resembled a giant uncooked pancake. Nest's store of apples from last year had been thrown everywhere: the only good thing was that they'd run out of time before they went up to the sleeping loft. Good because, hidden on a shelf right at the back of the loft was the bit of the Lady's staff. I scrambled up the ladder to check it was safe, and heaved a sigh of relief when I found it was. T.A.'s carrier bag was there, too, still bulging interestingly. Then I scrambled back down the ladder to pitch in with the big clear-up. By the time we had finished it was almost morning, and we decided to get a few hours rest before hunting down Astarte and Rhiryd Goch. Just before we fell asleep, T.A. waved Rhiryd Goch's red and black arrow at me. 'Up his nose!' she said, fiercely.

'And out his ear,' I finished sleepily. 'Kidnapping our Cariad!'

Next morning we ate breakfast—bruised apples, thanks to Astarte—and then Nest filled her scrying bowl with clear spring water.

Gwydion and I bent over it both at once and bumped heads. 'Ow!' I said, my eyes watering.

'I'll do it,' Nest said. 'We may be looking for a while, so we can each look until we get tired, and then someone else can take over.' She stirred the water with her fingers, and when it stilled, leaned over, her small, pointed face reflected in the dark surface, but there was no sign of Rhiryd Goch, who seemed to be hiding somewhere the scrying bowl couldn't reach.

'If he's shapeshifted with Astarte's magic,' I pointed out, 'how will we know what's him? If you know what I mean.'

Gwydion rubbed his bumped head thoughtfully. 'Maybe it would be better to scry Astarte instead,' he suggested. 'We know she can still shapeshift, but because Rhiryd Goch has most of her magic, she won't be able to do it too often, will she?'

Nest stirred the water again, and bent over. Quite quickly, she found Astarte, sitting disconsolately on a rock rubbing her feet as if they ached. A large red dog-fox sat beside her, its tongue lolling out, and Astarte, from the expression on her face and the way her jaw was wagging, was whining about something. The dog-fox barked, silently, and Astarte slapped it sharply on the muzzle.

'Gotcha!' T.A. breathed triumphantly. Rhiryd Goch snapped at Astarte's fingers, missing by a hair's breadth. 'They don't seem to be getting on too well, do they?'

After a while the fox nudged Astarte's legs and reluctantly she got up and began walking, while we watched them in the still surface of the scrying bowl. Soon, they were walking uphill, over rough stony ground. We couldn't see much of the mountain, but there wasn't much in the way of grass to walk on, just black stones and dark earth. They walked for quite a way, and I don't think Astarte's mouth stopped moving at all. Rhiryd-the-fox ran on ahead at one point, probably to get away from the sound of her nagging, but had to wait for her. Probably because he didn't know where he was going. Only Astarte knew that.

She suddenly turned left, Rhiryd Goch, his tongue lolling, trotting behind her. She seemed to be following a faint pathway in the rocky ground, and I held my breath waiting for a cave entrance to appear. And then, suddenly, Astarte vanished. Poof. Just like that, into thin air.

Rhiryd Goch scurried about, sniffing at rocks and barking furiously, scratching the ground and running in circles, but he was just as mystified as we were. We carried on watching for nearly an hour, but Astarte didn't reappear. Rhiryd Goch settled down near where she had disappeared, sharp nose resting on tawny paws, and waited.

And waited, and waited and waited. Almost all day, until the sun was sinking in the west. So did we, (wait, I mean, not sink in the west) but we took it in shifts. It was hours later when Astarte reappeared, just behind Rhiryd Goch, who had dropped off.

She tiptoed up behind him, and shouted in his ear, making him jump. Seconds later, Rhiryd Goch had shape-shifted, and was standing over Astarte, his fists clenched. But Astarte just walked calmly away from him and started down the rocky path.

We watched them until they went into a small hut deep in a wood. Rhiryd Goch lit a fire and Astarte fetched food (ours, probably, stolen from the *tŷ hir*) and they ate in sullen silence. When the light had gone from the hut, they lit rushlights (also ours, I suppose) and settled down, Rhiryd Goch lying on his side watching Astarte closely, Astarte ignoring him and brushing her hair so that it crackled with electricity and stood out all round her head, like a gingery dandelion clock.

'He doesn't trust her at all, does he?' I said. 'Doing that disappearing act sort of upset him. I wonder why she did it? Rhiryd Goch's supposed to be on her side, after all.'

'Rhiryd Goch is on Rhiryd Goch's side, Tanz, no one else's.' Gwydion was helping Nest get supper while the rest of us watched the bowl. 'Astarte knows that if he meets Merch Corryn Du, there'll be big trouble. He's still got most of Astarte's magic, after all. And because he's got that little bit of magic, Rhiryd Goch thinks he's strong enough to face the witch all on his own. He doesn't know how dangerous she is.'

I opened my mouth to ask 'How dangerous is she?' but then shut it again. I didn't really want to know. Yes, I had the Lady's powers, yes, I had the Lady's courage, but underneath all that was still little old cowardly me, who doesn't like spiders one bit. And Spiderwitch was much too spidery for my liking, *diolch yn fawr iawn*!

Gwydion knew exactly what was going through my

130

head. Later, when the others were clearing away, and Taliesin was scrying Rhiryd Goch and Astarte inside their dark hut, Gwydion came and sat beside me. 'Don't be scared,' he said, looking into my eyes. 'With the Lady's power, and with my—with everything else you've got going for you, you'll be O.K., honest. You'll get Cariad back and everything will be fine.

'That,' I said crossly, 'is all very well for you to say, Gwydion Dragonson. All my inner bits are telling me it's going to be me that goes in after old spider-knickers to get Cariad out. I know she's got to be saved, and I know the Lady has given me her powers, but every now and then I still come over all cowardly. I wish I was different, honest, Gwyd. But I'm not. I'm me, and you're stuck with it.'

Taliesin built up the fire so that it crackled and sparked, then fetched his harp and sat with us, stroking musical waterfalls from the glinting strings. 'I think,' he said, plinking a string thoughtfully, 'that we'd better watch them from here, and as soon as they make a move, follow them again. Sooner or later Astarte is going to have to go back inside the cave, and this time Rhiryd Goch won't let her get away. And also this time we'll be ready for her disappearing act. She must have just enough magic left to either shape-shift or place-shift.'

'Place-shift?'

'Yes. It's sort of thinking yourself sideways into another place.'

'Oh. Like "Beam me up, Scotty", on Star Trek?'

Taliesin sighed. 'Yes, sort of. Did I ever express the opinion that the youth of your day watches too much T.V.?'

I rubbed Garan's rough ears. 'No. But I expect you will.'

Flissy took over from Nest at the scrying bowl, and I took over from Flissy, and so on, so that watch was kept throughout the night. In between sleeping and watching, I worried about Cariad inside the cave with Astarte's Great-Great-Granny, and whether she was being looked after properly. I knew there was a wet-nurse in there, poor girl, but Cariad was used to nice clean disposable nappies, and central heating, and being played with, stuff like that. I hoped the wet-nurse was giving her lots of cuddles, at least. Garan and Brân were one each side of me, like furry, breathing blankets, and I hugged Garan for comfort, and Brân licked my knee. And somewhere during the night a small flea hopped off one of them and came to live on me.

'Ow!' I said over breakfast, scratching. 'That's all I need.' Something tickled inside my jerkin and I scratched that, too. 'When this is over, Nest, I'm going to borrow Aunty Fliss's bubble bath and your wash tub and have a nice bath. I really miss our power shower at home.'

'They're on the move!' Gwydion called excitedly. 'Come on! And we shapeshifted into merlins and hurtled towards Cadair Corryn Du.

Chapter 16

Their two small figures trudged up the mountainside. They didn't see the three birds hovering above them. Where Astarte had turned left on the mountain path, we flew lower, close above their heads. But yet again, one minute Astarte was there, the next she was gone. And once again, Rhiryd Goch was left alone on the mountainside.

Oh boy, did he have a temper! He hurled rocks, jumped up and down, swore, kicked stones, and went red in the face with fury. Then he sat down on a rock beside the path and sulked. Didn't do him any good, though: Astarte had gone. She reappeared, just as mysteriously. One minute the path was empty, the next she was there, tossing back her gingery, sandy hair, a smirk on her face.

Rhiryd Goch started leaping up and down again, and Astarte folded her arms and let him get on with it. But she looked different, somehow less nervous than she had before. Then I realised why. She had some more of her magic back! Her odd blue and brown eyes were narrowed, and there was an air of triumph about her. Either the 'lend it' spell was wearing off Rhiryd Goch bit by bit, and the magic was returning to Astarte gradually, or her Great-Great-Granny had given her a top-up to keep her going until Rhiryd Goch *had* to return it at the end of the month. Just as the idea occurred to me, she more or less proved it by zapping Rhiryd Goch with a spell. He stopped shouting at her, and grunted instead. He had to grunt, because he was a small, red, very, very cross pig. His little trotters beat an angry tattoo on the path. Astarte ignored him, and set off down the hill towards their hut, Rhiryd Mochyn Goch trotting crossly along behind her.

Some of Astarte's magic was definitely back: she zapped trees, making their leaves shrivel, changed small creatures unlucky enough to cross her path into other things, leaving some very unhappy mice thinking they were sparrows and frantically trying to take off and fly, and swiped the heads off flowers by magic, leaving clumps of sad stalks waving in the sun. She was checking, I suppose, to make sure everything worked.

We perched on a tree outside the hut. 'Tanz,' Gwydion squawked, 'you'd better go and sort out the damage she's caused. Taliesin and I will keep watch.'

I flew back the way we'd come, unshrivelling trees, restoring flowers, and took the sparrow spell off the upset and bewildered mice. They huddled together, shrieking with fear when they saw merlin-me hovering over their heads, and then relaxed as I flew away without swooping on them.

Taliesin scratched his head with a talon. 'I don't think there's any point in sitting out here all night waiting for them to set off again. We'd better go back to the *tŷ hir* and decide what to do. Anyway, I'm getting hungry, and mice for dinner always upset my stomach.'

So we flew back to the longhouse and human food. As soon as I shifted back to me again, I started to itch. Those darn fleas had been with me the whole time, nibbling away, and now I was me again I discovered their blotchy red bites. I scratched all the way through dinner, and then, while T.A., Nest and Flissy cleared the dishes, I borrowed Flissy's bubble-bath and washtub, filled it full of water (cold, unfortunately with just a cauldron-full of hot water heated over the fire to take the chill off—brr!) and dunked myself in it from head to foot, right underwater, in case any sporty little fleas were hiding in my hair. Afterwards, pale blue and with chattering teeth, I stood still while Nest anointed my bites with some stuff from a little bottle which took the itch away, and, wrapping myself in a huge linen towel I sat down to drink some hot herb tea to warm me up.

'We've really got a problem here,' Taliesin said. 'While Astarte's doing her disappearing act, we can't track her. We could follow her all night, but if she's just going to disappear as soon as she gets close to the cave, we're stuck.'

Nest was still scrying. 'They seem to have settled down for the night. Rhiryd Goch is getting more and more frustrated—although why *he* wants to meet Merch Corryn Du I can't imagine. I'd have thought he'd want to stay as far away from her as possible.'

'He certainly won't be flavour of the month,' I agreed. 'Refusing to give back Astarte's magic is not the way to win friends and influence people, is it?'

'The trouble with Rhiryd Goch is that no one, probably not even himself, half the time, knows what he's thinking. He's so crooked that whenever he goes for a walk, he's likely to meet himself coming back.' Gwydion rubbed Brân's ears and the hound yawned ecstatically. 'He must think Astarte owes him something, or that her magic will make Merch Corryn Du respect him. Rhiryd Goch wants Ynys Haf for himself. He wants to be DragonKing and will do anything to keep me from what is rightfully mine.'

'DragonKing will never be dead while you are alive, Gwydion,' Nest ruffled his hair. 'Your Time is here,

135

and soon he can rest. But first we must rescue the baby and rid Ynys Haf of Merch Corryn Du, Rhiryd Goch and Astarte. For ever, this time.'

'But,' I said glumly, 'If we can't follow Astarte into the cave, we can't get at her, can we? So until Spiderwitch decides she needs a bit of fresh air, we're stuck.' Brân, feeling left out, tried to climb into Gwydion's lap. 'Mind you don't pick up a flea, Gwyd. They're the devil to get rid of. I'm covered in—' I stopped. A huge grin slithered across my face. 'That's it!'

Taliesin looked mystified. 'What is? What are you on about, Tanz?'

'Fleas!' I crowed. 'We'll be fleas! If we can stick close enough to Astarte when she vanishes, you said, we'll be able to see where she goes. Well, what sticks closer than fleas?'

Gwydion began to laugh, and the others joined in. I hoped it would work.

Taliesin, Gwydion, T.A. and I got a good night's sleep while Nest and Flissy took turns watching Rhiryd Goch and Astarte in the scrying bowl. Next morning, as soon as they made their move, the three of us merlin-shifted again and hurled ourselves in the direction of the hut. At least, Gwydion and Taliesin hurled. Somehow I couldn't seem to get off the ground. I flexed my whippy brown wings, but nothing happened. I shut my eyes, thought the 'fly, fly, friendly-wind-beneath-my-wings-lift-me' spell over again, filled my speckled chest with air and hurled myself upward. And belly-flopped again. I changed to a peregrine, then a sparrow, then a kestrel. None of me seemed in a mood to fly: I couldn't get any of me off the ground. Flissy, watching from the doorway, was looking worried. I shifted back.

'What's going on, Tansy?'

'Blowed if I know, Fliss. I can shift, but I can't fly.'

'Try again.' I did. A seagull this time. Yellow legs, beady eyes, white feathers, black cap. Nothing. I checked my equipment: claws, beak, webbed feet, body, wings, all present and correct. So why couldn't I fly?

'Is someone else's magic interfering with yours? Is it Astarte?'

Shifting back to me, I thought about it. 'No. I feel more as if I've forgotten something. What, Fliss?' Then I knew. It was like a little voice inside my head. It wasn't a what, it was a who. 'It's T.A., Fliss! Something is telling me T.A. has to come with us. T.A.?' I hollered, and she came to the door, an earthenware jug in her hands.

'What?'

'You have to come with us. Don't know why, just know you have to come.'

Her face, as they say, was a picture. Half 'Oh, whoopee, I'm going on an adventure,' and half 'Oh, heck, I'm scared stiff'. She gulped. 'Oh.' Slowly, she put down the jug. 'O.K. Fine.' I'll say this for T.A., I can rely on her one hundred and one per cent.

Gwydion and Taliesin came back to see what was keeping me, circling overhead and then swooping in to land beside us, shifting back to themselves. Gwydion shimmered and grew tall, stretching his arms out from beneath the feathers. 'What's going on?' he asked. I explained.

'If you say we need to take T.A., then we take T.A.'

'Right, T.A. Get ready to—'

'Hang on a mo!' T.A. spun on her heel and rushed indoors. 'There's something I need,' she called over her shoulder. 'Won't be a minute.' I heard her scramble up the ladder to the sleeping loft and back down again. When she reappeared, the front of her jerkin was bulging suspiciously.

'What—?' I began, but then Nest called out from her place at the scrying bowl. 'Astarte and Rhiryd Goch are nearly at the cave!' and the four of us hurtled into the air, winging our way towards Cadair Corryn Du.

Far below, they walked along the path, one behind the other, like Red Indians. We swooped down behind them, keeping out of their line of sight, and once we were close enough, I quickly shifted T.A., dropping her onto Astarte's back, where she hopped quickly down inside her jerkin. Rhiryd Goch was hanging on very tightly to Astarte's sleeve: he obviously thought that if he hung on, she'd have to take him with her this time. Taliesin and Gwydion shifted and dropped onto him. Seconds later, I was flea-me, beside T.A. down Astarte's scrawny neck. It wasn't very pleasant down there: she was hot and clammy from walking. Nevertheless we clung on. I waved my front pair of legs at T.A., and she waved hers back.

I wondered what would happen when Astarte disappeared. I soon found out.

The last thing I heard before it started was Rhiryd Goch's howl of fury: obviously hanging on to Astarte's sleeve hadn't worked, because Astarte foiled him yet again. I hoped that, because she didn't know we were tucked away inside her collar, she'd think *us* sideways

138

at the same time as herself. I tried to forget that Taliesin and Gwydion were still with Rhiryd Goch: it was T.A. and me on our own now.

It was very dark, but then I imagine it usually is inside a thick felt jerkin. Then a tingle like a giant sneeze started at my six feet and rushed into my brain with a noise like the Swansea to Paddington InterCity going through a tunnel. I clung on grimly to Astarte's clothes, and then had a better idea. I sank my fangs into her back, and waved to T.A. to do the same. She did, and looked rather as if she was enjoying doing it. That tiny contact, I'm sure of it, got us into Corryn Du's lair. If we'd just clung to her clothes, we'd have been left behind when the wind began to howl around us.

That wind was so strong I felt like wotsisname, Michael Finnegan in that old song, you know the one: "he grew whiskers on his chinnegan; the wind came out and blew them innegan. Poor old Michael Finnegan." The gusting, roaring, terrifying gale seemed to go on forever, and then, just when I thought I'd have to let go, it stopped, and T.A. and I relaxed and unclenched our aching jaws. We were safely inside! I waved my legs at T.A. and we hopped off, leaving Astarte trying to scratch an itch she couldn't possibly reach, because I'd bitten her right between the shoulder blades. Oooh, I can be *nasty* when I want! Eventually she took off her jerkin and long skirt, and taking a robe from a peg on the cave wall, dropped it over her head. The robe was long, and black, with a spiderweb pattern all over it in silver thread, and there was a weird head-dress to go with it, with the black, beady eyes and large mandibles of a wolf spider fitting closely over her head just above her weird blue-and-brown eyes. T.A. edged closer to me as Astarte stepped into a dark opening in the cave wall.

So there we were, T.A. and me, all alone. Taliesin and Gwydion were outside with Rhiryd Goch, and we were inside. Just us, Astarte and the Spiderwitch. But was I scared? Of course I was! I was *terrified!*

T.A.'s first words when I shifted her back were 'I don't like spiders, and I don't like dark places, Tanz. If it wasn't for Cariad, I'd be straight off home, right now.'

'Me too.' I stripped off the long skirt I wore over leather leggings, and T.A. did the same. 'I don't know if we'll need to climb or anything, but we can run faster without our skirts. Don't forget, T.A., Astarte hasn't got a clue we've followed her, so if we're very, very careful we can get Cariad and escape without her knowing.'

'Except,' T.A. began.

'Except what?'

'Oh, never mind.'

'T.A.!' I warned.

'Well, it just kind of crossed my mind, Tanz. We don't know how we got in here, do we? So how will we know how to get out?'

Good question. Also *bad* question! Trust T.A. Then my pendant tingled around my neck, the Arianrhod ring squeezed my finger, gently, and the Lady's courage sort of kicked in. 'Don't worry about that now. Let's just find the baby and then worry about getting out. If there's a way in, there's a way out. If necessary, we can go out the same way we came in, riding on Astarte's back, all three of us.'

I sounded so confident! T.A. believed me, which

140

was one good thing. But deep down inside I had this horrible picture of us wandering round and round this dark cave trying to get out. Forever, and ever, and ever, and—oh, shut up, Tanz!

'Come on.' I looked at the dark patch of tunnel where Astarte had disappeared. 'Let's go find our baby.'

Chapter 17

Together (but not quite holding hands!) we approached the tunnel. And stopped. It wasn't just a tunnel. It was *eight* tunnels. Eight very dark tunnels. Eight very dark tunnels leading goodness knows where. Eight very dark tunnels leading goodness knows where and thank you very much I didn't want to find out!

'Ah,' T.A. said. 'Eight tunnels, Tanz! One for each of the spider's legs.'

'Oh, thanks a bunch, T.A. You really do know how to cheer a person up. I mean, gosh! I hadn't worked that out! Not at all! Eight tunnels! Wow!'

'There's no need to be sarcastic, Tanz. It just seemed—well, I don't know. Sort of *significant*, somehow, eight tunnels.'

I tried to calm down, but I was having a bit of difficulty not grinding my teeth. I took a deep breath. 'I think we should stick together, T.A. Not go haring off down a tunnel each, on our own or anything.' T.A. gave me a look which said that haring off anywhere all alone, never mind down a dark tunnel, had never even crossed her mind.

'If we start at the left-hand tunnel,' I suggested, 'and

explore that first, if we don't find anything we can come back and try the second tunnel, and keep going until we find Cariad.'

'Or Spiderwitch finds us,' T.A. said gloomily. 'What if the tunnels keep going round and round and we get lost, Tanz? And nobody ever sees us again, ever. Not until somebody finds our skeletons, all white and bony, lying on the—'

'Oh, shut up, T.A.! If we get lost, we get lost. There's no sense worrying about it. This is the only chance we have of finding Cariad—unless you've got one of your brilliant, world shattering, Olympic standard ideas?'

'Sarcasm,' my best friend said snootily 'doesn't suit you, Tanz. As it happens, I have.

'Oh, yeah?'

'Yeah. If we use a ball of string and tie it to this rock here, by the entrance, and then we can go down the tunnels one after the other and always be absolutely certain we can find our way back.'

'Except we haven't got a ball of string.'

'Yes we have.'

'You what?'

T.A. rummaged inside her jerkin and brought out a large ball of white string. 'Remember how much of that hemp twine Flissy uses in the garden of the *tŷ hir*? Well I brought her this as a going-away present. For when we go back. I thought it would make her laugh, cheer her up, you know.'

'T.A.,' I said, slowly, 'there is no doubt about it, the Lady knew what she was doing when she had second thoughts and sent you after me. Is there no end to your brilliance?'

'Probably not.' My friend sounded distinctly smug. She busied herself tying the end of the string to a rock, and, spinning it out behind us (*like a spider*, I thought, and shuddered) we set off down the first tunnel.

It was cold, and damp, and very, very dark. 'I don't suppose you've got a torch and some batteries tucked up your sleeve, T.A.?'

'No. T.A.'s voice was a bit wobbly. She doesn't like the dark.

Come to that, neither do I, much. Then I remembered the bit of the Lady's twig which was tucked inside my own jerkin. I pulled it out, the twig rough under my fingers, moving as if it were alive. Unfortunately, the tunnel was still dark. I sighed, and stroked the twig, remembering how it acted when sunlight fell on it. If there'd been one little ray of sunshine, maybe it might have worked. Except if there had been, we wouldn't have needed light anyway, would we? Twig, I thought, we could use a little light here. Honest, twig, we really, really need it. I concentrated hard and suddenly the twig twitched, and the cluster of blossoms at the top of it began to glow. It threw off a silvery, strong light that banished the awful darkness and made the way ahead quite clear. The tunnel branched in two, and we took the left hand way, paying out the ball of string as we went. Unfortunately, we then had to turn right, and came out of the second tunnel right next to the rock that our string was tied to.

'We went round in a circle,' T.A. said, helpfully.

'I noticed. So if we go back down there, and take the right turning instead of the left one, we should find another way through.' So we set off again down the

143

first tunnel, took the right hand fork—and found ourselves going right round in a circle. Back at the entrance, we chose the third of the eight tunnels and started walking. That tunnel went downhill, then uphill, then the tunnel curved to the right, and down again, then there was a flight of steps which we climbed and then—there we were back in the cave again—coming out of the eighth tunnel.

'I'm beginning to get cross,' I said, 'I don't think Spiderwitch wants to meet us.'

'That's fine by me,' T.A. was looking at me oddly.

'What do you mean, that's fine by you? Fine friend you are!'

'We don't want Spiderwitch, Tanz, remember? We want Cariad. Once we've got Cariad safely away, then we can worry about the Spider-Granny from Hell.'

'Oh, yes. Right.'

'The trouble with you, Tanz, is when you get ratty, you get this big sort of surge of courage. Not like you at all. It makes you all brave, but it also seems to stop you thinking.

'Right. Sorry.'

'Now, how can we get at Cariad? You've got the Lady's powers. Can you hear her?'

I hadn't even thought of listening. I sat down on a rock, untied the string and wound the bit we'd used back onto the ball, concentrating hard on sounds. And suddenly I could hear. Far away, far, far away, I could hear a very small baby with a very loud scream, and a soft voice trying to hush her, and not succeeding very well. And then, below that sound, I heard a noise that almost froze my bones! It was a shifting, dark, low, creepy-crawly sort of sound—together with the low

144

throb of a spiderweb being slowly strummed. Perhaps by something with long, black, hairy legs . . .

I shivered. 'I can hear Cariad, T.A.! She's here, and so is the nurse, thank goodness. At least there's someone to cuddle her and change her nappies and feed her.'

T.A. stared at me. 'I'm glad you heard Cariad, Tanz. But don't bother to tell me what else you heard, thank you very much. You went a very peculiar shade of green, just then. And your hands are shaking.'

I checked. They were. I ignored them. 'I can hear her shrieking, T.A., but I still don't know where she is.'

'What other powers have you got besides hearing?'

'My eyesight, my magic, oh, and that divining thing where you scry without a ball or water. But that's no good if I haven't got anything belonging to Cariad. I've got the bit of the twig, and— what are you grinning at, T.A.?'

T.A. groped in her jerkin and brought out a small blue furry toy rabbit with one terminally sucked ear. 'Recognise this?'

I gaped. 'Cariad's Blue Bun! What on earth made you bring that with you, T.A.?'

'Well, optimism. And soppiness. I wanted to bring Cariad something she'd recognise from home. But maybe it was the Lady helping us again.'

I took the bunny and held it against me, screwed my eyes up tight, and concentrated. I could hear Cariad shrieking, only louder this time, and a voice singing a Welsh lullaby, softly and soothingly, and the creak of a rocking chair moving on an earth floor. Suddenly the blue bunny twisted in my hands, wrenched itself free, and turning over and over in mid air, fell to the ground. And when it hit the ground, it was running . . . T.A.and I, open-mouthed, watched its pink furry tail disappear into the mouth of the sixth tunnel from the left.

'Did you see that? My toys never did that when I was small!' I gasped. 'That was a blue fuzzy bunny, that was!'

'And it's getting away!' T.A. shrieked, grabbing my hand and pulling me into the tunnel after the pink and blue rear end. We spotted it in the distance, and scuttled after it, running as fast as we could go, the Lady's twig lighting our way, Cariad's bunny leading us to—well, I hoped!—Cariad. It charged round a corner and skidded to a halt in front of a large wooden door.

'Is there a keyhole, T.A.?'

'No.'

The bunny, bright button eyes shining above twitching pink embroidered nose, scratched at the door and squeaked. Nothing else for it. I grabbed the huge iron ring handle, lifted it, and turned it slowly. A lock clicked, and the door began to move. I pushed harder, and the door swung open. Light flooded out, revealing the baby's wet-nurse, and—Cariad, purple with fury, struggling in her arms.

'My, Cariad, you've grown!' I said, startled. I'd forgotten that time was sort of elastic in Ynys Haf. Instead of being a tiny, helpless little scrap, Cariad was now large, wriggly, and even louder than before. The blue bunny hopped over my foot, ran towards Cariad, and sat at the wet-nurse's feet, whiffling its nose frantically. Cariad spotted it, stopped bawling and started crowing, stretching out her fat little arms for her toy. It hurled itself up into her arms and snuggled down. Cariad clutched it tightly, blowing joyful raspberries.

'Mind you don't—' I began, then stopped. The bunny was a stuffed toy again.

The wet-nurse stood up, looking bewildered. 'Oh, miladies. Have you come to take we away from here? I gets awful scared of that spidery old queen woman. She's not nice to we. She do whisper a awful lot. And the babby don't like her, neither.'

'We've come to take you both away,' I reassured her. I just hoped we could get out again! T.A. reached out and helped herself to a heaping armful of Cariad. 'Oo's a boofuls baby, then?'

Cariad chortled and grabbed a handful of T.A's nose. She grinned at me through watering eyes. 'We've got her, Tanz! She's safe now!'

Suddenly, with my extra-good hearing, I heard voices coming a long, long way off. Astarte's, and—the low, menacing tones of the Spiderwitch! 'Not yet she isn't. Look, we're going to have to get out of here, fast!'

The wet-nurse's eyes turned round and scared. 'Is that spidery 'oman coming?' She threw her pinny over her head and wailed.

'Stop it at once!' I said in my best Aunt Ant voice, and to my surprise, she did. 'Now, T.A., are you O.K. with Cariad?' T.A. clutched the baby to her chest and nodded. 'Right. Come on. Run!'

We shot out of the door, the others in front of me, haring back down the tunnel the way we'd come. Suddenly I had an idea, and rushed back to shut the heavy door to Cariad's room. Then I tapped it with the Lady's twig to seal it shut. That would occupy them for a while, give us a bit more time to get away.

147

We reached the chamber at the end of the tunnels out of breath and panting. 'We made it!' T.A. crowed.

'All we've got to do now is work out some way to get out of here,' I muttered. 'Remember?'

T.A.'s face fell. 'Oh. Yes, I'd forgotten that.'

'Quick. Everybody look for a way out. Anything that might be a door, a tunnel, a gate, a trapdoor, even a hole in the roof for goodness sake. There must be some way out.' Except, my mind told me, that Astarte didn't use a door to get in, did she? At the back of my brain I could hear Astarte and Spiderwitch shrieking at each other, their tempers utterly lost as they struggled to open the door I had sealed shut. We ran around the chamber like hamsters on wheels—covering what seemed like miles, but not actually going anywhere. At last, we gave up. There was no way out.

'The only way we can get out is the way we came in,' I said at last. 'I'll shift us all into fleas and we'll go out that way. It's risky, because by now Spiderwitch knows we're here.'

'What about Cariad?'

'Cariad will have to be a baby flea.'

'Please, Lady Tan'ith,' said a small voice behind me 'I don't want to be no flea.' The wet-nurse was green with fright.

'Look— what's your name?

'Megan, Lady.'

'Look, Megan, would you rather stay here and face Merch Corryn Du?' I asked. She shook her head. 'Right, then. Don't be scared. Being a flea is no different from being a human, only smaller. And faster. And you can jump higher.' She still didn't look convinced.

148

'And,' T.A. chipped in, 'you can bite Astarte as hard as you like.' That did it.

'All right. If you promises I can bite she?' T.A. nodded, solemnly. 'That be something to tell my husband, won't it? Being a flea and all!'

'I'll wait until the last minute to shift us,' I decided, 'so that Cariad won't get scared. All she'll be able to do is hang on, so I'll hang on tight to her, and then we ought to be able to get out when Astarte does. They're coming! Quick!' I shifted the four of us into three large and one very small flea, and held Cariad-flea tightly round the middle so she couldn't go hopping off.

Astarte and Merch Corryn Du rushed out of the tunnel and stopped.

Close up, the Spiderwitch was even more unpleasant. She wore a black robe like Astarte's, but because she was taller, and thinner, and nastier, hers looked even more scary, and the black mask on her head covered her eyes, which looked out through red-tinted eye-pieces, like slices of ruby, so that it looked as if the spider-mask was part of her own head. It was horrible, and I remembered suddenly that spiders like to eat insects. And that I was an insect . . .

'They must be here!' she hissed. 'Find them, Astarte, and bring that baby back. You bungling, stupid, useless excuse for a Witch! I regret the day I gave you any powers at all. If you ever get them back from that disgusting lout Rhiryd Goch, then I'll decide whether you keep them. You don't deserve magic! You are useless, just like your useless mother. AND your useless Grandmother!'

'Yes, Great-great-great-great-Grandmother,' Astarte muttered sullenly.

'Don't just stand there, you fool! Look for them!'

Astarte began rushing about, peering down tunnels, turning over stones, searching for us. The problem was, of course, that she didn't know what she was looking for. Corryn Du stamped her foot angrily. 'Somehow they've got out! But they can't have gone far. I can still sense them nearby. Get out and find them! Find them, I say!'

Megan-the-flea twitched. 'Keep still!' I said softly, watching Astarte strip off her robe and head-dress and put on her jerkin. 'Wait until Astarte comes close, and then jump for all you're worth, find a bit of Astarte, and hang on. As soon as she starts to vanish you'll hear a loud noise. When you hear that, *bite hard* and hang on.' Megan nodded. I clutched Cariad tightly, and as Astarte approached—

Chapter 18

—we jumped.

I needn't have worried about Cariad. As soon as we hit Astarte, she sank her fangs in.

With a last mutinous glare at Merch Corryn Du, Astarte fizzed and vanished, and we were outside again. I scrambled onto Astarte's collar and peered out at the rocky path, where a very cross and red-faced Rhiryd Goch waited.

'Where did they go?' she demanded before he had a chance to open his mouth.

The fox-haired man glared at her. 'Who? What are you talking about?'

'The Moonwitch and whoever she had with her. They've taken the baby, you fool! Which way did they go?'

'No one went past me.' (Too true, I thought. We're still here!)

'They must have. Granny said she could sense them close by.'

'Can't you? If Merch Corryn Du can tell, why can't you?'

Astarte looked angry. 'Because you haven't left me enough magic, you fool. It's all I can do to get into the cave! You've got to give it back. Now!'

'Nope! I told you I'd keep it until the moon's end. That was the bargain: I went through the Door of Time to fetch the brat, and I keep your magic for a month. A bargain's a bargain.'

'But I need it now! I'll give you anything. Gold! Land! I'll even build you a big castle!. You can be a great Lord once I've destroyed the Dragonson. Anything. Just ask.' Astarte looked coy. 'I'll even marry you, if you want.' She bared her teeth in a nearly-smile. 'Only I need my magic back now.'

Rhiryd Goch grinned. It wasn't a nice grin. 'While I've got your magic, Astarte, I've got everything I want. I don't want a wife, and if I did, I wouldn't want *you*!'

'But you can't keep it!' Astarte howled. 'It's mine! It will all come back to me in the end! I'm already getting bits of it back, thanks to Granny, and once I've got it all, Granny will flatten you like a—like a *bug!*'

'Which is why I need to meet your Granny!' Rhiryd Goch said. 'There's things I need to discuss with her. Once she's rid Ynys Haf of the Dragon King's brood, and finished off the Lady, then she'll need someone

151

reliable in charge, won't she! Someone strong enough to keep order. Someone not afraid of the *tylwyth teg*. Someone like me.' Rhiryd Goch strutted. 'I'm the perfect man for the job. You'll see.'

Astarte's mouth fell open. 'Don't even *think* about it! Granny would never—'

'Of course she would. Merch Corryn Du won't want to be bothered with keeping the peasants in order, will she? No, she'll need me for that. Just like you needed me, Astarte. To do your dirty work. I'm good at dirty work. You need me, Astarte, just like always.'

Astarte opened and shut her mouth like a goldfish. 'I—need—you?' she spluttered. 'You?'

'Me. Now, don't you think it's time you stopped arguing and looked for the brat? They can't have gone far.'

Astarte and Rhiryd Goch searched everywhere, but of course couldn't find us because we were still tucked away inside Astarte's (rather smelly) vest. When the sun was balanced like a great red ball on the horizon ready to tip over into night, Astarte gave up and stamped off down the path towards their hut. I scrambled back down inside Astarte's jerkin and found the others. Cariad had gone to sleep, and T.A. was clutching her so that she wouldn't fall off and get lost. Cariad even made a sweet flea!

'I think the best thing to do is to hang on until we get to the hut, then jump off, get outside and shapeshift. If we try to get off while she's walking, someone might get hurt.' So we all stayed close inside Astarte's clammy jerkin, hanging on for dear life. Megan the nursemaid was making the most of being a flea, and was managing about two bites of Astarte to the square centimetre in revenge for Astarte's earlier bad behaviour. Astarte would itch for ages! At last Astarte flung open the door of the hut and stamped inside.

'Quick!' I whispered, 'Jump now!' and four fleas scrambled over the top of Astarte's collar and hopped off onto the floor. Fleas are amazing jumpers—it was like having spring-heeled boots on!

Seconds later we were outside, and out of sight of the hut we shape-shifted and joined the other two merlins circling anxiously overhead. I turned Cariad into a fieldmouse, and carried her gently in my beak. I must have been getting really good at shape-shifting and still staying me inside the creature's body, because I didn't once want to eat her! Gwydion greeted me with a joyous squawk and we headed for the *tŷ hir*. Megan the nursemaid came with us, but we detoured and left her, shifted back to Megan, on the doorstep of her cottage, bouncing to get inside and tell her husband all about it.

Back at the longhouse we changed back and T.A. took Cariad from me almost before my wings had turned to arms. Honestly, she couldn't keep her hands off that baby! However, I had a feeling that once Flissy set eyes on her, T.A. would have to queue up and take turns!

The door flew open and Flissy and Nest rushed out. Flissy gazed at Cariad, her hands over her mouth. 'Well!' she said. 'Well I never. Hello, Cariad, *sidan fach*! Dear me, Tansy, she's the spit of our Heledd!'

'Crumbs, I hope not, Aunty Fliss!' T.A. and I said together.

'Well, she certainly looks like her,' Fliss said. 'She's her Mam, after all!'

She opened her arms and took Cariad into the *tŷ hir*. While Nest and Flissy cooed over the baby, I told Gwydion and Taliesin what had happened.

'So you still didn't find a way into the cave?' Taliesin looked worried. 'That's going to be difficult, Tansy. Riding on Astarte's back is all very well but it could get dangerous.'

'Dangerous?' T.A. and I said together. 'How, dangerous!'

'Tanz,' Gwydion patted my head and sighed. 'Everything you do in Ynys Haf is dangerous to some degree. Even walking down a pathway, for goodness sake, at least while Astarte and her unpleasant relative are about. But hitching a ride on someone else's spell is especially dangerous. They can go wrong and people sometimes reappear with—'

'What?' we said.

'Well, with bits attached in the wrong places.'

'You mean our arms and legs—' T.A said, horrified.

'Coming out of our ears?'

'Something like that, Tanz.'

'Thanks for telling us,' I said bitterly.

'If I'd warned you before, how would you have felt about doing it?'

'Not happy.'

'Well, then.'

'But you still should have warned us, Gwydion. I probably would have risked it anyway.'

'Oh, sure. I forgot the Lady's given you some bravery! Well, now I *have* told you. The safest thing is probably if you find a disappearing spell of your own and learn it properly—' he grinned at me. 'So that you don't end up with transistor radios and candlesticks.'

That made me cross. 'When I turned Astarte's family into those, I was only thirteen, and I hadn't been a witch for very long. I did my best. Now I've been practising, and I've got the Lady's power as well as my own, and if there's a vanishing spell inside me somewhere, I'll find it.'

Gwydion grinned. He *did* enjoy winding me up! 'I know you will.'

'The trouble is, Gwyd,' I went on, 'going inside Spiderwitch's cave puts us at her mercy: she knows the way around it, we don't. There were eight tunnels, and most of them seemed to go round in circles. If it hadn't been for T.A. bringing Cariad's blue bunny so that I could divine Cariad, then we'd have been stuck. If we go in looking for old spider-chops, we'll never find her. Unless she wants to be found.' I shivered. I didn't like the thought of that.

'Oh, she'll want to be found,' Taliesin said grimly. 'But only when *she's* good and ready. When she thinks she can beat us. That's why we've got to go in after her, and track her down and destroy her once and for all. She's the Dark Queen, Tan'ith. The cause of all the misery and cruelty and coldness in Ynys Haf. Until she has gone Ynys Haf will never be safe. And that is up to you and Gwydion.'

'What about Astarte? Won't she have to be destroyed, too? And Rhiryd Goch?'

'Rhiryd Goch's ambition will destroy him. He wants more than Merch Corryn Du is prepared to give. His biggest mistake was hanging on to Astarte's magic. If he'd given it back as soon as he'd taken Cariad, then she might have been a bit merciful. But not now. Nobody crosses Spiderwitch. Nobody with any sense, that is. As for Astarte, once Spiderwitch is finished, so will she be. Without her magic, she won't be strong enough to fight you, Tan'ith. You have the Lady's power.'

'But I'll have to give it back some time,' I said gloomily. 'Then what?'

'Wait and see!' Taliesin said. 'Wait and see.'

'The next thing you need to do—and quickly—' Nest chipped in from the other side of the *tŷ hir,* 'is try to find that disappearing spell. That's the most important thing of all. Until you find that spell, you can't do anything.' She busied herself putting blankets into a wooden box she had produced from the back of the *ty hir* to make a cradle for Cariad. 'One of us will have to keep watch tonight to make sure Astarte doesn't try to take the baby back. Then, tomorrow, Flissy and I will take her to the Dragoncave and stay with her. She will be safe there until this is all over.'

T.A. was hovering around Flissy, who was holding Cariad while Nest got her bed ready and prepared warm milk for her. Cariad was drowsy, and the warm milk tipped her over the edge so that she fell asleep in Flissy's arms. 'I'll watch her,' T.A. offered.

Flissy opened her mouth to object, then realised that T.A. could be trusted.

'She'll be fine, Aunty Fliss,' I said. 'T.A. is almost more besotted with that baby than Mam, for goodness sake!'

'You watch until midnight, T.A.,' Flissy said gently, 'and Nest and I will take the rest of the night. Tomorrow, Tansy has a spell to find, and a battle to fight and then— well, then it will all be over, one way or another.'

156

Funny, I didn't much like the sound of that!

Next day, I ate breakfast, said goodbye to Flissy, Nest and Cariad when they set off for the Dragoncave, then I got down to finding the spell while Taliesin scryed what Astarte and Rhiryd Goch were up to. Gwydion hovered between the two of us, as if he didn't trust either of us to do anything right.

I looked in Nest's spell book, but the spell wasn't in there. Of course, I knew exactly what was in the Emerald Spellorium, I'd learned it by heart, remember? But I couldn't find any disappearing spells anywhere! Every time I almost got the threads of one, it sort of hid itself behind some other spell, so that I couldn't get hold of it. It was almost as if it didn't *want* to be found.

Two hours later, I had a headache from trying. I was also getting very ratty. 'There must be one somewhere,' I groaned. 'There must be, or Astarte wouldn't have one, would she? And Astarte's definitely got one, right?'

'Or has she?' T.A. looked thoughtful.

'Well, she does a pretty good job of disappearing if she hasn't!' I said. 'What are you getting at, T.A.?'

'Rhiryd Goch has got most of her magic, remember?' T.A. had a piece of string in her fingers and was making absent-minded cats' cradles. She held out her hands with the string wound on, and I picked up the right loops for her, so she could finish her string pattern.

'So?'

'Well, she had to borrow some of Spiderwitch's, right? Or she wouldn't have been able to go anywhere or do anything, would she?'

'Right.'

157

'And true to her name Spiderwitch is a spidery sort of person. Right?'

'Right. What are you getting at, T.A.?'

'Well, just think about spiders for a minute. You know when you find one in the bathroom, what do you do?'

'Scream and run, usually. Or yell for Mam or Dad.'

'And if everyone's out, what do you do then?'

I shuddered. 'If everyone's out, I go and get my spider-catcher. A plastic tumbler and a postcard. And I slap the tumbler over the spider, slide the card underneath and lift spider and tumbler out of the window without having to touch it or hear it crunch if I squash it.'

'But when you go to get your spider trap—by the time you come back, what has usually happened?'

'The spider's usually disap—' I could see where T.A. was heading. 'Ah. Only of course the spider hasn't actually disappeared, has it? It's just—' I wiggled my fingers.

'It's just slid into the nearest crack in the tiling, or under a carpet, or behind a bend in the piping. So you *think* it's disappeared, and it hasn't at all, has it?'

Gwydion was looking puzzled. 'I don't understand what you're getting at.'

T.A. and I exchanged glances. Now *that* was a first, Gwydion not understanding! 'Don't you see? What T.A. is saying is that when Astarte disappears, she probably actually doesn't. She probably just shape-shifts into something very small like perhaps a money-spider—and crawls through a crack!'

Gwydion caught on. 'So if you're right, T.A., all we have to do is wait until Astarte disappears, and then shift into spiders and follow her. And then, once we're inside and we've seen the way in, we'll be able to get out again.'

'That would account for why I can't find a disappearing spell. I couldn't get a handle on the ones in the Spellorium—it was almost as if they were hiding from me because they didn't want to be used—and if the Lady hasn't given me one either, then she doesn't think I need one. So T.A.'s idea is probably right. Astarte hasn't been disappearing, just shape-shifting. Why didn't I think of that?'

'Probably because you've got so much important knowledge sloshing around inside your head that you've stopped looking for easy answers.' T.A. had her smug look on, which made me want to prod her hard in the ribs.

'I'm a lot happier about you shape-shifting than about you messing round with a disappearing spell, Tanz,' Gwydion said, stretching. 'I'd find it hard having you with an arm or a leg where your nose should be.'

'If I had a disappearing spell, Gwydion Dragonson, then I'd do it right. So there!' But inside me I was rather glad I didn't have to. He wasn't the only one who preferred my bits and pieces exactly where they were!

Chapter 19

When Flissy and Nest had taken Cariad to the Dragoncave, Gwydion and I prepared to shapeshift and head for Cadair Corryn Du. Gwydion's idea was to slip into the cave as soon as Astarte had left after her daily visit to her Granny. I must be honest: Spiderwitch wasn't the sort of Granny most kids would look forward to visiting! Grannies are supposed to be kind and cuddly, with a very high grandchild-spoiling factor and lots of sweeties concealed about their persons. Not tall, thin and spidery with a nasty temper and a fondness for weird puddings. I almost felt sorry for Astarte. Almost.

Gwydion was probably right. We'd have a better chance if Astarte wasn't around. I hugged T.A., thought 'red kite!' and shape-shifted, but yet again when I tried to fly, nothing happened. 'Oh, all right.' I said resignedly to no one in particular. 'Come on, T.A. Looks like we still need you.'

That girl looked definitely *smug*. 'Can't honestly say I'm surprised,' she chortled. 'Obviously, the Lady knows I'm essential.'

'Even if we don't know why. I've got to admit you've been sort of useful so far. Right, T.A. Is there anything you need from your Tesco bag before we go?' Actually, I was being sarcastic. But T.A. looked thoughtful.

'Half a mo.' She shot back indoors and up the ladder again.

'What did you get this time?'

She grinned. 'Never mind. Just something we might need, that's all. And something for us, too, after. Oh, and the ball of string.'

160

I didn't ask 'after what?' I knew. I shifted her and we soared after the others. She was getting almost as good at flying as me. Her pale-wing patches flashed and her reddish feathers glowed in the afternoon sun. We hung around the usual place and waited until Astarte appeared outside Spiderwitch's cave. She looked very cross, and her ears were bright red, as if she'd had a severe telling-off. She was also scratching a lot.

We shape-shifted to spiders at the place she'd appeared, and began to search for the entrance. Gwydion found it, and just in time, because none of us had noticed Astarte's hungry magpie hovering above us. He'd spotted us, though, and we just scuttled inside the tiny crack in the rock in time to avoid his sharp beak. I made a mental note to keep one eye aimed upwards if I shifted into a creepy-crawly again. I didn't want to be any bird's breakfast, especially not that one's.

It was strange being a spider: my legs had a tendency to tangle up, and once I accidentally triggered off my spinarets, and tied myself up in spider-silk. I had to concentrate very hard to remember where everything was, and what it was supposed to do. It was a bit like the first time I rode my bike without stabilisers. Well, I know what I mean, all right?

Once we'd crawled inside the cave, we shifted back to ourselves. I got the Lady's twig out of my jerkin and conjured light out of it. Taliesin, stretching arms and legs out of spider-shape, gazed around the cave and shook his head. 'Eight tunnels! Which ones are blind ends, Tan'ith?'

I tried to remember. 'The first two, definitely,

and—um—well, the sixth tunnel from the left leads to the room where they kept Cariad and the nursemaid. That's probably the right one, because I think the tunnel carried on going after we got to the room. Can you remember which tunnel they came out of, T.A.? When they followed us, I mean.'

T.A. shook her head. 'I think it was the fifth. Or was it the fourth? I wasn't really watching.'

'We'll go down the sixth tunnel,' Gwydion decided. 'And if we don't find Merch Corryn Du then we'll look down another one. We'll find her. I hope before she finds us.'

So we set off, Taliesin and Gwydion in the lead, T.A. and me following, down the sixth tunnel, the way ahead lit by the steady golden glow of the Lady's sprig. We passed the room where Cariad had been kept, and kept on going. The tunnel narrowed, and my little light seemed to get dimmer, somehow. I shook it, the way you do a torch when the battery is fading, which was pretty daft when I thought about it, because it wasn't a battery, it was magic. Surprisingly, though, it worked! The twig flared up and gave a stronger light, revealing that the tunnel ahead divided into two, leading off left and right, into darkness. We stopped.

'Which way?' Gwydion muttered.

'How do I know?' I said, crossly. 'I've never been here before either!'

'T.A. and I will take the left hand tunnel,' Taliesin suggested, 'and you two take the right hand one.'

'T.A.—where's that ball of string?' She produced it from inside her jerkin. 'Look, if we unwind it from the inside of the ball as well as the outside, we can take an end each and keep hold of it. That way, if some of us get lost, the others will be able to find them by following the string.' We took an end of string each, and left the ball at the junction of the tunnels. I broke the Lady's twig in half and gave a bit to T.A. so they could see where they were going. Then Gwydion and I set off down the tunnel on the right.

I held the twig above my head and our shadows leapt and swayed scarily on the walls ahead of us. We'd been walking for what seemed like ages when I heard a strange sound, like the bass notes of a very flat and badly strung harp. 'Listen!' I caught Gwydion's sleeve. 'What is it?'

Gwydion listened, his head on one side. 'Don't know. Unless—'. He stopped, suddenly.

'What?'

'Nothing. Never mind.'

'Gwydion, *what?*'

'You don't want to know.'

'I do.'

'You don't.' I fixed him with a Look.

'All right. Think spiderweb.'

I nodded. And remembered. Spiders are attracted by the movements their prey makes when it's caught in the web. If Gwydion was right, the noise we could hear was the sound of something moving on a large web. A very large web. The question was, what? I shivered. Maybe I'd better save that to worry about later.

Gradually, the sound grew louder, a regular, low, almost hypnotic 'brrrm, brrm'. I found myself walking in time to it, without realising what I was doing, and tried to stop. But if you've ever tried *not* to march in time with a street band, you'll know how difficult that

163

is! The beat seems to get into your brain and force you to march to it! It was bothering me, distracting me, worrying me.

Gwydion walked slightly faster, and I knew the sound was having the same effect on him. Then a glow appeared at the end of the tunnel, and we stopped.

'What is it?' I whispered.

Gwydion shook his head. 'Light of some kind. Shall I put out the twig?'

I nodded. 'Good idea. In case she sees it.' I took it back and blew on it. It fluttered, flickered and went out. I tucked safely it inside my jerkin for the journey back. I hoped.

The tunnel widened again towards the light, and the ceiling rose to arch above us into a great circular cave. A low, miserable drone came from a huge crystal tank on a shelf on the wall. It was full of beautiful orange and black bumble-bees, trapped inside. Mam used to say bumble-bees were fairies' pussy-cats. A jar of honey, a jug of cream and a dish and spoon stood on a table beside the tank, and I decided to make sure the bumble-bees went out with us—if we got out in one piece. *When* we got out, I told myself severely. Think positive, Tanz!

Gwydion nudged me, and pointed. At first I couldn't see what at, but then my eyes got used to the strange light inside the cave. A huge black spiderweb stretched from the roof to the floor, the neat strands as thick as silken ropes, and the strange, harp-like strumming sound came from them.

'Is she up there?' he whispered.

'Can't see her.'

'I think she is. She's probably watching us.'

I went cold all over. All the Lady's bravery disappeared. *I do not like spiders one little bit!* They scare me, O.K.? Yes, even after I'd just been one. I can't help it, it's the way they scuttle on their long, hairy creepy black legs. Ugh. And the thought of Merch Corryn Du, thin, black and *spidery*, up in that awful web, waiting to catch us . . . I really, really wanted to go home.

Gwydion prodded me. 'Come on, Tanz. Where's all that bravery gone? Remember that old Monty Python thing your Dad likes? The one about the Spanish Inquisition?'

I stared at him. Monty Python? Had he gone totally mad?

'Come on. Think!'

'We're the Spanish Inquisition. Our chief weapon is—' Suddenly I understood, and grinned.

'Our chief weapon is fear!' we recited together.

'Exactly. So if she can make us afraid, she's halfway to beating us. I know you're terrified of spiders, Tanz. But remember, she's only a baddie. And the goodies always win!'

'You hope!' I said, but my teeth weren't chattering quite so loudly. 'Where does it say that in the rules?'

'What rules, Tanz?' His teeth gleamed white in the strange light.

'Oh, thanks very much!' I was getting cross, but even that was an improvement on being terrified. 'Cheer me up some more, Gwyd!'

The web seemed to be strung at intervals with something that looked like tiny iridescent bulbs, like Christmas tree lights. It almost looked pretty, the way a spiderweb in a hedgerow traps dewdrops which flash like diamonds when the sun catches them. Then I looked closely at the nearest 'light' and realised that they were *tylwyth teg*—fairies—trapped by their wings on the sticky web, their radiance causing the strange light. They seemed to be breathing, but looked as if they were asleep—or unconscious. I thought of Nest, the half-fairy, and got really, really mad.

Fury shot through me like an electric shock. I started for the web. 'I'm going to find that spidery old rat-bag and tear her legs off! See how she likes being held prisoner! I'll, I'll . . .'

'You'll calm down and *think*, Tan'ith!' Gwydion hissed, grabbing my arm. 'If you go charging up that web you'll be doing exactly what she wants, remember? Merch Corryn Du isn't making the noise. It's her victims trapped in the web doing it, not her! We don't know where she is or if she can see us. So stay calm!'

I peered round, nervously. Nothing moved in the darkness. 'What can we do, Gwydion?'

Without a word he reached inside his jerkin, pulled out a pair of leather gloves and put them on. Then he stretched out his hands and gently grasped a strand of the web. Both gloves stuck fast. Careful not to make the web vibrate, he pulled his hands out of the gloves, leaving them dangling on the sticky strands.

'Just as I thought. If we try to climb up it—or even brush against it—we'll get stuck. We'll have to wait for her to come to us. She must be up there somewhere.' He gazed upwards at the thick strands of web disappearing upwards towards the cave-roof.

'We don't have to wait, you know,' I said. 'Spiders don't get stuck to the webs, do they? So why don't we be spiders and climb up?'

Seconds later, we were spiders again. Very large spiders, to cope with the very large web. We started up the strands, which were like the sort of ropes that ships get tied to docks with. It is much easier to climb with eight legs than two and two arms! We scrambled up to the middle of the web and waited. There was still no sign of Spiderwitch.

'She must be here somewhere!' I said, crossly. 'Why doesn't she show herself?'

'Let's encourage her!' Gwydion said, and began to strum the web with his front pair of legs, irregularly, like the struggles of a panic-stricken insect. My strange spider-eyes caught the first flicker of movement in the darkness at the top of the web. Something was testing the web, scenting the air, two front legs feeling its vibrations. 'She's coming, Gwydion!' I whispered. 'She's coming.'

'I see her.'

She wasn't Astarte's Great-Great-Grandmother now. She was all spider, huge legs, red eyes, fat, hairy body and fangs. It wasn't a face you'd find on a choccy box, that's for sure! Strangely, though, I wasn't afraid any more. I just felt cold, calm, and very, very angry. She climbed down a long strand of web, and saw us. When I realised how big she was, I thought 'bigger', and instantly I was the same size. And then she shimmered and changed, and Merch Corryn Du was back as herself, old Spiderwitch, lounging across the web as if she was resting in a garden hammock.

'So, Goodwitch!' Her eyes flashed behind the red crystal of the spider mask. 'At last. You finally found me. Though, what good it will do you, I can't imagine. Now I have you, and I have Ynys Haf.' She smiled,

167

showing sharp, pointed teeth, reached out a hand and broke off a dead butterfly's leg, its beautiful blue wings left glinting in the web. She crunched it like a cheese straw. 'Now that you are here, Goodwitch, you will certainly not leave. You can't, for instance, shape-shift into anything but a spider. Anything you could possibly think of, from ant to elephant, would instantly become entangled in my web. But I, on the other hand am at home here. And while my favourite food is bumble-bees and honey, I also enjoy a fat spider occasionally.' She licked her lips.

Gwydion scrambled closer to me, and whispered 'She's bluffing, Tan'ith. She won't eat her own kind.'

That didn't exactly cheer me up. Spiderwitch suddenly moved, the fast, creepy, scary way large hairy spiders move, and changed into the largest tarantula I've ever seen, in or out of a zoo. It was as big as a wolfhound . . .

Chapter 20

I closed my eyes and opened my mouth to scream, then suddenly realised that I needn't be terrified of her, because I didn't have to touch the sticky web. I threw myself backwards off it, and spun a long strand of silk behind me so that I could abseil down. Half-way, I shifted into a buzzard, flexing my wings and opening my beak ready to pounce on the tarantula. What I planned to do was fly down to the floor of the cave with it, change into an elephant and stamp it flat. Yes, I know goodies aren't supposed to think like that, but I don't like spiders, remember? The sight of the huge, hairy tarantula poised on the web scrambled my brains.

And then the tarantula leapt off the web, shimmered and was gone, and a golden eagle soared roofwards, gaining height, vicious curved talons stretched in my direction, tearing, ripping beak open and ready to pounce. It was bigger than me, and I knew when I was beaten. Hurtling up to the roof, too panicky to shift, I flew frantically in circles just ahead of the open beak, trying to get above it so that it couldn't drop on me and kill me with those awful hooked talons. Right up near the roof I found a small ledge, just big enough for me, and perched there, my heart thumping, trying to decide what to do next. The eagle hovered hopefully above me, and I cowered back into the small safety of the ledge. Whatever I turned into I'd end up with a problem. Like, a being eaten sort of problem. I shut my eyes and concentrated, and when I opened them the eagle had vanished. I craned my neck to see where it had gone, and just missed having my head chopped off by the huge bird dropping down from above like one of those jets that overfly Wales—in my time, that is, not over Ynys Haf!

Then my brain got into gear again. If Spiderwitch decided she wanted to be an eagle— well, so could I. I took a deep breath and threw myself off my safe perch, changing as I went, and swooped after Spiderwitch circling below me, huge splayed primary feathers almost touching the cave walls. Screaming with fury, Corryn Du struggled to gain height and get up above me, but each time she got close I attacked her, slashing with beak and claws and driving her back down to the

169

ground. I knew I had to keep her away from the web. There, she was safe and we couldn't get at her easily. Gwydion realised what I was doing, changed to eagle and helped keep her from reaching her web and safety.

At last she wearied of trying, landed on the cave floor, and changed back to Spiderwitch form. Gwydion shimmered back, and so did I.

Suddenly, out of the corner of my eye, I saw Taliesin and T.A. emerge from their tunnel. Merch Corryn Du had her back to them and didn't see them. Even if she had she probably would have ignored them. Gwydion and I were the real enemy.

'Now we are more equal, Spiderwitch.' I straightened my jerkin. 'You are away from your web and in the open.'

She opened her eyes wide. 'Should I be afraid? Look at me, Goodwitch. Am I trembling? Are *my* teeth chattering with fright?'

I felt my ears go pink. O.K., so my teeth had chattered. But they weren't chattering now. I was too angry to be afraid. One of the imprisoned *tylwyth teg* had woken and was watching us. I suddenly noticed that Spiderwitch wasn't looking at me any more, but very pointedly over my shoulder, instead. Ha! She couldn't fool me! I knew that old trick from all the old B-movies I watched on T.V. She was trying to make me think there was someone behind me.

Unfortunately, there was. T.A. suddenly shrieked, 'Look out, Tanz! It's Astarte!'

I swung round, and a fat, dirty grey spell just missed me, splattering messily against the web. Astarte and Rhiryd Goch, his sword drawn, had emerged from a tunnel behind me, and Gwydion and I were

170

sandwiched between them and Spiderwitch. Swiftly I shifted, becoming an ant, and disappeared, Gwydion following, under a small stone while I thought what to do. A long, sticky tongue suddenly probed under my stone a hair's breadth away from me. Astarte had turned into an anteater—which was a real improvement, actually. Gwydion became a pure white panther and, muscles rippling under his velvet pelt, gathered on his haunches to spring, just as Astarte disappeared and I shifted back to me.

Rhiryd Goch, meantime, was waving his sword around threateningly, and Spiderwitch had seized the opportunity to get back onto the web. Gwydion changed to a spider and followed her, and I concentrated on Astarte, whose Great-Great-Granny had obviously decided to let her fight it out with me while she took on Gwydion.

'Look, Astarte,' I panted, still out of breath after hurtling round the cave after Spiderwitch. 'You know you can't possibly win. Last time you ended up being a bush. And now, of course, I've got the Lady's power. Just think what I can do to you if I want!' And I hurled a spell at her which, had it collided, would have stuck her feet to the ground until I chose to free her. Unfortunately, it missed, and she threw back something dark green and fizzy. I ducked, and it hit the web, where it flared briefly and died.

'I see you've managed to get some of your magic back,' I said. 'Did Rhiryd Goch give it to you, or did your spidery Granny? Even with that, Astarte, you still won't be strong enough to beat me.' Oh, I did hope I was right!

'I've got it all back, Goodwitch. Every last spell.'

171

Astarte gloated. 'Granny took it back from Rhiryd Goch while he was asleep. He couldn't magic his way out of a paper bag, now, let alone go through a Door.'

This was obviously a surprise to Rhiryd Goch, who stopped glaring at me and glared indignantly at Astarte instead. He looked from the retreating figure of Spiderwitch to Astarte with a thoughtful look on his face. I wondered if he was about to change sides. They did rather keep playing dirty tricks on him. I think he'd just realised he wasn't going to be King of the Castle after all! Just to be on the safe side, though, I zapped him with a very heavy spell which hit him on the head and knocked him out. He slid down the cave wall and took no further interest in what was going on.

'And,' Astarte drew her arm back, ready to throw something at me, 'I've also got some of Granny's magic. Just like you've got some of your Lady's. So there. So you aren't stronger than me any more, Goodwitch, are you?'

Out of the corner of my eye I could see T.A. rummaging inside her jerkin. She took something out, gave it to Taliesin, and whispered something to him. Next thing, two large spiders were crawling up the web after Spiderwitch and Gwydion. They stopped at each horizontal strand of the web and—I wasn't quite sure what they were doing, but they seemed to be sort of *stroking* it. This is no time to admire the quality of the web, T.A, I thought, and turned my attention back to Astarte. She'd just launched another spell, which splattered on the wall behind me, harmlessly, although a bit bounced off and made a hissing noise as it whizzed past my ear.

I was searching about inside my mind for a suitable

172

spell—perhaps one that would give her galloping meagrot or thorple-pox, something permanent like that—when my brain suddenly seemed to turn icy-cold, and the Lady's voice spoke, clear as a bell, inside it.

'Tan'ith! Don't bother with small spells. You have to finish Astarte, and quickly. Now. Everything depends on it.' And into my brain filtered one of the forbidden spells. The ones from right at the back of the Spellorium, where the pages were stuck together with magic until I really, really needed what was inside. The only seriously, awfully permanent spells in the Book. I had glanced at them once, shuddered, and forgotten them. *You want me to use THOSE spells? Lady, are you sure?*

'Yes, Tan'ith! Astarte is no longer important. Merch Corryn Du is the one to be afraid of. Astarte is nothing. Don't tire yourself fighting her. Save your strength for Merch Corryn Du!'

'You're the boss!' I said, aloud, and took a deep breath. I retrieved the words of the spell from the attic of my mind, blew off the dust, sharpened it to a point and threw it. As it left my mind it became a spear of green light which hit Astarte right between her blue and brown eyes. Which crossed. And closed. She slid to the floor and lay there, fast asleep. I wandered across and bent over her. She was out for the count, a small smile on her lips, her gingery head pillowed on her arm. She was actually sucking her thumb! My spell had totally, utterly, de-magicked her. She would never do another spell as long as she lived. She was un-witched. She'd probably end her days as a cow-keeper's wife, or a washerwoman at the Castle. She didn't have the brains for much else. She might win an intelligence contest against a half-witted French poodle, but that was about it. If, that is, her Great-Great-Grandmother didn't defeat me, take away my magic and give it to her. The battle wasn't over yet, not by a long way.

I looked up at the web. I couldn't see Gwydion any more, and Spiderwitch had disappeared too, probably lurking in a crack in the cave roof, waiting until he got close enough to zap. I changed to a merlin and flew upwards, not wanting to climb the web and warn her that I was on my way. T.A. and Taliesin were crouched in the very centre of the web, where the separate vertical lines soared up and out. They were still stroking it with their front legs. Whatever they were doing, I hoped it would be useful.

I flew up into the arch of the roof and began to search for my enemy. I couldn't see her, but I knew she was there. I could feel her watching me. I fluttered in and out of small upside-down hollows, peered at ledges, flew frantically round and round but still couldn't see her.

And then, the way you spot, out of the corner of your eye, a spider walking across the floor when you're watching television late at night, I saw her. She had made the smallest of movements, perhaps just easing cramp in a leg, and I had her. As soon as she knew that I'd seen her, she shot down her web, lurking just above where T.A. and Taliesin were waiting.

'Ah, the Bard,' she hissed, changing into Spiderwitch-the-person, stretching down the web head first, like a bat. 'Good. You're all together. I can finish you off and then Ynys Haf is mine.'

'I don't think so, Merch Corryn Du,' I hovered

174

opposite where she clung to the web. 'Not if I can help it, anyway.'

'But you can't help it, can you?' She swung her legs down so that she was the right way up again, her awful eyes glittering behind the hideous spider mask. 'You aren't strong enough to do anything that could possibly harm me. You change, I change. You use a spell, I use a spell. But I am older, wiser, stronger and much, much nastier than you, Goodwitch. You are hardly a match for me. I should have preferred to fight your Aunt. What is her name? The one who thinks she is strong—ah yes—Aeronwy. Antonia. "The Ant", you call her, yes? How appropriate, since I could crush her under my feet just like a miserable ant. But I have to content myself with crushing you, instead.'

'Over my dead body!' I said, bravely.

'If necessary, yes!' Spiderwitch smiled. Her teeth seemed much more pointed than they had been, somehow . . . I found myself staring at them.

'Tan'ith!' Gwydion's voice startled me. 'Concentrate! Don't let her hypnotise you!'

I shook myself, and flapped my wings. I had begun to drift towards the web, where I would have been entangled. I looked around for Gwydion. I could hear him, but not see him.

'Looking for the Dragonson? He will not be any use to you. He is there, see?' Corryn Du waved her arms towards a dark shape at the top of the web. It was Gwydion, wrapped up like a parcel ready for posting, in sticky spider silk.

'Don't worry about me,' he called. 'I'm fine. Just concentrate. You can beat her, Tanz. Remember the Lady's powers! Remember them, Tan'ith.'

175

As if I'd forget! Then I realised he was trying to tell me something in particular. The Lady's special powers. Eyesight. Hearing. All my senses were enhanced. I used my eyes, peering into all the darkest corners, and came up with nothing special. Then I listened. I heard the scrape and thrum of the web, the sound of Gwydion breathing, Taliesin and T.A., their spidery legs rustling on the web. I heard a bird call outside, an earthworm tunneling—and then another sound. Tap. Tap. Tap-tap-tap-spatter-splosh-splosh.

What on earth? Then I knew. Rain! Heavy rain. The sort that soaked, and saturated, and—flooded. The Lady spoke again, her voice urgent, '*Nest is changing the weather. She is tired, it is a difficult spell, but if you act quickly, then she can keep going long enough. Quickly, Tan'ith. Before the rain stops.*'

Right, I thought. So it's raining. Nest has changed the weather. Whoopee. *So what, Lady?*

I heard T.A. call my name, softly. I fluttered down beside her. 'What, T.A.? Her spidery face had a definite grin on it. 'Can you hear the rain?'

'Yes, faintly. That's why I called you. I think I know what you can do. Think, Tanz!'

'I'm thinking, T.A. I'm thinking really, really hard. Only what should I be thinking about, particularly, please?'

'The nursery rhyme, Tanz! *The nursery rhyme!*' She was speaking in riddles, unable to say what she meant clearly in case Spiderwitch heard.

I looked at her blankly. And then it came to me. Of course!

Chapter 21

Of course! At last I knew what she was on about.

> *"Insy, winsy spider,*
> *Climbing up the spout*
> *Down came the rain and*
> *Washed the spider out . . ."*

Nest was making it rain. And if she could keep it up long enough to flood the tunnels, then Insy Winsy Spiderwitch would be trapped like a spider in a bathtub. But it would take ages to flood a cavern this size. Especially if it had to soak through that tiny crack where we came in and then down through the tunnels. If only I could make things a bit wetter at this end . . .

I flew up to the roof and perched on a largish ledge—large enough to take me in my human form if I didn't wriggle too much. I squirmed backwards, practically hanging on with my toenails, and fumbled very carefully in my jerkin for the twig, even more carefully raised my arm, trying very hard not to lose my balance and fall off, and touched it to the roof.

Spiderwitch was craning her neck upwards, trying to see what I was doing. She didn't want to leave the safety of her web, and her awful masked eyes glinted red in the dim light of the trapped *tylwyth teg*. I concentrated very hard on that small, frail, budding, blooming, fading, budding twig, putting all my magical powers into what I was doing, and at last the power shot up my arm, into my wrist, down my fingers and burst out of the end of the twig like a rocket from a launcher.

There was an almighty crash and a large hole

appeared in the roof of the cave, letting in a great gush of torrential rain—which instantly washed me off my shelf, swept like a leaf over a waterfall. While I was falling, I changed into a bird, wondering briefly as the rising waters rushed up to meet me, if it might be better to change into a fish instead. But then my magic kicked in, and merlin-me flew up and away.

Spiderwitch was still staring at me, her eyes glittering angrily.

'Do you think I am afraid of water, Goodwitch?' she shrieked. 'Don't be ridiculous! I shall just hold a bubble of air between my front legs and float to the surface. And then I shall come after you, and destroy you wherever you hide.'

The water gushed in through the hole in the roof. The cave floor was awash, but it would still take too long to flood the tunnels. Then I had an idea, flew down, changed, and splashed quickly round the walls, tapping them with the twig. Wherever I touched, springwater gushed white out of the cave walls until the sound of rushing, falling water filled the cave. Now it was beginning to flood properly—and quickly.

Then I heard T.A. call, 'She's getting away! Quickly, Tanz!'

I changed back into an eagle and flew up, harrassing her, worrying her, stopping her climbing, my flashing talons and tearing beak pinning her into the web so that she couldn't leap off and change, forcing her to go down, towards the water, instead of up to the hole in the roof and safety. She changed to spider and scuttled downward swiftly, avoiding my slashing beak. She rushed down the web, me following afterwards, worrying away at her.

178

'That's it, Tanz. Keep her going down!'

I wasn't sure why, but the excitement in T.A.'s voice made me do it. I drove Spiderwitch down past the level of web where T.A.- and Taliesin-spiders clung. Suddenly Spiderwitch stopped. And I mean *stopped*. Stopped the way you do when the brakes on your bike lock, going down a hill. Like, over the handlebars type stop. She jerked forward, almost falling flat on what would have been her face if she hadn't been a spider. She tried to lift a leg from the web, but it seemed to be stuck. She tried another, and another, but all eight were stuck solidly to the web. She was caught as fast as the *tylwyth teg*, in her very own spiderweb. She shimmered and changed back to Spiderwitch form, snarling with rage, but her arms and legs were still immovably stuck to the strands.

'Spiders don't stick to their own webs!' I said, feeling fairly confused.

'They don't, indeed,' Taliesin said. A small grin was lurking on his spiderish face.

'But this will do it every time,' T.A. crowed. She held up a squeezed and empty plastic tube. I craned my neck to read the label. It read: '**Supastik**'—**Sticks Anything, Anywhere.**'

'You used *superglue?*' I said. 'Wherever did you get superglue? The Lady told you to bring *superglue?*'

'Well, she didn't actually tell me what to bring. Not in so many words, anyway. I just wandered around the supermarket putting in things I thought might come in handy. And superglue was one of them.'

Taliesin grinned. 'I think the Lady might have given you a nudge towards the right shelf, T.A. In a manner of speaking.'

Gwydion's indignant voice came from above. 'When you lot've quite finished rabbiting, and patting each other on the back, would you mind unwrapping me?'

Gwydion! I started towards him, to free him, and then stopped. He was high enough above water-level to wait safely—if uncomfortably—until a bit later. 'Quick, T.A., Taliesin, we have to free the *tylwyth teg*. And the bumble-bees. And I don't suppose we can let Astarte drown now she's harmless.'

Taliesin changed to a merlin, shifted Astarte and Rhiryd Goch into (unconscious) mice and carried them out of the rapidly filling cavern, and I flew around the web, avoiding the superglued strands, gently untangling the *tylwyth teg*, careful not to damage their fragile, iridescent wings. In the meantime, T.A. splashed through the rising flood and broke open the clear box with the bumblebees in. One or two of them, flying upwards, stopped to buzz angrily round Spiderwitch.

Merch Corryn Du ignored them, watching us instead, her red, malevolent eyes staring, helplessly trapped in her own web. Once the *tylwyth* teg were all set free and were streaming in a joyful rainbow of colour upward and away from the rising water, I crawled up to Gwydion, and began to untangle the thick ropes of silk which tied him.

'So how come she managed to catch you, Gwydion?'

He scowled. 'I was so busy watching you that I didn't notice her sneaking up behind me.' He pulled his sleeve up, showing two small puncture marks on his wrist. 'She changed to a small spider—probably a venomous one, because I lost interest in what was going on altogether. By the time I came round, she had tied me up.'

I stared at the small red marks. 'Gwydion, she could have killed you! Suppose she'd been a really poisonous spider! One of those Australian redbacks or something! You'd be dead, now! She'd have killed you!'

He rubbed the marks. 'I think she tried. But I have enough of the Old Ones in me to resist the sort of poisons that mortals die from. Luckily. Otherwise Ynys Haf might be looking for a new Dragonson, and there isn't one.' Once he was untied, he shifted to spider, clambering past Spiderwitch, on the vertical strands of the web, which T.A. and Taliesin hadn't glued.

We surrounded our helpless prisoner. She glared and tried to wrench herself free, shifting from spider, to bird, to wasp, to cat, and back to herself again, but whatever she changed into, she was still hopelessly stuck to the web.

'The decision is yours, Dragonson,' Taliesin said, waving his front spiderlegs. 'Does she live or die?'

Gwydion stared at Corryn Du. 'If she will leave Ynys Haf in peace, if she will promise never to trouble the people of Ynys Haf or the *tylwyth teg,* or the creatures who live here. If she will promise to accept me as Dragonson and DragonKing, then she may live. I, Dragonson, ask for your promise of loyalty, Merch Corryn Du. Will you give it?'

'Never.'

'I ask for your promise never to fight against me again. Will you give it?'

'Never.'

'I ask for your promise to leave Ynys Haf in peace. Will you give it?'

'Never. Never, never, NEVER!' she shrieked.

'Then, Merch Corryn Du, you will have to stay in your cave forever. This is all you may have of Ynys Haf.'

'Who are you to command me, Dragonson. Would you drown me? If you do, you will break your own stupid laws. You are the Dragonson.' she sneered. 'You can't kill. Remember?'

'You are right, of course. I can't kill the way you and Rhiryd Goch do, in cold blood. But if you threaten the peace of my country, I, the DragonKing, can imprison you here under Cadair Corryn Du, until you swear to obey me. Until you grow old and die, if necessary.'

Spiderwitch smiled. It wasn't a friendly smile. It was the sort of smile you get from a guard dog just before it decides it would like your left leg for lunch.

'Yes, Gwydion Dragonson. You can do that. But you aren't DragonKing yet. And while I live, you will never be DragonKing. And you must, of course, let me live.'

'You're right, I must. But with the Lady's power, and the magic of Ynys Haf, I can defeat you once and for all by sealing you in here.'

'But you don't have the Lady's power. She is caught between worlds, and has lost her magic. She's finished.'

'Ah,' I said. 'Now you're only half right there, as it happens. The Lady *has* lost her powers. But didn't it occur to you to wonder where they went? I've got them, you artful old arachnid, you!' (I was quite pleased with that 'artful arachnid' bit: there's nothing like a bit of alliteration to make a good point!) 'The Lady may be powerless,' I said, 'but I'm blooming well not.'

Spiderwitch's face changed. For the first time, she looked ever-such-a-little-bit scared. Then the malevolence came back.

'You? You think you can threaten me, Goodwitch? What can you do to me? You may have the power, but do you have the courage to use it?'

I ignored this taunt and spoke calmly. 'I go along with Gwydion on this. You stay here. All alone in the cavern, for ever. If that is what Gwydion Dragonson wants.'

'And do you think I will stay here, once you've gone? What will you do, put me on my honour not to move? Don't be stupid.'

I mentally turned another of the forbidden pages of the Spellorium and winced. This spell was really nasty. It had a sort of *implacable* feel to it, you know? *Lady? Is it right to use this spell?*

'Use it, Tan'ith. She must be stopped.'

'I'd really like to chop her up in small bits and feed her to the lions, but I'm not allowed, am I? So I suppose we just seal her up in the cavern for ever 'n ever?'

'The choice is yours, Tan'ith. But think carefully before you decide. I advise you to use the spell.'

The trouble was that I still didn't like hurting people. I thought about the crunched-up bumble-bees, and wavered. I thought about Rhiryd Goch, stealing Cariad. But then we got her back, so that was O.K. I thought about locking up all the village men—and Iestyn Fawr—in the castle dungeons. But they were safe now, too. Yes, I'd really, really like to finish Spiderwitch for once and for all—but I couldn't bring myself to bump her off, so to speak. It wasn't my style. Gwydion was watching me, carefully, the way someone might look at an unexploded bomb. I took a deep breath. And decided.

'Merch Corryn Du, in the name of the Lady, I sentence you to stay for all eternity in your cavern. The openings will be sealed with magic, and the flood waters will remain at the level they are now. I won't let you drown, even though I'd really, really like to. And you won't starve. Plenty of insects and stuff will get into the cave, so whatever you shape-shift into, you can eat. It's up to you. But here you stay, for ever.'

She didn't say anything. She just smiled her terrible, pointy smile. Gwydion, Taliesin, T.A. and I leapt off the web and shifted, soaring up out of the water-filled cavern to freedom. Then, using the Lady's strongest magic, I sealed the hole I'd made in the roof and all the tiny cracks in the rocks, so that nothing could escape. When I'd finished, I heaved a sigh. Merch Corryn Du was trapped, and Ynys Haf was safe forever.

The evening sky was that wonderful deep blue that slips in between the sun going down and the moon coming up—not quite dark yet, but holding enough light for the blue to remain for a short while, streaked with pink on the horizon. Rhiryd Goch and Astarte lay on the grassy hilltop beside the hole I'd made in the roof of the cavern. Astarte still snored gently on, but Rhiryd Goch, groaning, was coming round. It had been a particularly heavy spell I'd socked him with. Nest had stopped the rain-spell, and the earth smelled wet and wonderfully fresh.

The four of us peered down into the hole in the roof of the cavern. There was no sign of Spiderwitch now, even though we got down on our hands and knees and peered into the darkness below.

'Well, we know she's down there somewhere. If I just chuck down a general superglue-melting spell, that should do the trick. She won't drown, anyway, not now the rain's stopped.' Even though the superglue should wear off in time, I felt I ought to unstick her from the web, so she wouldn't starve. I peeled off a bit of the Lady's twig, attached the spell to it, and dropped it down. There, she was un-stuck. Still trapped in the cavern forever, but able to move around it to find food. I turned away from the hole, and caught Gwydion's eye. He was looking at me strangely.

'What are you thinking, Gwydion?'

He grinned and ruffled my hair. 'Oh, only that if you'd decided to chop Merch Corryn Du into little pieces, I shouldn't have been a bit surprised. But I'm glad you didn't.'

'Why? I would have thought you wanted me to get rid of her for once and for all.'

'Part of me thinks that. The other part decided long ago that you are, underneath that obstinate and argumentative personality, too soft to hurt anyone. And I wouldn't have you any different.'

Naturally, I only heard the first bit. 'Obstinate! I am not obstinate! And I'm certainly not argumentative, Gwydion Dragonson! How dare you s—' I stopped, feeling rather stupid. Gwydion and Taliesin were holding each other up, snorting with laughter, and T.A. was looking sadly at me, shaking her head.

'Oh, Tanz. You walked right into that one.'

We gathered up Astarte and Rhiryd Goch to carry between us, and set off down Cadair Corryn Du towards the *tŷ hir*. When we reached the hut Astarte and Rhiryd Goch had used as a hideaway, Taliesin paused.

'I don't know about you, Gwydion,' he said thoughtfully, 'but I think this old place would make a pretty good bonfire.'

Gwydion nodded, and it seemed right to me, too. The quicker we got rid of all traces of evil from Ynys Haf, everywhere that Rhiryd Goch, or Astarte, or Spiderwitch had used to attack us, the better.

We dumped Astarte and Rhiryd Goch on the ground to carry on dozing, and Gwydion opened all the doors of the hut. Then he took a deep breath and sent a fire-spell whizzing like a comet into the thatched roof, which caught instantly, the dry straw burning with a crackle and a roar, sending flames leaping up into the night sky. Hunting bats wheeled in and out of the flying sparks, and a startled owl crashed into a tree, its night sight destroyed by the sudden glare. In the trees beyond, fox-eyes glowed green in the darkness, and smoke rose and curled against the moon.

There's something about a bonfire at night that is mesmerising. It really gets to you, doesn't it? It certainly got to us, because when we stopped watching the glow and feeling the warmth on our faces and turned round, there was no Rhiryd Goch: he'd legged it off into the woods.

'Rats!' I said angrily. 'We should have watched him. T.A., you and Taliesin go back to the *tŷ hir* and let them know everything's all right. Gwydion and I will go and look for him.'

186

We shapeshifted into owls and flew upwards. We searched the woods, the fields, even the slopes of Cadair Corryn Du, but there was no sign of him. At last we gave up, and headed back to the *tŷ hir*.

Chapter 22

I was so tired when I got back that I just crawled straight up the loft ladder and fell asleep with all my clothes on. I didn't stop to eat, and even T.A. coming up to bed didn't wake me. It was mid-morning when I woke. My boots had been pulled off and were standing side by side at the end of the straw mattress, so I tugged them on and peered over the rail. Only Flissy was downstairs, bustling around with her whisk broom. She felt my eyes on her and looked up.

'Good morning, Tansy! Come down and I'll get you something to eat. The others are all out doing various chores, but you were giving a good impression of a hibernating bear, so they left you to it.'

'Where's Astarte?'

'Oh, Nest took Astarte up to the Castle earlier this morning. She's quite harmless, now. No magic at all. They'll find her something to do, somewhere to live in the Castle, I expect. She's quite a changed girl without all that nasty magic sloshing around inside her. Almost pleasant. She even said 'please' and 'thank-you' once or twice!'

'Never!' I found it hard to believe Astarte had changed THAT much. I wasn't quite sure I trusted the new-style Badwitch! I scrambled down the ladder and went outside to splash my face and hands with cold water to wake me up. The sun was high, and the air was warm and full of sweet, woody smells. Oh, and bees. It was almost as if all the bees we'd freed from Corryn Du's cave the day before and all their honey bee cousins, had turned up to thank us. They buzzed in a small dark cloud a few feet away from me, followed me to the door of the longhouse, and then backed off.

'Aunty Fliss? There's thousands of bees outside. Do you know why? '

Aunty Fliss smiled. 'Bees are strange creatures, Tansy. Haven't you heard of the old tradition that when a bee-keeper dies, someone from the family has to go and whisper it to the hive? And when there's a birth, or a wedding? Bees like to know what is going on in their family, and after you set them free yesterday, they seem to have adopted you. They did the same to T.A. when she first went outside this morning. It won't do any harm to keep them posted about what's happening.'

'Should I do anything?'

'It wouldn't do any harm to have a word with them. Tell them everything is all right now.'

It felt fairly weird standing outside talking to a swarm of bees, but Flissy knew best. I cleared my throat and looked at the buzzing swarm. It came closer. 'Um,' I said 'I just wanted to say that I'm glad you weren't eaten. What Merch Corryn Du was doing with you was dreadful. I hope you'll be able to live in peace in Ynys Haf from now on, all right? Make nests in holes and burrows and stuff, and have lots of bee-babies and be happy. Um. That's all.'

For a minute, they hung there, buzzing, and then

the whole swarm turned and flew up into a tree nearby, and disappeared into a hole high up in the trunk. I watched until the last buff-coloured furry rump had gone, and then went back into the *tŷ hir*. 'Looks like Nest's got her very own swarm of bees, Aunty Fliss!' I picked up an apple and munched it, washing it down with gulps of sweet fresh milk.

'Oh, the bees will stay around now that they know they are welcome,' Flissy reached up to put a pot on a high shelf. 'Just as long as we keep them posted about what's happening.'

I laughed. 'Well, I suppose that now we've got Cariad back and fixed Spiderwitch, we can all go home! I don't really want to go, but T.A. and I've got G.C.S.E.s soon. And I still haven't got the hang of maths. Maybe Gwydion can give me a hand. T.A. was trying, but she isn't brilliant at maths either. Gwydion knows everything. Maybe he can help when we get back.'

Flissy picked up a jug and put it down again. 'Gwydion isn't going back, Tansy.'

I put my apple back on my plate, my appetite gone. 'What? Of course he's coming back, Fliss! He's mine! He lives with me! He always comes back.'

Flissy sat down opposite me, and took my hands in hers. 'He isn't yours, Tansy. He is the Dragonson, and will soon be the DragonKing. His time has come, and his duty is to stay here and rule Ynys Haf. His father must rest: he has lived a half-life ever since Rhiryd Goch's father had him poisoned by a treacherous servant. He can only exist in the Dragoncave, and he is existing only until Gwydion can take his place as DragonKing.'

I tried to imagine life without Gwydion. Even as Cat, he was still my most special companion. Yes, I know T.A. is my best friend, but Gwydion is different. Perhaps because he is magic, like me. Life without him would be—ordinary. Aunty Fliss watched my face, probably reading my feelings from the expressions flitting across it. I suppose I'd known all along that Gwydion wouldn't stay a cat forever. But I'd never imagined Gwydion not being there at all.

'Won't I ever see him again, Aunty Fliss?'

She patted my hand, and smiled. It was rather a strange little smile. 'Of course you will! You can pass through the Door of Time whenever you need to. I promise you'll see him again. You—' Then she stopped.

'What?'

'Nothing you need to worry about. Just trust me, will you? I promise you that you will see Gwydion again even though this time, you have to go back without him.'

That made me feel better—but I still wasn't happy about him staying behind. I finished the apple and chucked the core out of the door of the *tŷ hir* for the birds to pick at, then washed and changed my clothes. That was one thing I really, really missed about our time: hot showers! Cold buckets don't have nearly the same effect.

By the time I'd brushed my hair the others were back. I tried not to look too hard at Gwydion, because I still had that awful lump in the throat sort of feeling, as if I really wanted to have a good cry. When they'd had lunch, I said 'Right!' all brightly, so that no one would know anything was wrong. Of course, T.A. did, straight away, and she looked at me suspiciously.

'What's up, Tanz?'

'Oh, nothing. It's just that we've finished off

Spiderwitch, we've sorted out Astarte and even if Rhiryd Goch got away he's fairly harmless without the other two. So all we need to do is collect Cariad from the Dragoncave and go home.' I pulled a face. 'Back to G.C.S.E.s, remember?'

'Oh, don't! By the time we get back we'll have hardly any time left to revise.'

'Time's elastic, Tanz, remember?' Taliesin said softly, his knowing gold-flecked eyes meeting mine. 'It comes and it goes, and all that you need to do can be fitted in to it. You'll find Time to revise, I promise. But it isn't over yet, you know. You can't go back until after Gwydion becomes DragonKing. You of all people, as the Lady's representative, must witness that.'

'Is there going to be a party-thingy, after?' T.A. asked excitedly. 'There ought to be, didn't there?'

Taliesin roared with laughter. 'Can you honestly imagine Flissy and Nest letting a celebration go by without feeding everyone involved?'

I shook my head. 'Not really. When will it be?'

Gwydion, bending over Brân's head, nose to nose with the great hound, looked up. 'As soon as it can be arranged, Tanz. My father is tired, and it is time he was allowed to rest. But there is plenty to do before it happens.'

'There is?'

'There certainly is,' Nest said firmly. 'Flissy and I have to plan the banquet and get the cooks and maids from Castell Du to begin preparing it. You and T.A. have to go with Gwydion and Taliesin to fetch Cariad back, and—oh, loads and loads to do.'

T.A. jumped up, eagerly. 'Can we go and get Cariad now?' She couldn't wait to get her hands on the baby.

'All right,' Gwydion stood up and reached out his hand to pull me to my feet. 'We'll go the quick way, and shift. Then we can walk back.'

The four of us shifted to merlins, and headed towards the hills, blue in the distance, where the Dragoncave was hidden. I was bringing up the rear, and was a few yards away from the *tŷ hir* when I thought of something, and flew back to the longhouse, perching in the branches of a tree with a large hole in its trunk. I shifted back to me, and made the mistake of glancing down. Oops! Long way down, there, Tanz! I thought, and shut my eyes, quick. Then I opened them, cleared my throat politely and spoke loudly over the droning hum coming from inside the trunk.

'Excuse me, bees,' I said, feeling ever so slightly idiotic. Then I noticed that the steady buzzing had stopped. As if they were listening . . . 'I'm just— um—letting you know that we're going to the Dragoncave to get the baby, and after that Gwydion will be made DragonKing, there'll be a big party and then T.A. and I will go home. All right?'

There was a short silence inside the hole, and then the buzzing began again. 'Fine,' I said, shifting back to merlin and launching myself after the others. 'Just thought I'd tell you.'

Because the others were flying fairly slowly, I soon caught up, and together we landed on the mountainside just below the peak, where the huge round boulder hid the entrance to the Dragoncave. Shifting back, I turned to look down the side of the steep slope towards the woods below, and the sea beyond, glinting in the afternoon sunshine. A slight movement caught my eye in a clump of trees at the foot of the mountain, and something caught a stray sunbeam and flashed like a fragment of glass will sometimes catch light and reflect it. Then I heard the grating sound of the boulder moving aside, and turned, forgetting the brief dazzle of light. Out of the mountain came the muffled shrieking of a very loud baby.

'That's our Cariad!' T.A. chortled proudly. We went in through the entranceway and through the huge open stone dragonjaws of the gatehouse. I patted a huge stone fang as we passed through, for luck, marvelling at the amazing craftsmanship which had made the lifelike dragon coiling around the castle, its tail wrapped round the turret. We walked into the sunlit courtyard, where Gwydion's future people bustled about, smiling a greeting to us, and up the flight of steps to the castle door. Once again, Gwydion's father met us, and ushered us inside. I gazed back into the sunshine, wondering how it managed to be sunny, inside a mountain. Magic was an amazing thing: just think, mortals got excited about stuff like electricity, and here was all this impossible sunshine, deep inside a cavern!

We were welcomed into the great hall and serving maids brought us goblets of wine and small, crisp almond biscuits. T.A. was very taken with these, and demolished most of the plateful before she realised what she was doing. DragonKing, when we had all been served, sent a maidservant to fetch Cariad, and she scuttled off, her skirts stirring the rushes strewn on the floor.

'And what of Merch Corryn Du?' the King asked, eventually. 'If you are here she must be finished. Is she dead?'

Gwydion shook his head. 'No, Nhad, she isn't. But

she is sealed forever inside Cadair Corryn Du by Tan'ith's strongest magic. She will not trouble Ynys Haf again. Rhiryd Goch escaped, but without Astarte he is harmless, and Tan'ith, with the Lady's help, took away all Astarte's magic. So, you can rest, Father, if you wish.'

DragonKing sighed, massaging his forehead with long, transparent fingers. 'Rest! That sounds wonderful. Are you ready to take on the responsibilities of Ynys Haf, Gwydion?'

Gwydion didn't answer straight away. Then he took a deep breath and said, 'I think I have learned the lessons of Ynys Haf. With the help of the Lady, and Tan'ith, I am ready to become King.'

DragonKing then turned to me. 'And what about you, Tan'ith? Are you ready to face what lies ahead?'

'Me?' I was puzzled. 'Oh, you mean my G.C.S.E.s. Well, ready as I'll ever be. Trouble is, if I get lower than a C in maths, I've got to re-sit it in November. And I've been a bit too busy to revise, lately! Fighting old spider-chops and stuff, you know?'

The King looked puzzled. 'G.C.—whats? I don't—'

'DragonKing,' Taliesin broke in, 'Tan'ith has yet to learn the Lady's plans for her future.' He glanced at me, a curious expression in his eyes. 'But I'm sure she knows that in Time, she will return to Ynys Haf. And there is plenty of Time, my Lord. She is young yet.'

The King looked from Taliesin to me, and back to Taliesin, and nodded. 'I see. Well, when the Time is right, Tan'ith, Ynys Haf will welcome you back.'

The sound of a shrieking baby echoed down the corridor towards us, the door burst open and a harrassed-looking woman came in carrying a

194

struggling, red-faced Cariad. Cariad was beating the nurse about the head with a small blue stuffed bunny. T.A. leapt up and reached out her arms. Cariad, of course, stopped shrieking and snuggled into them.

'Thank you, Mari,' Taliesin said. 'You have taken good care of her. You can leave her with us, now.'

Looking as if she was mightily glad to be rid of Cariad, Mari curtsied and left. T.A. cooed and Cariad blew contented bubbles.

'That is a very loud child,' DragonKing said ruefully. 'She likes to have her own way. She has disturbed Our nights since she has been here. Such a temper in one so small!'

'But then, you've never met her mother,' I said, and then blushed, in case I'd been a bit cheeky. But the King laughed, and chucked Cariad under the chin.

'And now, Nhad,' Gwydion interrupted, standing up, 'I think it's time we let some fresh air into this place, don't you?'

The King looked up at his tall son. 'Oh, yes, my boy. How I have missed that.'

Chapter 23

Gwydion, T.A., Taliesin and I trooped outside, but DragonKing stayed behind. What I *thought* was going to happen was Gwydion was going to roll the boulder away for good so that the natural light could stream into the mountain. Boy, was I ever wrong!

Gwydion turned to me. 'You'll have to help me, Tan'ith. Break off a piece of the Lady's twig.'

Fairly mystified, I fished the sprig of the Lady's staff out of my jerkin and broke off a small piece.

'Now, hold your pendant with the Arianrhod ring, and with your other hand throw the twig as hard as you can. Try to hit the top of the mountain, all right? Just where that big round boulder is, up there. And at the same time, concentrate. Think "sunlight".'

'Sunlight?'

'Yes. I'll do the rest.'

I shrugged. I supposed he knew what he was doing. I clicked the Arianrhod ring against the pendant, and concentrated hard on the small twig in my hand, until I felt the Lady's power gathering in my fingertips, and then, obediently thinking 'Sunlight, sunlight', I threw it. It sailed through the air and landed on the huge boulder sitting on top of the mountain.

There was a small explosion, a puff of smoke, and the ground shook. Small stones rattled off the sides and rolled down the mountain, crashing down into the valley. A distant roaring sound, like a steam train in a tunnel, echoed far below our feet, and then the shaking got worse, and we had to brace ourselves on the ground like sailors in a rough sea not to be thrown off our feet. The boulder vibrated, and then shot upwards, hurtled through the air and flew down the mountain, bouncing all the way down, hurtling into trees and bushes. I made a mental note to mend them on the way back. I didn't like to think of us damaging Ynys Haf, even accidentally, and in a good cause.

Then I forgot all about the trees. Out of the hole in the top of the mountain (which now looked rather like a volcano) came another puff of smoke, then a sheet of flame, and in the next instant a massive, scaly head thrust upward into daylight, turning this way and that, great golden eyes searching, as if to get its bearings. Next, a crack down the side of the mountain appeared, and then another, and massive shoulders thrust their way into the sunlight, followed by two immense, red, leathery wings, and a long, scaly tail tipped with a sharp arrow-shaped point. As the great creature came fully free, the mountain crumbled all round it, revealing the shape of a mighty, sandstone castle. The dragon crouched on the battlements flapped its great wings, testing them, revealing a creamy underside contrasting with the dark crimson of its back and wings.

Beneath its talons the castle glowed red in the sunshine.

'Is that Castell y Ddraig?' I stammered.

Gwydion nodded, smiling proudly. 'My home, Tan'ith. The place where I was born. Out in the light of day, where it belongs, at last. Now that we've got rid of Merch Corryn Du and Astarte, it can stand free and proud again.'

'Um. That Castle. Castell y Ddraig,' I said, my knees wobbling. 'It doesn't seem to have a dragon gatehouse any more. It's just a plain, ordinary stone one. With a portcullis and stuff, instead of—' I gulped.

'Teeth?' Gwydion said, innocently. 'No, of course not. The dragon sort of wanted them back, Tanz.'

'Do you mean that every time I've walked through that gatehouse, *I've been walking inside that dragon's mouth?*'

He nodded. 'But it didn't bite you. It's on our side. Only the dragon could have hidden the Castle and allowed my father to live his half-life in the darkness until I was old enough to become DragonKing. The dragon is my ancestor; our protector.'

Funny, I still didn't feel any better. I remembered the huge jaws and sharp stone teeth. Those teeth, I thought, gazing upward at the sharp white points wreathed in smoke, hovering over my head.

The great glowing golden eyes gazed down, surveying the small band of people gazing up, at least two of us with our mouths open in wonder and disbelief, and then it gathered its four legs under it, flexed its wings, and flapped. As its wings grew stronger, its feet left the ground, and at last it was airborne, soaring up into the blue sky, the wind from its passing almost blowing us over. I shoved my dragon-blown hair back from my face. 'Where will it go, Gwydion?'

He shaded his eyes, peering after the dark shape majestically winging into the distance. 'Its home is the fastness of Eryri, Tanz,' he said softly. 'It will stay there, guarding Ynys Haf as it once guarded DragonKing. Until Ynys Haf needs it again.'

Only then I remembered T.A., and turned round. She was still clutching Cariad, sitting on a boulder looking totally, as they say, gob-smacked.

'O.K., T.A.?' I enquired.

'O.K.?' she muttered indistinctly, disentangling Cariad's fat fist from her hair, 'I've just seen a real, live dragon, and you ask if I'm O.K.?'

'That's all right then.' I turned to Gwydion, I was going to ask a question, but when I saw his face, it sort of got forgotten. His face was so sad.

I touched his hand. 'Gwyd? What's the matter? Shouldn't you be happy now? You're going to be

DragonKing, and your castle is back, and your father can rest. What is it? Please tell me.'

He turned, and put his arm across my shoulders. 'That's just it, Tanz. I knew it had to happen, once the dragon was out and Castell y Ddraig free again. But I shall miss him. He was always there. Well, more or less, anyway.'

'Miss who?'

'My father, of course. Now that his castle is back in the real world again.'

(Real world, I thought. Hah!)

'Everyone who served him has gone back to their homes, but my father's Time here has run out. He's really dead now, Tanz. It's a bit like having him die all over again.'

He looked so unbearably miserable I had to give him a hug. Where once I'd have been able to put my arms round his neck, now I could only reach his middle, he was so tall. 'Oh, Gwydion, I didn't think. I'm so sorry.' I looked up into his face, and he smiled back. A watery sort of smile, but a smile.

'That's the way of it, Tanz. The King is dead, long live the King.'

And there was I, hugging the King of Ynys Haf's bellybutton. I disentangled myself.

Taliesin, standing behind me, dropped to one knee. 'Highness,' he said softly, bowing his head. Gwydion slapped him on the back, and Taliesin stood up.

'Am I supposed to curtsey or something?' I said.

Gwydion chuckled. 'Probably not. You'd only fall over, knowing you.'

I got indignant. 'I can curtsey as well as anyone.

Watch.' However, my knees were still wobbly from the earthquake, the dragon-rising and stuff. I fell over.

'See?' he said, smugly.

'You may be the next DragonKing, Gwydion,' I said crossly, dusting off my rear end, 'but you're still a lousy know-all at times.'

T.A. was going purple in the face trying not to laugh. 'It's O.K., T.A., you can laugh. I mean, you're only my best friend. Why shouldn't you laugh at me, just like—GWYDION, LOOK OUT!'

I threw myself forward, shoving him out of the way. A flung spear hissed past his ear and bounced harmlessly off the castle wall. The setting sun caught a gleam of reddish hair slipping back into a clump of trees. 'Rhiryd Goch!' I said. 'Quick! T.A., get Cariad inside the Castle. Gwydion, Taliesin, come with me.'

And, shapeshifting into red kites we curved our white-patched red wings, hurtling down the mountainside after Rhiryd Goch.

The wood, after the bright sunlight outside, was gloomy, and we flew from tree to tree, trying to find him. He was well hidden, and although we searched the small copse from end to end, there was no sign of him. Like the fox he resembled, he had gone to earth.

Eventually, we landed and shimmered back to ourselves. 'He's gone,' Taliesin said, 'but we have to find him. If we have to spend our lives looking behind every bush in case treachery lurks behind it, Ynys Haf will never be safe. But this time, we must make sure that he is finished.'

'What,' I said uncertainly. 'Kill him? We can't *kill* him, Taliesin. 'We don't—'

'Do that sort of thing. I know. But we can make sure that he doesn't bother us again.'

Suddenly, something small, furry and striped shot past the end of my nose. Followed by another, and another, and—

'It's the bees!' I yelled. 'The bees have come. They'll find him!'

And find him they did.

They spread out, thousands of them, searching every leaf, twig, damp hole beneath the roots of trees, until they discovered him. He was hiding in a discarded badger sett, covered in dried leaves and mud where rain had seeped in. The bees drove him out, like tiny sheepdogs worrying a huge sheep, and, flying in a cloud around his head, pushed him towards us. Then they flew off a few yards and hovered in a dark, droning cloud, watching.

Gwydion stood tall and stern, his arms folded. Rhiryd Goch, mud-spattered and sullen, still clutched a short bow, and the quiver on his back was filled with the familiar red and black striped arrows. Taliesin stepped behind him and took them away. Rhiryd Goch clutched his bow as if he'd like to strangle Gwydion with the bowstring, but they left him that. Gwydion was big enough, if he felt like it, to tie Rhiryd Goch in a knot round the nearest tree.

'Rhiryd Goch,' Gwydion said sternly, his deep voice echoing in the stillness of the wood, 'you have been a thorn in Our side since the day you were born. Your mother was a trouble-maker, your father had mine poisoned, and you were raised to cause Us trouble.'

Do you know, he sounded so stern he almost scared me!

'Whatever trouble I caused you, DragonSon, was nothing to the trouble you and your father caused me. You took away my lands when you killed my father. I only want what is mine.'

'Nothing was taken from you, Rhiryd Goch. Despite your father's evil, my father showed you nothing but kindness. He had you educated, fed you, made sure your mother wanted for nothing. He had no reason to do this: your father had him poisoned, a coward's weapon, and died in battle rebelling against him. And you, his son, sacrificed Ynys Haf to Merch Corryn Du in the hope of taking my place. For crimes against DragonKing, it is in my power to forgive you. But for your crimes against Ynys Haf, you must be punished.'

Rhiryd Goch shook back the rufous hair hanging over his eyes. 'Punish me? How? You can't kill me. I shall fight you to my last breath, DragonSon! So how will you punish me?'

Gwydion smiled. 'Oh, I'm sure the Lady Tan'ith can think of something!'

Who, me? I stared at him. 'Me?'

'Think about it, Tan'ith. How can we be sure that Rhiryd Goch can do us no further harm?'

I thought about it, and while I was thinking, tuned in to the Lady's powers. Birds rustled in the leaves around us, a fox cub yipped in the distance, earthworms tunnelled tirelessly through the brown earth beneath our feet, interrupted only by the occasional slither-chomp-stretch-byoinnnng-slurp when they found themselves in a mole run by mistake. A mole run . . .

'I think I've got it!' I said, and grinned. Rhiryd Goch was staring warily at me, ready to run. I took out the Lady's twig, tapped him firmly on the head with it, even though he struggled to get away, twisting and turning his head to avoid it, then I closed my eyes and concentrated.

There was a strange whistling, sucking sound, and Rhiryd Goch disappeared. At my feet, blinking in the brightness, was a small creature with a bright pink nose, whiskers, and big, pink spade-like hands . . .

'Now then, Rhiryd Mole,' I said, crouching down to hold it before it could burrow into the earth. 'Just about the only damage you will be able to do in future is to make mole-hills on the castle lawn. Off you go, there's a good creature.'

With a last, malevolent glare, the small, dark creature thrust its pointed nose into the ground and, digging with its spade-like hands, disappeared. Gwydion absent-mindedly flattened the scattering of newly dug earth it left behind.

I grinned at him. 'There. Nothing remains now but to get you DragonKinged, have a totally amazing rave-up, and then we can all go home. Right?

'Right!'

Amazing how I managed that smile. I didn't feel like smiling. I couldn't bear the thought of going home without him.

Chapter 24

Everyone joined in the preparations for the coronation: messengers on swift horses were sent all over Ynys Haf with invitations I had to help write because, of course, word processors hadn't been invented yet, and if we'd left it to the King's Scribe we'd have been there until Domesday, because he insisted on illuminating every capital letter in gold and painting little red-and-silver dragons round the borders!

It felt a bit odd when I put the one marked "Gwyddno Garanhir, Cantre'r Gwaelod" in the envelope. I remembered the legend which told of Cantre'r Gwaelod's drowning. Maybe I'd get a chance to warn him about his sluice-gate keeper. Gwydion needn't know, and Taliesin, with luck, wouldn't find out. Maybe I could save Cantre'r Gwaelod from its watery grave single-handedly.

I should have known better. The night before the ceremony Taliesin sat me down and had a few quiet words. 'Tan'ith,' he said sternly. 'This is both Taliesin, Chief Bard of Brython, and Mr Howard, Music, speaking, so please listen to both of us. Many of the people you will meet tomorrow will have familiar names. Names from history, and legend. If you, by one word, hint to any one of them that you know what is going to happen to them, I will personally turn you into a bluebottle and swat you. Understand?'

I pulled a face.

'Look, let me give you a for-instance. If Owain Glyndŵr was coming—which he isn't, by the way— and you decided, just because you knew how it all

204

ended, to tell him that his great and righteous uprising was doomed to failure from the start, he might not even attempt to fight, no matter how great the injustices heaped on Wales. And then, if he didn't even try, Wales would lose one of her greatest heroes. Do you understand? *You can't change history.* You could destroy Ynys Haf, and you would even have a terrible effect on Your Time Wales as well. What will happen must be allowed to happen. O.K.?'

I could see his point. But I had to try, didn't I? 'Not even a little, little, very hard to puzzle out hint? Please?'

'NO, Tan'ith! You'll behave? Promise?'

I sighed, and scuffled my boots in the rushes. 'All right. I promise.'

It did seem a shame, though. Then people started to arrive, and I found myself so totally gobsmacked by some of the people I was meeting—I, me, Tanith Williams, from Heol y Bryn, Glanllyn, Sir Gaerfyrddin, Wales. Like who? Well, Gwyddno Garanhir, of course, and minor and major Lords and Princes from all over Ynys Haf, ranging from the big, bearded and noisy to the small, dark and musical. Heroes, legends, Kings, Princes, all jumbled together out of my history books. All together, from different centuries. Where else would they be, but Ynys Haf? Some of them had a sort of fragile, ethereal look about them, as if they had sent their spirits and left their bodies sleeping in a cave somewhere, but some of them, like Gwyddno Garanhir and his son Elffin were very much alive—for the time being, at least, I thought glumly. Then I caught Taliesin's suspicious eyes on me and tried to cheer up. They wouldn't actually *die*. If they lived on in legend, they'd live on in Ynys Haf, wouldn't they? Like Hywel Dda, and Llywelyn the Last, and Owain Glyndŵr.

But best of all was the one I *wasn't* expecting. Can't think why. Logical, really, when you think about it! And when I met him, I didn't even recognise him. That's the trouble with reading about someone for years and years—you think you know what they should look like. And then, when you meet them, they don't. With the Lady's hearing, I could pick up the sound of someone arriving long before anyone else did, except the dogs, of course, but even I didn't hear this guest arrive. We were all in Castell y Ddraig, helping to decorate the great hall ready for the feast afterwards. Outside on the battlements were two Very Enthusiastic trumpeters. Whenever they spotted anyone coming up the mountain, they tootled away until everyone had assembled in the courtyard. At first they did this for everyone, so several kitchen maids, men-at-arms and laundry-carriers got a welcome that turned them scarlet with embarrassment, and a lot of time was wasted by busy people having to rush out into the courtyard every five minutes to wave their hats and shout '*Croeso!*', and 'Well, goodness me, look who's here!' and other stuff like that. This time, however, the person arrived so fast that all the trumpeters could manage was a sort of strangled squawk. And the strangled squawk was mainly because they didn't know exactly what had arrived! By which time he was already inside the courtyard.

I saw him first, although I didn't know it was him, if you see what I mean, because, like I said, he didn't look the way I'd imagined he would.

206

'Gwydion,' I said, sort of thoughtfully, 'there seems to be a condor outside. A Very Large one.'

'A what?' Gwydion peered through the open doorway. 'So there is. Oh, good. He's here.'

'Who?' I asked, but he was gone.

I followed him out, and arrived at the foot of the steps just in time to see the condor shimmer and shape-shift. Some sort of a magician, then.

He was tall, and thin, with round, thick-lensed glasses which slid down his narrow nose. He wasn't exactly handsome, but he had a kind sort of face, but an absent-minded one, as if he was trying to remember the eighth item he had written on a very long shopping list he'd accidentally left at home. His thick white hair was tied at the nape of his neck in a pony tail fastened with a rubber band (which hadn't been invented yet), but then neither had his denim jeans, T-shirt with 'Ynys Haf is Magic!' on the front, and ratty old trainers.

Gwydion waited politely until whoever it was had straightened his T-shirt and pushed his glasses up his nose. The stranger looked up.

'Good Grosmont, Gogerddan and Gwbert, Gwydion! You've grown up, you nasty little monster!'

Gwydion's ears went pink. 'I am honoured that you could come, Sir. Your gracious and wise presence would have been sadly missed,' he said, stiffly. I think his teeth were gritted. 'It wouldn't have been the same without you.'

The person peered at him through his glasses, which were smeary, as if he'd forgotten to clean them for a week or so. 'Well, I should just think it wouldn't be the same, you nitwit. It can't happen without me, can it?'

Gwydion went redder. 'No, sir. I forgot, sir. Sorry, sir.'

By that time, Taliesin had arrived. 'Oh, leave him alone, Merlin, you old grouch. He's a grown man now, and will be DragonKing tomorrow. Try having a bit of respect, if only for the title.'

Merlin? Where was the long beard? The pointy hat? The gown with the moons and stars on? The wand? This Merlin looked like a chemistry master we'd once had. Sort of absent-minded and a bit bad-tempered.

Gwydion, who by this time was bright scarlet, turned round, saw me, and picked on me to cover his own embarrassment. 'Close your mouth, Tanz, there's a bus coming.' I shut it. 'Merlin, I'd like to introduce—'

'I know, I know. The Lady told me about this one. Tan'ith. It's rather short, isn't it? And have you noticed its freckles? And its hair is—'

'If you say ginger, it'll throw a tantrum,' Taliesin advised solemnly. 'Say dark red. It doesn't mind that.'

'But I do mind being talked about as if I was some sort of bug that isn't here,' I said coldly. I put my nose in the air to stalk inside, tripped over my feet and fell flat on my face. Gwydion picked me up and turned me round. Merlin peered at me. His eyes glittered behind the smeary lenses.

'Good. She's not afraid to stand up for herself. Just what you need, Gwydion. Someone to let you know when you're being a complete idiot.'

That was better. I was almost beginning to like him. 'He can be, can't he?' I said. 'He's getting better, but he still has a way to go, I'm afraid.'

Gwydion had begun to splutter. 'I—'

I shrugged Gwydion's hands from my shoulders. 'My Lord Merlin,' I said politely. 'May I offer you a cup of tea and a Welsh cake? My Aunt Fliss makes the best Welsh cakes in Ynys Haf—and in our Time Wales, for that matter.'

'Welsh cakes? I haven't had a decent Welsh cake for centuries. I tried Marks and Spencer's once, but they weren't the same. And I remember Flissy's from the old days.'

We left Gwydion and Taliesin open-mouthed at the foot of the steps. At the top, I turned round. 'Just make sure Lord Merlin's chamber is properly aired and tidy, Gwydion, will you?'

That'll show you, I thought!

Aunty Fliss and Nest flew at Merlin with cries of delight, and whisked him away to fill him full of goodies. I had to go and try on the dress I was supposed to wear for the crowning. Three seamstresses had been working for days to get it right. It had lots of green lacy stuff, and bits of silver in it, and even if I say so myself, I looked kind of good in it. T.A. had a deep red one, which set off her curly dark hair. Lord Ceredig of Ceredigion was rather taken with T.A., and was following her around like a puppy-dog, but I reminded her that he was a sailor, and probably had a girl in every port. Well, every port between Fishguard and Cricieth, anyway! However, I noticed that T.A. wasn't exactly discouraging him, despite my warning!

All that remained to be done to my dress was to sew up the hem, and I was standing on a stool while plump Anwen, her mouth full of bone pins, pinned it up to the right length, ready for the seamstresses to sew. The door opened behind me, and someone came in. I glanced over my shoulder and caught a glimpse of a girl carrying a tray with beakers of tea and a dish of Welsh-cakes on it. Then out of the corner of my eye, I saw something move, high up on the wall. A huge wolf spider crouched in a web up near the ceiling. I shivered, remembering. 'Do you think someone could get rid of that spider, please?' I asked. 'And the web if you can reach it.'

Anwen, her hands busy pinning up the hemline, spoke indistinctly through her mouthful of pins. 'You, Astarte. Do as Lady Tan'ith says and shift that spider. Quick with you, now!'

Astarte? I nearly fell off my perch like a dead budgie, with shock. The familiar blue-and-brown eyes glanced at me. Then up at the spider. She balanced carefully on a stool, reached up, and caught the spider between her cupped hands. It ran between her fingers and up her arm, sitting on her shoulder next to her face, stroking her cheek affectionately with its long, hairy legs. I shuddered.

She saw my shiver, and smiled. The smile said 'Still don't like spiders, Moonwitch? Good!'

She might have lost her magic, but she still didn't like me much. With the spider still nestled against her face, she quietly left the room.

'She's a strange girl, that one,' the seamstress said.

You're telling me, I thought. Still, without her magic, she was harmless. I hoped!

The evening before Gwydion became DragonKing was strange. We were all half-happy, half sad, because after tomorrow, everything would change. Gwydion would have to stop being Gwyd and would have to be

King, responsible for all the people in Ynys Haf; all the creatures, and all the land and everything growing on it. He had spent a long time during the day shut up in a chamber with Merlin, and came out looking very serious and a bit worried. But when we'd eaten supper, and were all sitting around, the dogs at our feet, exchanging stories and remembering things that had happened to us in Ynys Haf, the feeling got a bit lighter, with almost a Christmas Eve-y feel to it. You know, that fizzy-bottle-of-pop in your middle feeling?

'Gwydion,' I idly tugged Garan's ears, 'now that you have Castell y Ddraig, what will happen to Castell Du? It's a sinister old place, but it's got a lovely view over the sea. Will anyone live there?'

'I've been thinking about that,' Gwydion shifted in his seat, reaching for another of Flissy's Welsh cakes, the pig, even though we had just finished dinner. 'I thought I'd fill in the dungeons, and make the arrowslits into nice big windows, and put in a solar at the top of the turrets and then it could be my sort of summer palace—my Llys Haf, you know?'

Merlin cleared his throat. 'A good idea, my boy, in theory. But it is a fortress, and fortresses are built for a purpose. Don't forget that it occupies a valuable position of sea-defence. Even though Ynys Haf is peaceful now, don't make the mistake of thinking that it always will be.'

I glanced at Gwyddno Garanhir, who was dozing fatly off, and at his son, Elffin, who was lying on a sheepskin rug with dogs all round him, making sheep's eyes at T.A. All that history, waiting to happen. I sighed.

'You're right, Merlin,' Gwydion agreed. 'But just

211

for tonight, let's not worry, shall we? Tomorrow I become *Brenin Ddraig*. Tonight I don't want to think about the future. I'll do it tomorrow. Right at this minute, there's no need to worry, is there?'

I remembered Astarte, and wondered. No. She didn't have any magic left at all, did she?

'Tanz?' T.A. was sitting on my left. 'What's up?'

I grinned, and punched her arm, gently. 'Nothing, ratface. Except I saw Astarte today. She may have lost her magic, but she still doesn't like me.' I told T.A. what had happened with the spider, and how Astarte had let it run all over her. 'It's horrid, but it doesn't mean anything, does it?'

'No, I suppose not.' She took a swig of her wine. 'I nearly forgot. I've got a treat for us tomorrow. I'm fed up with drinking all this mead and wine and stuff. I've got two whole cans of you-know-what,' she whispered, 'so we could have them the night before we left Ynys Haf. A sort of cheering-up operation. It won't be ice-cold out of the fridge, but it will still be cola.'

I could almost taste it—all that unhealthy sugar. Yummy! 'Oh, mega-blissful, T.A.! You know, you're amazing? Only you could have have behaved with such utter unselfishness and resisted drinking them.'

She pulled a tragic face. 'Ain't it the truth, toadface. It was so totally, totally hard. But I've got to agree. I am totally, amazingly amazing!'

Chapter 25

I didn't think I'd sleep too well that night, but I did, and was quite surprised when the noise of the castle birds shrieking in the eaves woke me at first light. I lay there for a bit, drowsing under the patchwork quilt. There was a knock at the door, and I yelled 'Come in'. Then I saw who it was, and wished I hadn't. It was Astarte, carrying a breakfast tray. 'Oh, it's you.'

'Yes, it's me. I begged the cook to let me bring it up to you. I smiled, sweetly, and said please and thank you, and yes, ma'am and no, ma'am, and it would be such an honour, ma'am.' She glared at me, her odd eyes blazing hatred. 'It doesn't take much to fool the peasants. But you know differently. You know I haven't changed. I'll fight you as long as I can. You may have taken my magic, Moonwitch, but I'm still here.'

'But you can't do anything now, Astarte, can you?' I said reasonably, struggling to disentangle myself from the quilt. 'It's all over. Just accept it, O.K.? Spiderwitch is stuck in her cavern forever, Rhiryd Goch is finished, so there's only you, and you haven't got any magic left, so there's no way you can do anything to hurt Ynys Haf or Gwydion, is there? Nothing at all.'

She smiled. 'No, you've taken my magic away, I haven't forgotten. I hate you for that. But one day, when you aren't looking . . . Sharp knives and dark nights, Tan'ith. You'll never know where, or when.' She put the tray down on the end of the bed and picked up the apple that lay on it. She showed her pointed teeth. 'Or maybe poison. That would be so easy, wouldn't it?'

'Except that I shall be in my Time, Astarte, and you will be here in Ynys Haf. And without magic, you can't reach me there.'

'You won't always be there, Moonwitch. Sooner or later, you'll have to come back. And then . . .'

'It's no good, Astarte. You can't do anything. So you might as well settle down and enjoy Gwydion's crowning. Go on. I know it's hard. Just try to accept that you're beaten.'

She strolled to the door and opened it, then turned, 'Don't be too sure of that, Moonwitch. And remember—watch your back.' She grinned, evilly. 'Oh—and *do* enjoy your breakfast.' She closed the door softly behind her.

I looked at the tray she'd brought: large speckledy brown boiled egg, bread soldiers, herb tea, and the apple. Didn't look poisoned. But then, how could I tell? I decided to do without breakfast.

Down in the great hall, everyone was panicking. Cooks were rushing around, Kings, Princes and Aunty Fliss were shouting at servants, and men-at-arms were polishing armour as hard as they could go. Gwydion was nowhere to be seen. Taliesin was tuning his harp, and the silvery sound made a pleasant counterpoint to the awful noise.

'Where's Gwydion?' I asked, sitting beside him on the bench.

'Gwydion, believe it or not, must be still asleep. I'd have thought he'd be down by now, and getting in a twist about the ceremony. Merlin will want to spend some time with him beforehand: he'll probably get Merlin's number one lecture on being a Good Little DragonKing.'

214

'Merlin doesn't have to worry about that. Gwydion will be the best DragonKing ever.'

'I know that, and you know that, and Merlin probably knows it too, but he does love to lecture people. In your Time——'

'He'd have been Professor Merlin, Science!' I said, and laughed.

Bored, I went for a walk, and found my swarm of bees, so I brought them up to date on what was happening. I quite liked having someone to talk to that didn't answer back, just listened. I told them all about Astarte and her threats, and they buzzed angrily. Then it was time to get dressed, and I said a polite goodbye and went indoors.

Gwydion still wasn't awake, and by this time Merlin was looking slightly testy, and tapping his foot. Taking the hint, Taliesin went up the spiral stone staircase to wake him. Seconds later, he was back.

'He's gone!'

'Gone?' I was mystified. 'He can't have!'

Merlin was on his feet and racing upstairs to Gwydion's chamber. It was empty, the bed-hangings pulled back and the bed-clothes rumpled. Gwydion's leather trousers were in a heap on the floor, together with the green jerkin he'd worn the day before. If his clothes were there, where could he be?

Taliesin searched the garderobe and the little turret on the battlements, and I looked under the bed, but he wasn't in any of those places. I looked up at the hangings over the four-poster, wondering if he could possibly be hiding on top of it, to give us all a scare. But deep down I knew that wasn't Gwydion's style.

Then I saw it.

A thick dark spider-web stretched from the top left-hand pole of the bed hangings to the bottom right hand pole. Right across the bed. If the sun hadn't caught the thick strands of silk, I'd have missed it.

'Spiderwitch!' I breathed. 'She's taken him. I just know she has!'

'I thought Merch Corryn Du was safely sealed in her cavern.' Taliesin reached up a hand and angrily dragged down the web, wiping his hand on his jerkin. 'We should have finished her when we had the chance.' He paced the floor, his gold-flecked eyes glittering with rage. 'There are people who don't deserve to live. This time, we will make sure.'

'We can't kill her, Taliesin,' I repeated. 'The Lady would not want that.'

'Right at this moment, Tan'ith, Lady or not, I could tear Merch Corryn Du limb from limb. Where do we begin to look?'

And then the bees arrived. They buzzed in through the arrowslit in a steady black and yellow furry stream, hurtled around my head like small, droning missiles, and then shot off down the stairs. When I didn't immediately follow them, they came back, buzzing impatiently, and did it again.

'I think they want us to follow them!' I said, belatedly catching on. I hadn't watched all those T.V. re-runs of *Lassie* for nothing! 'Come on, quick!'

We pounded down the stairs, Taliesin, Merlin, and I, to be joined at the bottom by T.A., clutching her Tesco carrier bag. I decided I didn't have time for the failing-to-take-off routine, so when we shifted into red kites to follow the bees, I shifted T.A., too, to make sure we didn't lose any time having to go back for her.

I vaguely noticed her shoving the carrier inside her jerkin as she shimmered and changed.

The four of us hurtled upwards after the bees, which for such bumbling little creatures, could certainly move when they put their minds to it. We zoomed down the mountain, across the valley, over the roof of the *tŷ hir*, skimmed the tops of the trees and the village huts. I think I knew all along where we were headed, and I was right.

Castell Du crouched on its cliff above the sea, black, sinister, and silent, because all the people who had been inside had moved themselves to Castell y Ddraig for the ceremony. Even Rhiryd Goch's army, once they knew for sure he had gone, had defected and sworn an oath of fealty to Gwydion, and the Castle was still and silent. But as we grew closer, I realised that something else was different about the Castle. It had taken on a greyish appearance, as if it was covered in fine dust. Except that it wasn't dust, it was spiderwebs. The whole Castle was covered, from turrets to drawbridge, in a fine network of webs. Merch Corryn Du couldn't have done it all herself: she must have called in an army of spiders. Well, there were plenty of those around any Castle. I squawked a warning to the others just in time to prevent them landing and getting stuck to the web, then followed the bees round to the seaward side of the castle.

And there was Gwydion. Tied up tightly in thick strands of sticky web, wearing only his white under-breeches, dangling over the side of the battlements, spinning helplessly in the wind from the sea, his black hair blowing across his face. Down below, the waves crashed hungrily on jagged black rocks. Above him on the battlements was Spiderwitch, and in her hands was a large knife.

The bees buzzed angrily round her head, distracting her, and she threw back her head, laughing horribly, plucked a bee in mid-flight, tossed it into her mouth like a peanut and *crunched*. The bees backed off, then, and shot off in all directions out of range. Taliesin, Merlin, T.A. and I flew as close to the battlements as we could without actually touching them. She knew at once who we were.

'You came! I knew you would.' She sneered at me. 'Did you honestly think your puny magic could keep me trapped anywhere?'

Well, yes, actually, I had. 'How did you escape?'

'You made three mistakes, Moonwitch: first, you didn't kill Rhiryd Goch, who still believed that he was due some reward for his bungling. Secondly, although you sealed all the entrances to the cavern, you forgot to seal the earth beneath. And then, in your relentless and mistaken *good*ness, Moonwitch, you changed Rhiryd Goch into the very creature that could burrow down and release me.'

I groaned inside. 'And where is Rhiryd Goch now?'

'Rhiryd Goch? Dead, of course. The foolish creature forgot that burrowing into a cavern half-full of water is a good way to drown.'

'You didn't save him? After he helped you?'

'Save him? Why? He had outlived his usefulness.'

A gust of wind blew Gwydion against the wall, and I winced. He'd be covered in bruises at this rate. However, if we couldn't work out how to release him, then he would crash onto the rocks below as soon as Spiderwitch cut the web that kept him hanging there. And she would . . .

I flew down level with his face: his eyes were closed

but he was breathing, thank goodness. I noticed the two small puncture wounds on his right arm: she had bitten him, paralysed him with spider-venom to get him here.

Spiderwitch was playing with the knife, and with us, putting it to the web and pressing, and then withdrawing it. 'He will die, you know. And then there will be no Dragonson, and no DragonKing. I shall have Ynys Haf.'

'No, you won't. The Lady won't let you.' I flew up level with her face.

'The Lady! What can she do to stop me? She has no magic!'

'I have it all, and *I* won't let you.'

'Don't you know yet, Moonwitch, that I am stronger than you? Evil is darker, richer, heavier than good. If you are lucky, you will die, soon. If you are not . . .' She shimmered and changed to a monstrous spider, great fangs dripping venom. Inside my feathers, I shuddered. And then knew what to do. I flew a little way off, beckoning the others to join me. 'Quickly. Change to spiders—big ones, like her—and rip away the web surrounding the battlements. A spider made it, and only a spider can undo it. *Quickly!*'

Hovering in the air above the web-covered battlements, we changed, dropped down, and all together hurled ourselves at the web, ripping, tearing, making a place where we could stand as humans, face to face with our enemy.

She fought us, trying to drive us away, but we were too many. At last the battlements were clear, and we shapeshifted and stood, panting, a few feet away from her. She shimmered and shifted back to her human form, the knife poised over the rope.

'Touch me and he dies,' she spat. 'I cut the web and he falls. The rocks are very sharp, Moonwitch. Will you be responsible for the death of the last of the DragonKings?'

Over her shoulder, I could see what she couldn't. From everywhere, all over Ynys Haf, great clouds of bees were coming. Millions and millions of angry insects. Then she heard them, and turned. She raised the knife and slashed through the rope holding Gwydion— but he didn't fall, because the packed bodies of a million bees formed a thick cloud that lowered him gently to the ground and laid him on the sands above the tideline a little way away from Castell Du.

Spiderwitch, screaming hoarsely with fury, was backed into a corner, knife in hand. We watched her closely in case she decided to shift. Whatever happened, this time she mustn't be allowed to get away.

Merlin drew himself up to his full height. 'It is my considered opinion,' he said, 'considering all the various considerations and taking account of the unusually malevolent maliciousness of the mis-demeanours of this miserable miscreant—'

'Oh, for goodness sake, Merlin!' Taliesin interrupted. 'Say what you mean for once!'

'I think we should bump her off,' Merlin said, pushing his glasses up his nose.

'Me too,' I said. And then I heard the Lady's voice.

'No, Tan'ith. To kill her would make us as evil as she is. Tell the bees, Tan'ith, tell the bees.'

Tell the bees? All right, if that's what the Lady wanted. 'Just a mo',' I said. 'The Lady has spoken, and she wants me to tell the bees.' I cleared my throat, and walked to the edge of the battlements.

'Excuse me, bees?' I called. Strangely, I didn't feel as daft as I had before. I told the bees what our problem was, that we had Merch Corryn Du at our mercy, but the Lady didn't want to finish her off. The small creatures buzzed angrily, and then did a strange thing. Half of them shot off out to sea, towards where the mountains of Eryri reached to the skies, and half of them hung around Spiderwitch, but safely out of munching range. Every time we got close, she waved the knife at us. And whatever we shifted into, a knife stuck into us would do us damage.

'Now what do we do?' T.A. asked.

I shrugged. 'Wait, I suppose.'

I was beginning to worry about Gwydion. 'Taliesin, I think you and Merlin should go down and check on Gwydion,' I suggested, and they shifted into gulls and screaming, soared off the battlements. That just left T.A., me, Spiderwitch—and the knife. The sun was getting hotter: it was almost noon. As I watched her, Spiderwitch began a sort of hypnotic weaving movement with her body, and the knife glinted in the sun. I kept watching it. I tore my eyes away, with difficulty. 'Crumbs, I'm hot! I'd kill for a drink!'

'How about a nice cool cola?' T.A. said.

'Oh, shut up, T.A. Don't torture me.'

'Da-daaaa!' With a flourish T.A. produced a familiar red can from inside her jerkin. 'If we have one now, we can still share the other after Gwydion's ceremony.'

My tongue was hanging out! But just as T.A. held out the can and I took it, Spiderwitch made her move, lunging at T.A., who was nearest, and grabbing her round the waist.

'Help! Tanz!'

Now I ask you. What could I do? And then matters got worse. Astarte, who without magic hadn't been able to shapeshift, must have followed us on foot, and pounded up the spiral stairs just in time to see her Great-Great-Granny grab T.A. She skidded to a halt just inside the arched doorway, and smiled.

'Oh, well done, Granny!' she shrieked, and clapped, simpering and tossing her gingery hair.

Creep, I thought.

'Ooh, Granny! Stick the knife in her! Kill her dead, Granny!'

Spiderwitch glared at her descendant for a long time before speaking. Then,

'Astarte. You are utterly, utterly useless. You have made a complete mess of every single thing I've asked you to do over the last seven years,' she hissed. ' Now, shut up.'

'But, Granny, I—'

'SHUT UP!' Spiderwitch turned her attention to me. 'Now, Moonwitch. You are going to stand there, and I—' She coiled her arm round T.A.'s throat. T.A. gulped, and looked sick. '—I shall leave. But first I shall kill this meddling little mortal. Then I shall kill you. I do so hate loose ends!' And she raised the knife, watching me, still smiling her dreadful smile, the black hair coiled on her head like a great snake.

Now it's an amazing thing. Instead of going to pieces, and screaming and shouting, I used the only weapon I had. I gave the can of coke a good, hard, quick shake, and pointed it at her, and half-ripped off the pull-ring. It was probably already fairly fizzy anyway, what with all the flying around and shapeshifting it had done inside T.A.'s jerkin, but when I yanked the ring-pull, the brown liquid shot out of the little opening like a guided missile, straight into Spiderwitch's eye. Hooray for me! What a shot!

'Aaaaagh! I'm blind!' She dropped the knife, let go of T.A., and put both hands over her eyes. Which might have been a good thing, because at that moment the bees came back, accompanied by . . .

Chapter 26

. . . the dragon. I'll say this for it, it didn't mess about. It flapped in, did what it came to do, and flapped off.

I saw the vast shape skimming in low and fast like a jet-plane across the sea, and (not being all that used to seeing dragons flying around), didn't recognise it at first. But then, as it drew closer, its great wings and tail, and vast, red, scaly head gleaming in the noon sun, there was no mistaking it. Close to, it was so huge that it almost blotted out the sun, its shadow falling across the battlements like a great dark cloud. It balanced on the upward thermals from the sea below, and then lowered one great, red talon, wrapped it round Spiderwitch's waist, and flapped off towards the distant blue peaks of Snowdonia. Spiderwitch screamed a lot, and thrashed about, but there was no way the dragon was going to let her go. Ever. I shuddered. Boy, was I glad the dragon was on our side!

Merch Corryn Du was gone. And this time, it looked like forever.

Astarte gazed open-mouthed after the dragon. 'Granny?' she shouted crossly, 'come back at once!

Don't go without me! Stop playing silly games, Granny! Grann-eeeeee!'

We'd got rid of Merch Corryn Du, but there was still Astarte to think of, and even without magic, she was still a threat. Rhiryd Goch's ancestors had treacherously poisoned Gwydion's father, and I didn't want to risk that happening to Gwydion. Or to me, for that matter. I studied Astarte, racking my brains for something to do with her. She glared back.

I wouldn't make the mistake I had with Rhiryd Goch, by turning him into a mole so he could let Spiderwitch out—even if he had wound up dead. Anything I changed Astarte into must have no talent at all for making mischief. A cabbage might be good, but that, I felt, was taking it just a little too far. Nothing with a sting, nothing with teeth, nothing, in fact that could do anything at all except—

Except sit on a lily-pad and go 'Ribbit Ribbit'? And, maybe, have a tadpole or two. Perhaps. If she could find a male froglet who fancied her. Or a handsome Prince to give her a kiss (which was unlikely, since handsome Princes aren't known for their frog-kissing talents).

I said the spell, and there on the stone floor was a large brownish-green frog, with one cross blue eye and one cross brown one.

'Now, Astarte,' I said, picking her up. 'I'll pop you in the fishpond as we go past. But behave yourself, or I'll send you to France. And I'm sure you know what French people like to do with frogs!'

Astarte blinked, and her throat swelled with air. 'Ribbit!' she said. She wasn't a happy froggie!

When she'd splashed into the fish-pond outside the

castle walls, I shifted T.A. and we flew down the cliff-face to Gwydion's side. He was conscious, thanks to Merlin's ministrations, and sitting up, groggily, although the spider-bites on his arm were still red and angry looking.

I shifted us back, and crouched beside him. 'Are you all right, Gwydion?'

'I'll live. My arm is throbbing a bit, and my head aches. And I'm so thirsty, I could drink the well dry.'

'I can think of something that might help.' T.A. twitched. 'Hand it over, T.A.'

'I suppose we can share it three ways,' she said glumly. 'Not that I begrudge it, seeing as it's you, Gwydion.' She reached inside her jerkin and produced the last, precious can of cola, popped the ring-pull and handed it to Gwydion. We didn't share it three ways. The future DragonKing chug-a-lugged the entire can, straight down, the greedy pig.

Merlin frowned through his glasses. 'You young people! Don't you realise that it's been scientifically proven that that stuff is bad for your teeth? Dental caries! Cavities, to you! Toothache! Gingivitis! And we haven't invented decent dentists, have we? It's all barbers with pliers for a couple of hundred years yet! I suppose you know there's—'

'We know,' T.A. and I chorused, 'two thousand spoonfuls of sugar in every can. It'll rot our teeth.' Then we fell about laughing, partly because it was funny, and partly from relief that none of us was harmed.

When Gwydion was strong enough, we shifted and flew back towards Castell y Ddraig. The ceremony had been planned for noon, but it was closer to four o'clock when it began.

I wore my lovely green dress, T.A. wore her red one (and don't think I didn't notice Prince Ceredig and Elffin of Cantre'r Gwaelod mooning over her. How come no one ever moons over me?)

And Gwydion . . .

You might have thought he would wear something posh, with a lot of gold thread and jewels, stuff like that, but you'd have been wrong. He wore the colours of Ynys Haf. Soft brown, earth-coloured boots; trousers the green of a stately fir-tree; a flowing shirt that matched the summer skies, his dark hair blowing about his face, because this coronation wasn't held in some stuffy abbey packed with Knights and Barons in coronets and ermine. Gwydion's crowning was in the open air, with a counterpoint of birdsong accompanying Taliesin's harp-music.

Merlin, of course, was in charge, and he changed his jeans and T-shirt for a white robe which reminded me a bit of the one the Great Druid had worn—except that Merlin's didn't have egg-stains and greasy patches all over it.

'Dragonson,' Merlin began, in a thrilling, sonorous voice. He sounded like dark chocolate might have sounded, if dark chocolate had a voice. 'Dragonson, I offer you the Crown of Ynys Haf. Do you swear to protect Ynys Haf, her people, her creatures and her land? Will you fight for her, administer her Laws justly, and treat all who call on you for aid and comfort with compassion and patience?'

Gwydion didn't speak. He looked around at the rustling trees loud with birdsong, up at the sun, sinking in a red blaze towards the West, tinting the pewter sea with liquid fire, looked at the faces of his friends and his people gathered around him and smiled. I followed his gaze, and realised that it wasn't only the humans of Ynys Haf who had gathered to witness the crowning of their DragonKing: the ethereal, rainbows-dancing shapes of the *tylwyth teg* wove their way in and out of tree-branches excitedly, and behind every bush lurked an animal. Deer loitered shyly in the shade, badgers poked their noses round trees, foxes lay down with wary rabbits, even wolves drifted like grey smoke through the trees, their eyes glowing red as they watched. The whole Island of Summer fell silent, waiting for Gwydion's reply. No one was even breathing, waiting . . .

Then: 'I will!' he said, joyously, and Merlin turned to the small, puffed-up-with-importance pageboy waiting patiently behind him bearing the Dragon-Crown on a blue velvet cushion. Merlin took the crown, raised it high so that the soft, mellow sheen of silver flashed in the sunlight, and placed it on Gwydion's dark head. And the breath-held silence was broken by cheering, shouting, slapping-on-the-back, cap-throwing in the air, trumpeters trumpeting, drummers drumming, bees buzzing, everyone talking and laughing and crying at once. Was I the only one who noticed the two almost transparent figures in the darkness between the trees? Side by side, one tall, with close-cropped hair, the other tiny, fragile, wearing flowing robes, her dark hair bound by ribbons of starlight. My eyes widened, and I opened my mouth to greet them. They saw me, and smiled. The King shook his head. Then he and the Lady were gone.

Merlin raised up his hand majestically, and the noise gradually faded. 'Hereby I do proclaim you, Gwydion,

Son of Ynys Haf, Child of Light, Son of the Dragon King of Blessed Memory, in the sight of all gathered here and all in the whole discovered world, DragonKing.'

'Oh, I wish Mam and the Aunts could have seen this!' I whispered to Flissy, who was dabbing her eyes and leaning on Iestyn Mawr, who was patting her awkwardly, the way I'd seen him pat his carthorse, and beaming proudly at the same time.

'But they have, Tansy!' Aunty Fliss sniffled, 'they will have scryed it all!' She was right, of course. I pictured them gathered round the scrying ball, and grinned. Mam, by now, would be howling her eyes out. I felt a bit sniffy myself.

Then came the banquet. As the Lady's representative, I sat between Merlin and Gwydion at the top table, with T.A. on the other side of Gwydion. We ate, and ate, and ate. There was venison, and beef, and lamb, and pork, and chicken, and fish, and for pudding—oh, it was enough to make a dieter *die*! As far as I was concerned, and probably T.A. as well, there was only one thing missing . . .

I sipped my wine, and sighed. Merlin heard me. And grinned. He pushed his glasses up his nose, snapped his fingers, and the air in front of me shimmered. And there, on the table, was a two-litre bottle of—you've guessed it! So cold that condensation formed on the outside, and little chilly droplets oozed down the dark brown sides . . . T.A and I reached for it at the same time.

'Remember your teeth, young ladies!' Merlin said.

'*Dim problem*, Merlin,' T.A. said cheekily. 'Where we're going, there are dentists!'

228

Where we're going . . .

Where we were going there would be no Gwydion. Suddenly, I lost my appetite.

There was lots of entertainment, jugglers, fire-eaters, tumblers, a choir of minstrels that sang several (rather rude) songs which made everyone laugh and one or two of the maidservants blush, and lastly, Taliesin.

Taliesin, of course, as Chief Bard of Ynys Haf, was saved until last—sort of 'topping the bill'. When everyone was silent, he ran his fingers across the silver strings, making a liquid sound like falling water, and he sang a song about Gwydion. First of all, he sang about his birth, and how proud his Mam and Dad had been; then he sang about his childhood (here, Merlin scowled, perhaps remembering an episode involving cabbages and socks!) and his youth, when he was sent to Other Wales to be my companion. And then, to my awful, dreadful, red-faced, toe-curling, eye-lash cringing embarrassment, he sang about me! There was lots about my bravery and resourcefulness, and a funny bit about my "spotty dapples and red and shorten hair" which made everyone (except me) laugh, and then he got serious again:

'Tanith, daughter of the Moon
Child of Other Wales
and Daughter of Ynys Haf
Your proud Destiny linked with
DragonKing'

Well, up to now it had been. But tomorrow, when we went back, that would be that. Except for occasional visits. Taliesin carried on

'When you return to Ynys Haf
You will be the Lady
and your Children shall
wear her Stars.
In Time.'

I wasn't quite sure what it all meant, but it sounded good. I suddenly felt my hand squeezed, and looked up into Gwydion's eyes. The slender circlet of silver about his head made me feel shy. He didn't seem like my Gwydion any more. He seemed to have moved away, grown up. He had to stay behind and rule Ynys Haf, and I had to go home.

And sit my G.C.S.E.s. It was all over.

Gwydion rode with us to the Door in Time, Cariad cradled in his arms. Surprisingly, she didn't scream, but gurgled happily at him, and tried to stick her fingers up his nose before she fell asleep. At the Door in Time he dismounted, and handed the sleeping baby to T.A., who was still carrying her Tesco carrier, which surprisingly, still bulged. Since she'd used more or less everything she'd brought with her, I couldn't think what was inside—unless it was her Ynys Haf leather jerkin, which she'd fallen in love with. Or maybe some of Flissy's left-over Welsh cakes. I didn't care. I had other things on my mind.

Gwydion helped me down from my horse (as if I wasn't capable of doing that myself!), and with the horse shielding us from the sight of the others, took both my hands in his.

'Please don't say anything soppy or sentimental, Gwyd,' I said firmly. 'I shall cry if you do.'

230

'I won't. But look, Tanz,' he said seriously, gazing into my eyes, 'when you come back next time—'

'Goodness knows when that will be,' I chirped brightly, 'I've got my G.C.S.Es to do, you know!'

'Shut up, Tanz.'

'Yes, Gwydion. But—'

'Shhh. Oh, *Merlin's Nightshirt!*' Then he grabbed my ears, as if I were a spaniel, and kissed me. Smack. On the lips.

Now I've been kissed before. I have, stop laughing, T.A.! Well, Bryn Jenkins when I was eight, and that spotty boy, at that party, and—well, maybe not too often. But this was the first real one. And the best. Even if he did grab my ears first. Then he shoved me away, and I kissed Flissy, (my toes still tingling) and hugged Iestyn Fawr (my ears burning) and shook hands solemnly with Merlin (my face bright pink) and flung my arms (grinning like an idiot) round the neck of Taliesin, who wasn't coming with us either, because a DragonKing needs a DragonBard.

Then I grabbed T.A.'s hand and towed her and Cariad through the Door in Time without looking back. I couldn't have seen anything if I had, because my eyes were filled with tears.

And that's it, really. I did my G.C.S.E.s, and when the results came out in August (the wait was *torture!*) I'd done really well, as if a tiny bit of the Lady's magic (which had disappeared during the time I was travelling through the Door, leaving me with just my plain old ordinary magic) had hung around long enough to get me As and Bs in everything. Except

231

Maths. In which I got a D. Which means I've got to re-sit in November. Sigh.

But that was The End of the Adventure. No more Merch Corryn Du and her spider's webs. No more Astarte. No more Taliesin/Mr Howard (the new Music teacher isn't nearly as good) and no more Gwydion. Except . . .

When I went to bed on the night I got back, I found out what T.A. had brought back in her carrier bag.

She left the Tesco bag on my pillow. Inside, wrapped in dark red velvet, was a beautiful, slender silver coronet. I tried it on. It fitted as if it had been made for me, heavy and solid around my forehead. The bright silver gleamed with intricate designs of birds, animals, insects, moons and stars—and at the front, in the centre, a strangely shaped design, like a relief map of Wales, but with Cantre'r Gwaelod lying, for the time being at least, safely above the waves. The coronet of Ynys Haf.

A coronet fit, one day, perhaps, for a Dragon-Queen.

Gwydion's DragonQueen.

Here ends the third Book of Gwydion